Turning to her, he asked, "Shall we begin?"

Eliza started, as if pulled from abstraction, then darted a look at him. As their gazes caught, Giles saw in her eyes the same reluctant attraction he felt.

So he'd not been imagining that subtle tension in her body—or the fact that it indicated she too was aware of the pull between them.

As he pushed away the disturbing implications of that fact, she said, "I'm ready when you are."

Shaken more than he wanted to be, he nodded and focused back on the score. "Then let us start."

As they played the piano, Giles forced his concentration to remain on the music, which was indeed difficult enough to require full attention. Just below the level of consciousness, though, he remained aware of the attraction buzzing between them.

Author Note

Most authors who write historical fiction are, I suspect, history nerds like me. Although my stories always start with the characters, as I discover their interests and pleasures, I'm usually soon plunging down the rabbit hole of research to explore how they would pursue those interests during the Regency period.

For heroine Eliza and hero Giles, a shared interest was playing piano duets. It's hard for our instant-music-on-your-phone-whenever-you-want-it world to imagine a time when the only way to hear the music you loved was to play it yourself or listen to someone else play. Musicales were a prime source of entertainment, and with organized symphonies just beginning, most musical evenings featured enthusiastic amateurs.

But what would they play? To decide which duet my hero and heroine might have performed together, I was "forced" to listen to a number of music videos. Treat yourself to Franz Schubert's Piano Sonata in C Major or Beethoven's Sonata in D Major op. 6. You will see why, despite Eliza's doubts about Miles's professed interest in her, sitting side by side on the piano bench performing these pieces, they fall in love.

I hope you will enjoy their (musical) journey.

JULIA JUSTISS

The Wallflower's Last Chance Season

HARLEQUIN
HISTORICAL

HARLEQUIN®
HISTORICAL™

Recycling programs
for this product may
not exist in your area.

ISBN-13: 978-1-335-59564-5

The Wallflower's Last Chance Season

Copyright © 2023 by Janet Justiss

For questions and comments about the quality of this book,
please contact us at CustomerService@Harlequin.com.

Harlequin Enterprises ULC
22 Adelaide St. West, 41st Floor
Toronto, Ontario M5H 4E3, Canada
www.Harlequin.com

Printed in U.S.A.

Julia Justiss wrote her own ideas for Nancy Drew stories in her third-grade notebook and has been writing ever since. After publishing poetry at university, she turned to novels. Her historical Regency romances have won or placed in contests by the Romance Writers of America, *RT Book Reviews*, National Readers' Choice and the Daphne du Maurier Award. She lives with her husband in Texas. For news and contests, visit juliajustiss.com.

Books by Julia Justiss

Harlequin Historical

Least Likely to Wed

A Season of Flirtation
The Wallflower's Last Chance Season

Heirs in Waiting

The Bluestocking Duchess
The Railway Countess
The Explorer Baroness

The Cinderella Spinsters

The Awakening of Miss Henley
The Tempting of the Governess
The Enticing of Miss Standish

Sisters of Scandal

A Most Unsuitable Match
The Earl's Inconvenient Wife

Visit the Author Profile page
at Harlequin.com for more titles.

To the wonderful authors (some of them now good friends) who have taken me on journeys of adventure, romance, inspiration, heartbreak and delight my entire reading life. Thank you!

Chapter One

London—May 1836

Eliza Hasterling tucked back into her reticule the needle and thread she'd used to repair the tear in her skirt where the hapless Mr Alborne had trod on her hem. Hopefully it wouldn't show; her meagre allowance wouldn't allow replacing the gown. Giving her feathery curls one last look in the mirror, she left the ladies' withdrawing room and headed for the stairs back down to the ballroom.

Her forthright friend Lady Margaret would say it was her own fault for dancing again with Alborne, she thought with a sigh. But with his spotted face and eager, puppy dog eyes, she found it impossible to fob him off as Maggie—and so many other young ladies—did. Being neither handsome nor rich, and clumsy into the bargain, he was hardly considered a desirable parti. Knowing what it was like to be overlooked and disparaged, she couldn't help feeling sorry for the young man. Which meant, as she didn't snub him, he repeatedly sought her out.

Even she might have to start refusing him if he were going to destroy her limited wardrobe.

She'd descended the stairs and begun to cross the room when the older gentleman to whom she'd nodded as they passed uttered a sharp cry of dismay. She turned to see the cane on which he'd been leaning skid off the first step and clatter to the floor. Losing his balance, he pitched sideways.

She rushed over to grab his arm, not strong enough to prevent him staggering to his knees, but at least able to keep him from falling full-length on to the floor. After she helped steady him back to his feet, she knelt to recover the cane.

She'd just handed it back to him when two matrons entered the passageway and stopped short, eyeing them curiously—the gentleman leaning on his cane, looking down at her, and Eliza beside him on her knees. Seeing the flush of embarrassment on the gentleman's face, Eliza held her hand out to him, saying quickly, 'How clumsy of me to stumble! I do thank you for offering to help me up.'

Catching on, the man took her fingers and pulled them as she rose to her feet. Belatedly recognising one of the matrons as the imperious Lady Arbuthnot, Eliza braced herself.

'Lord Markham, how condescending of you to lend her a hand,' the lady said before turning to Eliza. 'You should be more careful, Miss Hasterling. You might have careened right into Lord Markham.'

'No harm done, Your Ladyship,' Markham said.

Giving Eliza a disdainful glance, Lady Arbuthnot nodded to the Viscount, then linked her arm with her friend's and proceeded past them up the stairs. As they reached the top of the stairway, she murmured—but quite loud enough for them to hear—'A *clergyman's* daughter. No grace or poise—but then, what can one expect?'

Her companion sniffed. 'Gracious of Markham to even acknowledge her. She ought to know her place and keep silent!'

Eliza pressed her lips together, feeling her own face redden but determined to ignore the remarks. Once the women walked out of earshot, she said, 'You are unharmed yourself, Lord Markham?'

'Yes, thanks to you—Miss Hasterling, was it? So very generous of you to spare my blushes—at the cost of bringing down the unkindness of Lady Arbuthnot on your own head. I've half a mind to follow her and put her straight!'

'What, and undo my good work?' Eliza said with a smile. 'You mustn't concern yourself about Her Ladyship. As she considers a mere clergyman's daughter far beneath her notice, she is unlikely to trouble me further. I'm just glad I was here to prevent you suffering an injury.'

'Have we been introduced? You seem to know me, but I'm afraid I don't recall meeting you. A terrible lapse, not to remember so fetching a young lady.'

'We were introduced last Season, but it was just before…' She hesitated a moment before continuing, 'Just before you lost your lady wife. Quite understandable that much of that sad time became a blur. My condolences, by the way, on your loss.'

The smile faded from the Viscount's face, a look of haunted grief replacing it, and Eliza chided herself for reminding him. Why could she not have just said they'd been introduced, and left it at that? She knew Markham, having finished a year of mourning, had only just re-entered society. By all accounts, he and his late wife had been very close, and he'd been devastated by her death.

'I'm so sorry!' she cried. 'I didn't mean—I shouldn't have—'

Markham waved her to silence. 'No need for apologies, child. It was a grievous loss, but I'm coming to terms with it…gradually. After my unexpected meeting with the floor, I should probably not strain my knee further tonight by dancing. But may I escort you to take some refreshment, in thanks for your kind and timely intervention? Had you not come to my aid so quickly, Lady Arbuthnot would have found me sprawled out on the parquet, a humiliation she would have excused at the moment and afterwards delighted in describing to her friends.'

Eliza chuckled. 'So she would have! I'm happy I was able to prevent that.'

'Shall we have a glass of wine to celebrate that felicity?' Markham asked with a smile.

Smiling back, Eliza had just allowed Markham to tuck her hand on his arm when a tall, dark-haired man hurried into the passageway. 'Father, is everything all right? You've been gone rather long. Withram is asking for you.'

'Just chatting with this lovely young lady. Do you know my son, Miss Hasterling?'

Eliza stared up, fascinated, at the handsome, rugged face of the man who was regarding his father with concern. Dressed in simple, understated black evening garb, he was whipcord lean, with dark hair curling on to his forehead that he brushed back impatiently, and intense dark brown eyes. When he reached his father's side, she noted the marked resemblance, the newcomer a younger, stronger, more vital version of the gentleman she'd rescued. A strong current of attraction rippled through her as he halted beside them.

'N-no, we've not been introduced,' Eliza said, pulling herself from her scrutiny of the gentleman.

'Let me do the honours. Miss Hasterling, may I present my son, Baron Stratham? Stratham, Miss Hasterling.'

After bows and curtsies were exchanged, Markham said, 'I'm about to escort Miss Hasterling to the refreshment room. You can tell Withram I'll look for him afterwards.'

Bedazzled at first by Stratham's virile figure and handsome face, Eliza only then realised that he hadn't returned her smile of greeting. Instead, he was staring, stone-faced, at the hand she had rested on his father's arm.

For a moment, she thought he would remark on it— though what could he possibly say? Although there was nothing remotely improper about a lady taking a gentleman's arm, Eliza none the less felt a flash of discomfort, as if she had been caught doing something she shouldn't.

'Shall we go, Miss Hasterling? With the ball ending soon, you'll want to return to the dancing, and I wouldn't wish you to miss that treat.'

Markham nodded to his son, but instead of leaving to deliver his father's message, Stratham said, 'I believe I shall have some wine as well.'

A look passed between the men—gentle resignation on the part of the father, determination from the son. 'Accompany us if you wish,' Markham said mildly.

As they strolled, the Viscount said, 'You must let me repair the lapses in my memory of meeting you last Season. Where does your family reside? I don't recall being acquainted with your father. He's a clergyman, you said?'

'Yes, but it's not surprising you have not met. He seldom leaves his parish in Saltash, near Plymouth, where he resides with my mother and the rest of my family. I'm staying in London with my older sister, Lady Dunbarton, who has been kind enough to act as my chaperon so Mama can remain at home with my younger siblings.'

'Have you a large family, then?'

'Quite large. I have two married sisters; my only brother is still at home, being tutored by my father, who is a notable scholar, while Mama tends to the little ones.'

As she answered the Viscount's questions, Eliza was all too conscious of his son walking behind them, seeming to tower over her, still unsmiling. Disapproving, it seemed?

But of what could he disapprove? He hadn't encountered Lady Arbuthnot, so he couldn't have been regaled with an account of her 'clumsiness'.

Or—did he think she had *designs* on the Viscount? Markham was, she knew, a wealthy widower—if he'd not been titled, he'd be just the sort of *parti* her friend Maggie was urging her to beguile into marriage, the sooner to become a rich widow in charge of her own life. Not a goal to which she aspired, though she was trying to give Maggie's Grand Plan a fair hearing.

Still, she had to suppress a smile at the ridiculous notion that anyone would suspect lowly Eliza Hasterling, daughter of an obscure county clergyman, of having designs on a *viscount*.

Less amusing and more irksome was the unusual experience of encountering someone who seemed to view her with disapproval. She was accustomed to being treated with kindness and courtesy by her friends and family, while with her modest dowry and undistinguished connections, she was usually overlooked or ignored by society gentlemen.

Taking another quick glance at Stratham's sombre expression, she wasn't sure she liked being noticed.

By now they'd arrived in the refreshment room. Eliza accepted the glass of wine Markham obtained for her, trying to ignore the scrutiny of Lord Stratham, who continued to hover nearby. Recalling her friend Lady Laura Pomeroy's advice that the best way to engage a gentleman in conversation was to enquire about his interests, she said to Markham, 'You have lately been in the country yourself, have you not, my lord?'

'Yes, at our main residence in Hampshire, Stratham Hall.'

'Do you have other children residing there with you?'

'No, alas—all but my son have married and moved to homes of their own, one daughter residing outside York, another near Portsmouth and the youngest recently wed to a gentleman from Northumberland.'

'Do you plan to stay long in London?'

'The rest of the Season, probably. I grew…lonely in the country.'

'London will certainly cure you of that! Always something to do and people to see! What are you most looking forward to in the city?'

'I enjoy seeing old friends and visiting the theatre, but especially love perusing the King's Collection at the British Museum.'

'Ah, you are a scholar, too, my lord?'

'Probably not on the order of your father. I do enjoy philosophy, poetry and the classics.'

An avid reader herself, Eliza exclaimed with delight, 'The classics? Which do you like best? I'm no great scholar myself, but Papa did teach me Latin and a little Greek. I particularly enjoy Petrarch.'

'Do you indeed?' Markham said, looking impressed. 'As do I! You must allow me to call on you, so we might discuss our favourite passages.'

Shaking her head, Eliza held up a disparaging hand. 'You mustn't be thinking me erudite! I only know the poems for which I had Papa's help with the translations.'

'I should be interested to discover which ones he felt worthy of you reading.' After a slightly exasperated look at his son, who contributed nothing to the conversation but still hovered at his elbow, Markham said, 'I must let you go back to the dancing. But you will allow me to call on you tomorrow?'

So he might thank her again for assistance, Eliza suspected, which he did not wish to do with his son listening in. He wouldn't want to admit his embarrassing near-fall in front of Stratham.

'I'd be honoured,' she replied. 'As I mentioned, I'm residing with Lady Dunbarton at Holly House on Brook Street.'

Markham waved to a waiter to take their empty glasses, then offered her his arm. 'Let me escort you back to your chaperon.'

Putting aside his own glass, Stratham once again followed them. Like a knight vigilantly protecting his king from danger, Eliza thought, suppressing a smile.

As they entered the ballroom, Eliza spotted her sister chatting with friends. 'My sponsor is over there,' she said, pointing.

'I'll walk you over,' Markham said. 'You will introduce me—us,' he added with a rueful glance at the man trailing them, 'won't you?'

'Of course.'

Just before they reached Lady Dunbarton, Stratham paced forward to walk beside them. 'You enjoy dancing, Miss Hasterling?'

Behold, the sphinx speaks, she thought. 'Very much, Lord Stratham.'

'Would you do me the honour of standing up with me for the next waltz?'

A hollow feeling swooped in her stomach at the thought of being held close to that lithe, powerful body, her hand in his, his other hand clasping her waist. Then her brain caught up with her overexcited senses and reminded her he seemed to look on her with disfavour.

Besides, she should know better now than to let herself be carried away by a strong physical connection. One humiliating rejection should be enough for a lifetime.

But if he disapproved, why had he asked her to dance?

However, she was not promised for the waltz, and as usual, couldn't quickly come up with a convincing reason to refuse. 'It would be my pleasure,' she said reluctantly.

Her sister noticed her approaching, her look of annoyance changing to surprise as she took in Eliza's escorts. Smoothing her expression to one of welcome, she curtsied to the men, who bowed in return.

'I return your charge to you safely, Madam,' Markham said.

'Thank you, Sir! I'd been wondering where she'd got to.'

'I had to repair my hem,' Eliza explained.

At her sister's frown, Eliza realised she shouldn't have brought attention to the slightly shabby state of her gown. As Lady Dunbarton would doubtless later point out, she should instead have simply said that she'd gone to the retiring room.

Would she ever master the art of social chit-chat, where one automatically refrained from doing or saying anything that might show one in an unfavourable light?

'The delay is my fault,' Markham was saying. 'I encountered her in the passageway and persuaded her to brighten my first ball in a year by taking a glass of wine with me.'

'Maria, you will remember Lord Markham—and his son, Lord Stratham? My sister, Lady Dunbarton.'

'Of course. It's good to have you back in London, Lord Markham. And I don't believe I have previously met your son.'

'Stratham never had much interest in larger society,' Markham said, a marked dryness in his tone. 'Then over this last year, he's been taking much of the burden of managing the estate off my shoulders, which has kept him in the country.'

'Always a delight to have another handsome gentleman in town,' her sister said, giving Stratham a bright smile.

'As it is pleasant to renew our acquaintance, Lady Dunbarton. And yours, Miss Hasterling,' Markham said.

'I'll be back to claim my dance,' Stratham said. With another bow, the two strode away.

Her sister's gaze followed them across the floor before she turned back to Eliza. 'What happened?'

Briefly, Eliza recounted her meeting with the Viscount —although she didn't mention that she'd saved him from falling, instead inserting the fib that he'd recognised her, then asked her to accompany him for a glass of wine, where they encountered his son.

'Two very eligible *partis*,' her sister said, nodding approvingly. 'And the younger one coming back to waltz with you! Well done, Eliza!'

'He asked out of politeness only,' Eliza insisted, not wanting to reveal more of the complicated undercurrents that flowed between them. Attraction on her part, regrettably. Enough scepticism on his that she really wasn't looking forward to him claiming that dance.

No matter how aroused her silly senses were at the prospect.

'I know you've been cautioned to be more…reserved in society than you are among family, and often have little to say to young gentlemen,' her sister observed. 'But with Stratham coming for a waltz…what a sterling opportunity! You must make a determined effort to converse with him.'

'I do converse…some,' she protested. 'I'm just not comfortable voicing the sort of fawning flattery, or worse, clever but critical observations about others that seem to make up most of the conversation between young society ladies and gentlemen. I have no trouble talking with older men, who like Papa generally have more wide-ranging interests.'

'Mature men like Lord Markham? He'd be an excellent catch, if a bit old for you. Gossip is that after mourning his wife, he's now decided he wants to find a congenial companion to brighten his golden years. Though I would think you would prefer the son. What a handsome devil he is, to be sure! Stratham has a good deal of money in his own right, for after his mother's death, he inherited the estates that had been her dowry. Already a courtesy baron, he'll be viscount after his father.'

'Let's not be marrying me off to either of them yet,' Eliza said quickly. Heaven help her if the already suspicious Stratham sensed from her sister's demeanour that Eliza was setting her cap for his father!

'Well, you need to put your mind to attracting *someone*,' her sister reminded. 'You know Papa can't afford to give you another Season. Dear as you are to me, my pin money wouldn't extend to funding another one for you, either.'

'I know. I appreciate you taking the time to squire me about again this year,' Eliza said.

She was all too aware that this would be her final Season. If she didn't find a husband before society dispersed for the summer and she returned to the wilds of Saltash, she likely never would. And would end up sharing the unhappy fate of other well-born but indigent spinsters, shuffled from one family home to another to help with children, ailing relatives or the elderly.

Much as she enjoyed her sisters' children, she still cherished hopes that one day the babes she tended would be her own. And that she could be mistress of the home in which she lived, supported by a husband whom she loved and admired.

She would take her sister's advice and make best efforts to converse with Lord Stratham—if he did in fact come back to claim his dance.

Though she was quite sure that her as yet unknown husband would be neither Viscount Markham nor his handsome, suspicious son.

Chapter Two

As they traversed the ballroom, Giles Stratham braced himself for a scold from his father over his playing gooseberry during the Viscount's interlude with Miss Hasterling. Perhaps he was overreacting, but the proprietary hand the young lady had placed on his father's arm had immediately roused his alarm.

He knew his father was still emotionally fragile, by no means fully recovered from losing his childhood sweetheart and lifelong companion. He was also lonely, having just weathered his first winter without his wife and dearest friend. Giles had provided what comfort he could, but congenial as their relationship was, he was an inadequate replacement for his father's beloved spouse.

He keenly missed that sweet and energetic lady himself. And despite his father's loneliness, he didn't want to see her over-hastily replaced.

'Where did you say Withram was waiting for me?' his father asked at last.

'In the card room.'

'I'll join him there, then. Until later?'

Giles watched his father walk off and drew a relieved breath, glad the Viscount had chosen not to discuss the touchy subject of potential courtship—or Giles's interference in it. With his father safely ensconced in the card room, he could let down his guard.

Not ready yet to return to the ballroom, he strolled down the deserted passage, glad to have some time alone with his thoughts. It wasn't that he resented on his beloved mother's behalf the *possibility* that his father might marry again; Mama would have wanted her dear Markham to go on with his life.

Giles just worried that his lonely father could be vulnerable to some scheming miss eager to weasel her way into becoming a rich viscountess.

By asking solicitously about the gentleman's home and family, teasing out his interests, then expressing surprise and delight at sharing them, perhaps?

He'd be very interested to hear Miss Hasterling discourse about Petrarch.

She'd not be the first female to give chase. A mere six months after his mother's death, hopeful mamas from all over Hampshire began paying calls on the Viscount, expressing their eagerness to lighten his burden of grief by inviting him to a 'quiet family dinner'—the dinner company always including some comely, unmarried female.

The campaigns had intensified once the Viscount's mourning year ended and he returned with Giles to London. Within hours of their arrival, invitations began pouring in—particularly to parties at which his father would be introduced to attractive unmarried ladies, from ingenues straight from the schoolroom to widows with grown children of their own.

Miss Hasterling's Petrarch ploy had impressed Markham enough to induce him to promise calling on her, Giles thought uneasily. Which was why Giles had asked the chit to dance, giving *him* a valid excuse to call on her, too. Along with his father, if he could finagle it, or if that was too unsubtle, at least allowing him to linger at her sister's house until the Viscount called, when he could keep a protective eye on him.

Miss Hasterling seemed nice enough—if how she'd presented herself reflected her true character. He had to concede, too, that while she was no Diamond, she was attractive. With her slender frame, heart-shaped face and enormous brown eyes, she certainly looked the part of the sweet innocent, an appearance that would inspire gallant men like his father to want to shelter and protect her.

A sweet innocent…like Arabella.

The old pain seared him, deepening his disquiet as he recalled the wide-eyed ingenue who'd captured his youthful heart—before abandoning him while he was away at university to wed an older, wealthier, already titled gentleman.

Like Miss Hasterling hoped to?

Not if he could help it, Giles thought, setting his jaw in a grim line. He'd protect his father from the sort of anguish he'd suffered at the hands of scheming females— be they young innocents or sophisticated beauties.

In a flash, the image of artless Arabella segued into a vision of the dazzling Lucinda…reclining on the sofa in her sitting room, draped in a negligee designed to emphasise her voluptuous figure, admiring the diamond bracelet that adorned one slender wrist. So absorbed had she been in admiring it, she hadn't attempted to hide it until after he'd walked in.

Anger, distaste and a deeply buried ache escaped to reverberate through him.

He hadn't learned much from his first heartbreak, he thought bitterly. From the moment he'd met the newly widowed Lady Evans when he came down from Oxford eight years ago, he'd been captivated.

He'd pursued her ardently, been thrilled to finally possess her—and made himself ignore the fact that she sometimes entertained other men. Pressed on by believing he'd lost Arabella by not early securing a promise to wed, he'd even impulsively asked Lucinda to marry him. To which she replied that she'd been married, and it was boring.

It had been a disaster of a union for her—shackled practically out of the schoolroom to Lord Evans, an older admirer with grown children. Lord Evans, whose deep pockets after they wed had, not incidentally, alleviated her family's pressing financial woes. She'd been hauled out of London and isolated at her husband's country estate until his death freed her to return to society.

Giles met her that first triumphant Season. Of course, he'd agreed, after her long exile, she deserved to have time to be fêted and admired as the Beauty she was. Of course, she deserved to flirt and tease and thrill at working her way into the inner circles of the politicians at the peak of power in Parliament and the Court. He'd hoped, as she'd assured him, that after a time in the limelight she would have her fill of acclaim and be ready to settle down with a single, faithful love.

That little display last week, when he'd caught her admiring the diamond bracelet another gallant had given her while he'd been in the country tending his estate, would once have filled him with jealousy. In an angry exchange, he would have wheedled out of her the name of her paramour—Melbourne, in this case, who though he had many flirts, wouldn't have gifted her with a diamond bracelet just in thanks for her political advice. Then after an acrimonious parting, determined to re-establish his pre-eminent place in her life, he'd have immediately hared off to his jeweller and commissioned something even more magnificent to adorn her.

This time, the next bauble he chose would be a farewell gift.

He wasn't sure the exact moment when his patience had finally become exhausted, when he realised that all the care and devotion he'd lavished on her these last six years wasn't enough. That she would never be ready to settle for just one man. And that he was, finally, tired of the game.

Would she seek to ensnare him again, once she realised he was actually walking away? Did he want her to try?

He didn't know the answer to either question.

Lucinda hadn't bothered much in the past with admirers who ceased to pay her court. There were always newcomers eager to take their places.

What would fill the void giving her up would leave in his life?

He suppressed an empty, hollow feeling. Running Stratham would keep him busy enough. With his father incapacitated by grief last summer, he'd assumed the reins out of necessity. As the Viscount gradually recovered his spirits, Giles had offered to turn the day-to-day management back over to him, but his father had declined. The estate would be his to run soon enough anyway, his father said, and in the interim, the Viscount would be able to devote more time to his music and his books.

A rising swell of melody roused Giles from his reflections. The musicians had completed their break; he must return to the ballroom and claim Miss Hasterling for the dance she'd promised him.

Perhaps she *was* the sweet innocent she seemed, genuinely interested in his father rather than simply calculating how to ensnare a rich husband. Although getting what she wanted from a man was what all women schemed to do, wasn't it?

This time, he'd keep in mind the hard-won truth that a female's primary concern was securing for herself the most advantageous situation possible—whether that was a rich husband, or a succession of wealthy, generous lovers.

He'd ensure his father wasn't as taken in by some heartless female as he had been. Keep watch until the Viscount recovered enough presence of mind to be able to discern whether a woman valued him as much for his person as she did for his wealth and position. Once convinced his father had recovered that capacity, Giles could withdraw and leave him free to choose a companion to brighten the rest of his life.

He would then do what he'd once believed unthinkable—abandon London, settle permanently in the country and concentrate on managing the estate.

As heir to both the property and the title, however, he couldn't escape his duty at some point to find a wife himself. Thankfully, that unpleasant chore could be put off until later.

Steeling himself to his task, Giles entered the ballroom and went in search of Miss Hasterling. He found her chatting with a tall, auburn-haired lady and an older gentleman, neither of whom he recognised. Which wasn't surprising. Though he was nearly a decade out of Oxford, over those years he'd spent little time at society functions, Lucinda preferring the intimate gatherings of her political friends and Court events rather than the crush of balls beloved by most society women. And having no interest in any woman but Lucinda, he had resisted as much as politely possible being introduced to other ladies.

'Miss Hasterling,' he said, bowing as he reached her. 'You are promised to me for the next waltz, you will recall.'

'So I am,' she replied, curtsying to his bow. 'Before we go, may I make you known to my dearest friend? Lady Margaret D'Aubignon, this is Lord Stratham, son of Lord Markham, who has recently returned to London. Stratham, Lady Margaret and her friend, Mr Fullridge.'

As the parties murmured the appropriate greetings, Giles wondered if Fullridge was another older gentleman Miss Hasterling was trying to entice. From the unfriendly look given him by that gentleman, it seemed the man resented him bearing her off.

'Mind you return after the dance. Mr Fullridge has hardly had time to converse with you,' Lady Margaret said, giving some credence to his suspicions about the other man's interest in his partner.

'As you wish, Lady Margaret,' she replied tranquilly.

Giles tried to covertly study the girl he was escorting on to the dance floor. She seemed neither eager to claim his escort nor impatient to return to the older courtier. Nor did she immediately try to engage him in conversation—as if she didn't care whether or not his attention remained focused on her.

Which seemed odd. Being as prime a matrimonial candidate as his father, on the handful of times he had ventured solo into society, he'd been sought after and flattered by a bevy of eligible maidens and their hopeful mamas. Although Miss Hasterling must certainly be aware of his position, she seemed…indifferent to the possibilities of being singled out by him.

Though such a phenomenon was foreign to his own experience, perhaps not all females felt compelled to try to captivate every man they encountered.

Still, he was surprised to find himself a bit…*piqued* by her obvious lack of interest.

Perhaps she preferred older suitors? he wondered, his unease intensifying. He must use the opportunity of this waltz to learn as much about her circumstances as she had been trying to dig out of Father about his.

'Have you been in London all Season?' he asked as they took their places.

'We arrived shortly after the beginning of the Season, yes.'

'You must have enjoyed a number of balls by now, then.'

'Not so many, actually. My sister brought her children, and some of them have been unwell. It was necessary to tend them, of course.'

'They were too ill to be left in their nurse's care?' Giles asked, surprised.

'Not seriously ill, thank heaven. But fretful enough that they appreciated a doting aunt's care,' she said, her face warming at the mention of the children.

Most society matrons either left their offspring in the country, or if they bothered to bring them, consigned their care to the nursery staff. He couldn't remember hearing that some lady had missed an entertainment to care for a sick child. Was Miss Hasterling *required* to act as unpaid help for her sister?

He would have to discreetly enquire about her circumstances. He hadn't needed her comment about repairing the hem of her gown to notice that the frock she wore was neither new nor in the latest kick of fashion. Having accompanied Lucinda on numerous forays to her favoured modistes—and paid for many of the gowns—Giles knew more than he cared to about current styles.

If Miss Hasterling were in financial straits, she might be even more desperate to land a husband than most girls. Desperate enough to settle for an older, wealthy husband rather than the passionate, handsome younger one such a lady would probably prefer.

'How very…compassionate of you to nurse them,' he said at last, trying to keep the scepticism from his voice. 'You must enjoy the entertainments you have been able to attend even more, then.'

She gave him a sharp look, as if she'd noted his tone. 'I enjoy music, dancing and the theatre. But I most enjoy the opportunity the Season allows to spend time with my friends, Lady Margaret and Lady Laura Pomeroy. Since my family resides near Plymouth, Lady Margaret's family estate is in Somerset and Lady Laura's in Warwickshire, during other times of the year we must settle for correspondence.'

'How did you come to be friends, if you hail from such widely dispersed locations?'

'We met during our debut Seasons last year.'

'So this is your second Season. And have none of you yet found a gentleman to your taste?'

A look of annoyance passing swiftly over her face, she opened her lips as if to respond, then hesitated before saying, 'Not yet.'

He waited in vain for her to continue. Exasperated by her silence, he was about to speak again himself when, with a determined smile, she seemed to rouse herself. 'And you, my lord?' she said at last. 'Although I met your father last Season, I don't recall seeing you at any entertainments then. Or this year, until today.'

He hadn't been present at many, happily deferring to Lucinda's preference for political gatherings. He'd gritted his teeth through the few balls they had attended together, for with her dazzling beauty, she immediately became the focus of every gentleman in any room she entered. It was annoying enough at small events, for she enjoyed the attention and responded by flirting with any man who caught her interest. And a *ton* crush contained far too many.

Such occasions had frequently led to quarrels afterwards. She'd mocked his jealousy even as she exploited it, telling him no one would ever lock her away again as her first husband had, but that shouldn't cause him any concern. She would always choose him over any other gallant.

Several times, she'd dallied with another man before choosing to come back. He'd agonised over the lapses until, with her seductive charm, she'd soothed him into forgetting them. Or rather, succeeded in getting him to force them from the forefront of his mind, though the memories—and the hurt they caused—always lingered just beyond the edge of consciousness.

Soon, he'd put an end to that bitter, fruitless cycle.

He suddenly realised that while he'd been silent, lost in memory, Miss Hasterling had been patiently awaiting his response, her large dark eyes fixed on his face. Vexed with himself for letting thoughts of Lucinda distract him yet again, he said shortly, 'No, I've not gone about in society very much.'

'Your father mentioned you'd taken over supervising the family estate, which has kept you out of London. Do you prefer the country?'

'Until recently, I've preferred the city.'

She gave him a tiny frown. 'Then I'm surprised I've not encountered you—oh, but of course. Your father did say that you don't much favour society events. One can hardly blame you, when there are so many other entertainments available to a single gentleman. Gatherings and performances at musical, theatrical, sporting and philosophical societies, Tattersall's, gentleman's clubs. Do you share your father's enjoyment of theatre and books, or are you more given to sporting pursuits?'

He could hardly admit that his primary activity had been the ardent pursuit of a beautiful, capricious lady. 'Though I enjoy reading, I'm no scholar, not like Papa. Though I do attend the theatre, I would prefer to be outside, riding in the park or driving in the country.'

Lucinda wasn't much of a horsewoman, but she'd always enjoyed having him take her on drives outside the city. Especially to snug little inns for an afternoon tryst. The ghost of a bittersweet smile curved his lips before he realised that Miss Hasterling was doing more interrogating of him than he was of her.

Determined to refocus on his need to learn more about the lady, he said, 'And you, Miss Hasterling? Do you enjoy riding, or are you completely absorbed in your books?'

He tried to keep the scepticism from his voice, but she gave him another sharp glance, as if she suspected him of doubting her self-proclaimed scholarship. Beneath that innocent ingenue façade, she possessed a keen discernment, he noted grudgingly.

She didn't take him to task for his mistrustful tone, though, responding simply, 'I love to ride and very much miss having a daily gallop. But it was much too expensive to bring my mare to the city.'

Noting that further evidence of her limited means, he continued, 'What other activities have you found to take its place?'

'Just the usual round of social events. As those do not interest you, nothing worth mentioning.'

He paused, but again she'd fallen silent. Annoyed that apparently he was going to have to keep the conversation flowing, he continued, 'Come, tell me more. I'd like to hear about your pursuits.'

She raised her eyebrows. 'I can't think why. You would doubtless find a description of the teas, musicales, and soirées I've attended only a little less tedious than my nattering on about my delightful nieces and nephews. Surely it would pass the time more pleasantly if you were to tell me about your own activities.'

A female who didn't want to talk about herself, even when pressed? That was, in his experience, also rare. His interest sharpened in spite of himself, he said, 'You seem very much involved with your family. Tell me more about them.'

At this, her eyes brightened, though her expression remained wary. 'Only if you are quite sure you wish to know.'

With his desire to discern how pressing was her need to marry—and discover as much as he could about her preferred suitors—he could certainly promise her that. 'I do indeed. A lady who misses social events to tend her sister's ill children, who prizes time in the city more so she may visit friends than to attend parties, must spring from a remarkable family.'

'Well—if you insist. They are very dear to me. My father Robert, as I've said, is a clergyman and cousin to the Earl of Winterstone. My mother, the former Esther Lyons, is a clergyman's daughter—her uncle is

Lord Lyons of Lyondale. My sponsor is my eldest sister, Lady Dunbarton, who married Sir George Dunbarton of Farnworth; they have the three children over whom I dote. Her husband, a confirmed countryman, prefers to remain at home tending his property, though he does pay us frequent visits.

'My next eldest sister, Mrs Abigail Needham, is recently married and lives at her husband's estate near Bath. Still at home in Saltash are Samantha, Agatha, Anna and little Penelope. As you can imagine, Papa was delighted after all those girls to finally have a son, my brother Timothy, whom he tutors along with several other young gentlemen.' She smiled. 'Even if school fees weren't ruinous, Papa has such a reputation as a scholar that the boys receive a far better education from him than they would at Eton or Harrow.'

Perhaps so, but they wouldn't be making the friends and connections that would help ensure their futures, Giles thought—and her father must know it. With such a large brood to support, funds would be short, especially if, as Miss Hasterling's dated attire suggested, there was a limited amount of family money to draw upon beyond his clergyman's stipend. With numerous sisters waiting in the wings to be fired off, her parents were doubtless eager for her to wed as soon as possible.

Following the tune dimly in his ear, Giles recognised the music would soon draw to a close. He had only a few moments left to press for as much information as he could. 'Shall I return you to Lady Margaret rather than your sister when the dance ends, as she bid me?' He smiled. 'I'm sure Mr Fullridge would appreciate it. He looked cross with me for leading you out. Did I steal the dance he'd wished to claim?'

'He had not yet asked me to dance, so I cannot know,' she said—but her fair face coloured.

So there was something going on there. 'Are you inclined to favour the gentleman?'

She swung her gaze up to his. 'That is an impertinent question.'

He gave her what he hoped was an ingenuous smile. 'You ladies always say we gentlemen are worse gossips than you are.'

'Not holding with gossip, then, I shall return you no answer.'

The dance ended, perforce requiring him to walk her back to her waiting friends. A transit during which, as she had when he'd led her on to the dance floor, she seemed content to let silence reign between them. Not sure how next to proceed, this time Giles didn't try to make conversation either.

A moment later, they reached her friend, who was still chatting with Fullridge. After giving Giles another suspicious look, the gentleman smiled at Miss Hasterling. 'You must be thirsty after the rousing efforts of the waltz! Allow me to escort you to take some refreshment.'

'Yes, do,' Lady Margaret encouraged. 'I know Mr Fullridge is longing to talk with you.'

Miss Hasterling hesitated—about to confess she'd recently had a glass of wine, and didn't need another? But then she said, 'I should be honoured,' and offered the older man her hand.

As he claimed it, she looked up at the man and smiled—a genuine smile which, he had to admit, enhanced her Madonna-like features into something damnably appealing. With her appearance so different from Lucinda's—her beauty subtle rather than showy, her stature petite rather than tall and willowy, her soft curls brunette rather than blonde, her large eyes deep brown rather than pure spring bluebell—he'd not at first paid much attention to her physical attributes.

The surprising strength of the attraction that tightened his body now brought home that along with her unspoiled, English rose sort of beauty, she possessed a subtle sensual charm.

No wonder that combination of innocence and muted sensuality intrigued his father.

As Fullridge led her off, he called after her, 'I shall look forward to calling upon you tomorrow.'

She gave him only a nod—not another of the charming smiles she'd bestowed upon Fullridge. Giles found himself once again unaccountably piqued.

She certainly wasn't trying to charm *him*. Or did she consider trying to entice a younger gentleman with no interest in society too unlikely of success to bother? Did she intend to focus on older gentlemen? Both Fullridge and his father had seemed quite amenable to being enticed.

She'd neatly avoided answering his final question about whether she smiled on Fullridge. Which showed her to be clever as well as perspicacious. This was no naive ingenue relying solely on her youthful appearance and sweet amiability to charm, able only to chatter about gowns and soirées. If she were setting her cap for the Viscount, she'd be a formidable opponent. The task of protecting his father might prove even more difficult than he'd feared.

If she *had* set her cap for him. Or was she tossing a wider net, encompassing men of wealth but lesser position, like the older Mr Fullridge?

His indelicate probing of her family situation showed

that she probably needed to marry as soon as possible. The Viscount would be a much bigger catch. And was therefore more likely to become the focus of a determined campaign.

If his father seemed as inclined to be conquered as he'd shown himself tonight, Giles was going to be seeing a good deal more of the cryptic, not-as-unworldly-as-she-appeared Miss Hasterling.

Chapter Three

His father left soon after his waltz with Miss Hasterling, allowing Giles to relax his vigil. He remained until Lady Dunbarton and her party departed, slipping into the card room to avoid the dancing but keeping track of which gentlemen *she* stood up with.

Fullridge, twice. A spotty-faced youth who displayed more enthusiasm than skill. The Earl of Atherton, though that gentleman's attention seemed more focused on her friend Lady Margaret. For quite a few of the dances, she remained on the sidelines with the chaperons and other wallflowers.

Which didn't surprise him. Her responses in their conversations indicated that despite her wide-eyed appearance, she didn't lack wit—but society prized idle, flirtatious chatter over silence or short responses. Her beauty was subtle rather than the dazzling sort that would see her celebrated as a Diamond. Prized as much or more was a hefty dowry, and the lack of interest in her on the part of the younger gentlemen suggested hers must be modest indeed.

Which would prompt her to focus her charms on older, wealthy men more interested in a pleasant companion than an exacting Beauty with a large dowry. At least until he learned how intent she was on attracting such a man, he would have to keep watch.

The Viscount having already retired by the time Giles arrived back at their town house on King Street, it was not until breakfast the next morning that he was able to talk with his father.

Well aware that he would need to tread carefully, lest his father take affront and close him out, Giles chatted first of inconsequential matters. Not until after they had both finished their beefsteak did he take a deep breath and broach the topic that concerned him.

'Will you be calling on Miss Hasterling this afternoon? Having danced with her, I owe her a call as well. We might take the carriage together.'

The Viscount raised his eyebrows. 'You have an interest in her?'

'She seems sweet, but quite intelligent,' he answered carefully. 'Somehow…different than most society ladies I've encountered.'

His father laughed shortly. 'If you are comparing her to the lady I think you are, "different" is a compliment.'

Resentment—and a mingled pain and discomfort—flared, but he stifled it. His father had never tried to interfere in his romantic affairs, although the oblique comments he sometimes uttered, like this one, made it clear he'd never approved of Lady Evans. Although Giles should probably admit that his father's misgivings had been wise, the whole matter was still too raw for him to want to discuss.

Irritated to have once again allowed thoughts of Lucinda to distract him, he looked over to see the Viscount regarding him with a speculative expression.

'I grant you, society would never consider Miss Hasterling a Diamond,' his father observed. 'But as a man gets older, he realises there are qualities more important than dazzling beauty. Such as kindness. Empathy. Discretion. Qualities Miss Hasterling appears to possess in abundance.'

Alarm over the warmth in his father's tone drove all other thoughts from his head. The Viscount seemed even more taken by the girl than he'd suspected.

'You believe that on the basis of a single chat? She certainly impressed you!'

His father smiled. 'She did. Are you interested in the maiden? If so, I certainly approve.'

Was his father angling to play matchmaker for him? Eager to discourage that line of thought, he said, 'I'm not ready to set up my nursery yet.'

'More's the pity! I won't live for ever, you know, and I should like to have your children to dandle on my knee before I shuffle off this mortal coil. But if you worry that I'm anxious to set up my own nursery again, you needn't.' Angling his head at Giles, he said mildly, 'You seem to think I'm a doddering old fool who will fall for the first pretty face that offers a lonely old man some sympathy.'

That was close enough to the core of his anxiety that Giles felt himself reddening. 'I don't think that at all. But I would like you to take your time to…to heal before you form any romantic attachments.'

'I shan't jump headlong into anything. I'm not looking to replace your mama, Son. No woman could. I'm not even sure I'm ready to look for a companion. But I have healed enough to at least consider the possibility.'

'Just…be cautious. Make sure you know the lady well before making any commitments.'

'Oh, I shall. Now, I must choose a bouquet to bring

Miss Hasterling.' With the hint of an amused smile, he added, 'Would you like to accompany me to the florist?'

His father's invitation reminded him that, though not required, it was considered courteous for a gentleman to bring flowers when he called on a lady with whom he'd danced. Having never waltzed with anyone but Lucinda, he'd forgotten the protocol.

But most gentleman would simply send a footman to purchase flowers and have them delivered. That his father wanted to choose the blooms in person revived his concern.

'Yes, I should like to join you. We could pay the call afterwards.'

So I can see how you present the bouquet and how she receives it.

'My man of business is visiting here first. I'll let you know when I'm ready.'

'I shall be in the library, going over some estate records.'

His father nodded, then set down his coffee cup and rose. Pausing on the threshold, he looked back to give Giles another curiously speculative look. Shaking his head with a little chuckle, he said, 'Until later, then.'

Giles frowned, not sure what his father's odd expression meant, but the Viscount walked away before he could decide whether or not to ask him. Dismissing the matter, he poured himself another cup of coffee.

He didn't usually go out early. Lucinda wasn't an early riser, so he was always able to accomplish whatever errands he needed in the afternoon before calling on her in the evening.

A call he hadn't made since the incident of the brandished bracelet. By now, she would probably be expecting him, well aware of how, in the past, she'd drawn him back to her even after he'd vowed to keep his distance.

Once in her presence, she somehow always managed to beguile him into abandoning that resolve—though her attentions never fully assuaged his frustration and pain. Which was why, though he was pretty certain this time he *could* successfully break with her, thus far he'd avoided seeing her again.

Could she beguile him anew? Clear as the need to end their relationship seemed to him now, he wasn't yet sure enough of his ability to withstand the hold she always exerted over him. He'd continue to avoid her a while longer, not making the final visit until he was sure he would be able to resist any blandishments she might offer.

He would need to see her one more time to break off the relationship for good. They had meant too much to each other for too long for him to take the coward's way out and send her only a farewell note accompanied by a bauble. She deserved to hear his decision from his own lips.

In happier matters, after his chat with the Viscount just now, he felt more confident about his father's situation. He was still certain the Viscount had not yet fully recovered emotionally, but Markham seemed to realise it was too soon for him to press forward with any relationship.

Giles would observe him during their call today to see if his behaviour with Miss Hasterling confirmed that assessment—and observe hers, to determine whether she seemed to be trying to entice his father. If not, he would feel safe abandoning his watchdog role—at least with Miss Hasterling.

He'd still need to keep watch to counter the potential

moves of any other predatory females who might seek to take advantage of his father.

Later that afternoon, Eliza sat on the sofa in her sister's parlour, only half listening while Lady Dunbarton talked with the several friends who had called. She was fairly certain Lord Markham would follow through on his promise to visit today…but would his son accompany him?

She'd be quite happy to greet the Viscount again. Whether or not he might harbour romantic inclinations—which she doubted—with his easy manners and enthusiasm for scholarship, he reminded her so much of her beloved papa, she felt quite comfortable in his company.

The same could not be said for his son.

Just thinking of the Baron sent a nervous prickling over her skin and set off discomforting eddies in her stomach. Because his subtle sense of suspicion unsettled her? Because the strong attraction he aroused reminded her too keenly of the unfortunate episode with George? Or because, despite his unspoken disapproval and the common sense that warned she must resist him, when he was near, she had trouble concentrating on anything but his physical appeal?

Her disjointed attempt at conversation with him had been proof enough of that, she thought, her face warming as she thought how disappointed her sister would have been with that performance.

Hopefully, she wouldn't have the need to repeat it.

She'd just settled her unease with that soothing conclusion when the butler bowed himself in and announced, 'Viscount Markham and Lord Stratham.'

Her heart skipped a beat as an almost painful shock shot through her. Meanwhile, Lady Dunbarton smiled in delight and her other two guests looked towards the doorway, avid curiosity in their gazes.

Fortunately, the exchange of curtsies, bows, and conventional greetings gave her time to repair her shattered composure—which she did while giving herself a stern rebuke. Nothing about a simple call should upset her, she chided herself. Calling upon a lady with whom a gentleman had danced was a common courtesy, while Markham had previously indicated he meant to visit.

She would converse with their guests like the intelligent female she liked to consider herself and not embarrass her sister by acting like a ninny. No matter how much the air between herself and Stratham seemed to almost crackle with electricity, like the atmosphere after a nearby lightning strike.

Smoothing her expression into what she hoped was a serene smile, she accepted the cheery bouquet of late daffodils and forget-me-nots offered by Lord Markham and one from Stratham with an assortment of pure white blooms.

Apparently her sister's guests knew Markham well, for they greeted him fondly and immediately drew him into conversation. Which left her to entertain Lord Stratham.

Trying to eradicate the unpleasant sensation of swallows thrashing about in the cage of her stomach, she dawdled as long as possible over the bouquets, giving the maid she summoned unnecessarily detailed instructions on how to trim the blooms, what sort of vase in which to display them, etc. Finally finding no further excuse to postpone it, she dismissed the maid and turned back to Stratham.

Dredging up another smile, she said, 'The flowers are lovely. How very thoughtful of you to bring them.'

'Nowhere near as lovely as their recipient.'

Surprised at the praise, she frowned, suspecting him of mockery. Though she was woefully conscious of how strongly he attracted her, he'd previously given her no reason to believe she affected him. But disputing the comment might cause a confrontation she'd rather avoid, so she said only, 'You are most kind.'

She then struggled for words, trying to resolve the desire to not appear a monosyllabic featherhead with the contradictory impulses to at once curtail and on the other hand prolong the conversation.

As she dithered, after giving her a rather exasperated look, Stratham said, 'The ball was very enjoyable, did you not think?'

Hardly a brilliant beginning, but better than she had managed, and one that finally shook her brain out of its paralysis. 'Y-yes. Lady Eversham's entertainments are…are always enjoyable. Excellent refreshments, superior musicians, and an agreeable mix of guests.'

'So there were. I was honoured to meet your friend Lady Margaret. She seems a most exceptional lady; Lord Atherton certainly appears to think so.'

The mention of dear Maggie eased her nervousness and prompted the wisp of a smile. 'I believe he does,' she confirmed, relaxing a bit.

'Perhaps one of your debut friends has found her spouse, then.'

'Not necessarily. Lady Margaret emphatically does not intend to marry, and as a widower with an heir and several spares, Atherton doesn't have much interest in wedlock, either.'

'Indeed! Is your other friend—Lady Laura Pomeroy, I believe you named her—also so opposed to marriage?'

'Not at all,' she said. Though she was still intensely

conscious of Stratham, thankfully, speaking about her friends calmed her and made it easier to ignore the disturbing feelings he evoked. 'Lady Laura surprised us by falling in love with a banker's son, the brother of a young lady she's befriended. She just yesterday confided that they intend to wed soon.'

'A banker's son?' he echoed, sounding shocked. 'Is her family's position powerful enough for her to avoid being ostracised by society for making such a misalliance?'

Eliza shook her head. 'Although she's a marquess's daughter, her father comes from a junior branch of the family, and she wasn't raised to occupy a high station. She's also quite unique—a mathematical genius who attends philosophical society lectures and talks enthusiastically about Mr Babbage's Difference Engine. She intends to marry quietly, withdraw from society and assist her husband in his banking business.'

Stratham's eyes widened. 'One a mathematician, the other a female set against marriage? Do you share your friends' unusual opinions?'

Eliza laughed. 'I'm afraid I'm quite ordinary, with no exceptional talents.'

'Not even reading Petrarch?'

She gave him a suspicious look, once again suspecting him of mocking her. Choosing her words with care, she replied, 'Perhaps I enjoy scholarship more than other young ladies. Only because, despairing of a son after the arrival of five daughters, my father found me the most receptive of my sisters to sharing his love of literature, and was eager to teach me. But I've no aspirations beyond the hope that I may marry a man I can love and respect.'

'Regardless of his age?'

So he did still suspect her of trying to entice his father! Trying to restrain a growing anger that happily further blunted his physical appeal, she said stiffly, 'I hope to find a loving relationship such as my parents share, based on similar background—he is a clergyman, she was a clergyman's daughter—and mutual interests. It's not essential that a prospective husband be of an age, but preferable, probably. I would like children of my own.' Not that it was really any of *his* business.

Before Stratham could continue his impertinent questioning, the butler entered the drawing room to announce the arrival of Mr Fullridge and another of Lady Maggie's prospects for her, Mr Garthorpe.

Irritated to find herself as much regretful as relieved that the newcomers' arrival would prompt an end to her solo chat with Stratham, she rose to curtsy and sent them a welcoming smile. 'Good to see you, gentlemen.'

After responding in kind, the two men walked over to pay their respects to their hostess. Their greetings to Stratham had been noticeably cooler, Eliza noted. Neither could truly consider Stratham a rival—could they?

While she wondered, the Viscount detached himself from the group around her sister and approached them. With a nod to Stratham, Markham said, 'Your sister tells me this property boasts a charming garden. Would you care to stroll there with me, Miss Hasterling?'

Markham would want more privacy than was offered by her sister's drawing room to thank her again for her ballroom rescue, Eliza figured. Firmly dismissing any lingering regret at ending her conversation with Stratham, she gave Markham a bright smile.

'A stroll would be delightful.'

Then, with a nod to his son, she took Markham's proffered arm.

As they walked away, she felt Stratham's sharp gaze like a beam of sunlight burning into her back until the footman closed the door behind them.

Chapter Four

The next morning, Eliza was happy to answer Lady Margaret's unexpected summons to call on her in Portman Square. The visit offered a welcome opportunity to unburden herself about her troubling situation.

She hadn't wished to discuss her agitation with her sister; Lady Dunbarton would only urge her to encourage all potential courtships. But with her friend, she could speak with candour about Markham's unexpected attention, which led to Stratham's curious blend of courtesy and veiled disapproval.

If it was disapproval. Stratham's presence affected her so strongly, she knew her normal equilibrium was disturbed whenever he was near.

Maggie, a keen but disinterested observer, could advise her on how best to deal with both father and son. Undoubtedly, Eliza thought, a smile lightening her sense of unease, while pressing her to give more consideration to Fullridge and Galthorpe, Maggie's preferred candidates.

She'd have to be careful how she worded her request, though, for she didn't want even her dear friend to realise how effectively Stratham aroused her senses and confused her thinking. Especially when Maggie would

surely point out that after Eliza's distressing experience
with George, she should know better than to let herself
be attracted to a deviously charming aristocrat.

Maggie jumped up to meet her as Eliza followed the
butler into the morning room, giving her a hug before
instructing Viscering to bring refreshments.

'Are we not going to wait for Laura?' Eliza asked. 'I
assumed you'd asked her to call, too.' She gave Maggie
a wry grin. 'Which is fortunate! I can talk to you both
about my…situation.'

'No, Laura isn't joining us, although she is the reason I asked you to come with such urgency,' Maggie
answered as she led Eliza to the sofa. 'I received a note
from her this morning, informing me that Mr Roch-
dale has already procured a special licence. They plan
to marry in two weeks' time and wish afterwards to
establish their own household, rather than remain with
her father. In the interim, she expects to be fully occupied hunting for a suitable property and making ar-
rangements for furnishings and staff.'

'All this to warn us she is withdrawing from any further participation in the Season?' Eliza guessed.

Maggie blew out a breath. 'Sadly for us, yes.'

Lady Margaret fell silent, nor could Eliza think of
anything to say. The sudden realisation that Laura's
marriage would take their friend away from them hit
her like a blow to the stomach. 'Do you feel as…bereft
as I do?' Eliza asked after a moment.

Maggie wiped at what looked suspiciously like a tear.
'I do. Oh, I knew in my head that when the two of you
married, your husbands and families would displace our
friendship. I just hadn't expected it to happen this soon.'

Eliza pressed her hand. 'Nothing will ever *displace*

our friendship! But with husbands and families, priorities, and the amount of time one can devote to friends, must change.'

'But she did write that if our social engagements allowed, she would appreciate our accompanying her and advising her on her selections.'

'We shall make the time! I'd enjoy immensely helping her set up her household.'

'As you have better domestic instincts than I, your advice will be of more value. Caregiver that you are, I expect you will be in your element.'

Eliza shrugged. 'I shall never be a force in society, like you are, and I'm certainly not a genius like Laura. I'm just…ordinary. My sole hope is to establish a home of my own and nurture a family I can make happy and comfortable. Even if that is not a very elevated aspiration.'

Maggie pressed her hand back. 'Nothing a female can do is more important than creating a strong, loving family and raising confident children to lead the next generation. As I, who grew up amid conflict and chaos, can certainly attest. But enough about Laura and marriage! When you first arrived, you said something about needing to talk about your "situation". What situation?'

Maggie's eyes brightened. 'Are you finding Fullridge attractive? You did have a rather long chat with him. I should be ecstatic if at least one of my friends were to follow my advice to marry a rich older man who might soon make her a rich widow.'

Eliza laughed. 'Fullridge seems nice enough,' she admitted. 'But…that was not what I wanted to ask about.'

'What, then?' Before Eliza could decide how to phrase her answer, Maggie frowned. 'Is it Markham? He seems congenial, but possessing such high rank, he's rather above your touch, as well as being the sort of titled man I'd have you avoid. And surely you're not attracted to Stratham! He's as arrogant and assured of his own worth as every other aristocrat. And after your unfortunate experience…'

'You needn't worry,' Eliza assured her. 'George cured me at a young age of ever again trusting the intentions of a high-born gentleman.'

Maggie gave a disdainful laugh. 'I should think so! "How presumptuous of you, Miss Hasterling, to claim you thought my regard serious,"' she mimicked in a high-pitched voice. '"An earl's son and a vicar's daughter? Absurd!" I wonder that you didn't plant him a facer on the spot.'

Eliza smiled wryly. 'An excellent idea—if I hadn't been too disbelieving and devastated to do more than gape at him. I was only sixteen, after all, and thoroughly convinced after all our rides and talks that he was as much in love with me as I was with him. And once the disbelief faded, I was too humiliated. Indeed, had we not happened upon him last Season, I would never have confessed the unfortunate affair, even to you.'

Maggie pressed her hand, sympathy in her gaze. 'When I saw how dismayed you were when we encountered him, I had to know the reason. What are friends for, but to help one through the bleak times?'

'It was long ago, and I'm over it now,' Eliza said stoutly, firmly suppressing the hard knot of misery and humiliation she'd never quite succeeded in eradicating.

Although that experience didn't seem to have made her immune to Stratham's appeal.

'If it isn't Markham or Stratham disturbing you, what is?' Maggie asked.

'Well, it is them, but not in the way you're prob-

ably thinking.' Quickly Eliza summarised her rescue
of the Viscount, his gratitude for her timely intervention, and the call paid on her by both father and son.
She described the walk in the garden with Markham
during which he thanked her again for the assistance
she'd rendered and the deception she'd engaged in to
spare him embarrassment.

'I should think he would be grateful,' Lady Maggie
said. 'Having Lady Arbuthnot observe one in an embarrassing situation? That dragon would have gleefully
spread the story all over the *ton* before the night was
out. And clever of you to come up with an excuse so
readily—even if it did give the woman the opportunity
to criticise you. Well done, Eliza!'

Blushing a little at her friend's praise, Eliza said,
'Stratham has become rather attentive, but only, I suspect, to figure out whether I have designs on the Viscount. Since I imagine his father did not confess his
near accident, it must seem suspicious to Stratham that
his father suddenly began singling me out. You should
have seen his response when Markham asked me to
walk with him in the garden!'

She laughed. 'I half expected he would catch his father's sleeve to prevent him leaving with me. I'm not
sure whether to be insulted Stratham thinks I'm conniv-
ing enough to try to entice a gentleman or flattered that
he thinks I'm attractive enough that I might succeed.'

'How presumptuous of Stratham to suspect you on
such slim evidence!'

'What do I do now, though? If I want to disabuse
Stratham's suspicions, I shall have to avoid Markham,
and I've already agreed to him paying another call. I
don't want to slight or insult him just because his son
harbours a false impression of my intentions.'

'Stratham has no more right to challenge your behaviour than he does to question his father's! Even if you did have designs on Markham, that's the Viscount's business. It's not for his son to interfere.'

'Perhaps you could take Stratham aside and advise him of that fact?' Then she held up her hand. 'No, don't, I beg you! I was only teasing…and you might truly do so.'

'So I might,' Maggie said stoutly. 'Especially if Stratham continues to bedevil my dear friend. Though I still hope to interest you in Fullridge or Garthorpe. Oh, I know you aren't much taken by my strategy of marrying an older, wealthy man, but only think, Eliza, how much you could do for your sisters when they debut, for your whole family, if you were a wealthy, well-placed society wife! Think what you would be able to do for yourself, eventually, as a wealthy widow.'

'You may think me a poor honey, but I'd still rather end up merely comfortable, married to a good man I can love and respect.'

'They always say it's as easy to fall in love with a rich man as a poor one. And you've not yet found anyone you particularly favour, have you?'

The vision of Stratham's tall form and compelling dark eyes flashed into her head. Firmly pushing it away, she said, 'That's true enough.'

'Well, we shall not settle this now. If you will not let me confront Stratham, how would you like me to help?'

'There's nothing you can do if Stratham attaches himself when Markham next calls on me. But I did inform the Viscount when we walked in the garden that I would be attending Mrs Chiverton's musicale not tomorrow but the night after. After he told me that playing pianoforte duets was one of his family's favourite evening activities, I... I said I'd consider performing one with him.'

Maggie raised her eyebrows, and Eliza felt her face heat. 'I begin to understand Stratham's concern,' she said archly. 'You could have found some excuse to demur. Are you sure you don't want to encourage the Viscount?'

'It seemed impolite to rebuff him, and I do very much enjoy playing. And you know I'm hopeless at finding the words to avoid accepting invitations I have no compelling reason to refuse.'

'Which is why Alborne trips all over your hem so often,' Maggie acknowledged with a despairing shake of her head. 'Besides, your sister would doubtless have chided you if she learned you had rebuffed a prominent potential suitor whose attentions might encourage other men to notice and then pursue you. Well, there's nothing to be done about it now. Do you want me to lure Stratham away if he tries to hover over you?'

The thought of the Baron loitering at her elbow as she played—looming over her, filling the air beside her with the subtle scent of his shaving soap, making her acutely conscious of his silent presence—sent a surge of excitement and trepidation through her. With him looking on, how would she not stumble over all the notes?

Swallowing hard to calm the agitation produced by such a vision, she said, 'Yes, please, don't let him hover. I'd play every note wrong.'

'I'll do my best. Perhaps I'll put a bug in his ear about leaving his father to make his own romantic decisions.'

Imagining the forthright Maggie lecturing Stratham, Eliza grinned. 'You would have to do that within my hearing, though. I'd love to see his reaction.'

'You know I don't let any man intimidate me,' Maggie

said with a sniff. 'If my father and all his threats couldn't deter me, I'll hardly be cowed by a mere baron's drawing room rebuttal. Very well, I shall mark the musicale in my diary. Now we need to decide when we can meet to help Laura with her house plans. Would you be free tomorrow afternoon?'

Eliza nodded, then felt the sadness begin to steal over her again. 'I shall be happy to help Laura…start her new life.'

Would she ever have the chance to do the same?

'She won't be totally leaving us behind, remember. Perhaps she and her new husband could give me such good investment advice that I can make a handsome profit at the stock market. Enough to engage you as my companion, if I don't succeed in marrying you off! I know your family can't afford to give you another Season, and I refuse to have you settle for marrying someone you cannot respect or becoming a drudge at the beck and call of needy relations.'

Touched, Eliza felt the burn of tears. 'That's very kind, but I'd not want to become a burden on you, either.'

'Friends would never be a burden. What a pair we would make, two eccentric spinsters setting society on its ear! But amusing as I find that prospect, it isn't what you want for your future. The Season isn't over; there's no reason to concede defeat yet. Perhaps upon further acquaintance, you will find Fullridge as charming as he already finds you.'

Eliza wasn't as sanguine about that possibility as Maggie. Might some other young man come along to charm her? She'd not given up hope—but after a Season and a half, those hopes had dimmed. Alborne paid her particular attention, but though she might take pity and dance with him, she'd rather become a spinster than marry him. Other young men had occasionally flirted with her or asked her to dance, but with her modest looks and even more modest dowry, none was attracted enough to pay her serious court.

And none save one impossible Baron made her pulse race or prickled her skin with awareness.

Should she abandon the dream of a young husband and give Fullridge and Maggie's other candidates serious consideration, thanking her family for their gift of two Seasons by ending this one wed? Could she be happy pledging herself to a kind and admirable man in a marriage of convenience? Or was it wiser to resist a loveless union and repay her family by offering them a lifetime of service?

Sighing, she shook her head. She still could not make up her mind which alternative would be better. And time was running out.

Chapter Five

Two nights later, Eliza accompanied her sister into Mrs Chiverton's drawing room. 'Since our hostess made it known that all attendees should be willing to perform if called upon, young ladies with only rudimentary skills will not be present,' Lady Dunbarton said. 'Which means you, with your superior abilities—'

'Will face much less competition,' Eliza inserted with a grin.

'Will have an opportunity to shine, regardless of the competition,' her sister amended with a reproving look.

After greeting their hostess, they joined the rest of the guests, who were chatting and enjoying light refreshments. Just after them, Lady Margaret walked in with her mother, the Countess of Comeryn, escorted by Mr Fullridge.

While Eliza walked over to greet her friends, Maggie halted, gazing around her. 'I don't see Markham or Stratham,' she murmured as she exchanged a hug with Eliza.

'They've not arrived—yet. Just as well if they don't! Or at least, not Stratham. I'll be much more comfortable if I don't have to play under his gimlet stare.'

Fullridge left his place beside the Countess, who was

now chatting with Eliza's sister, to approach them and bow. 'I hope to have the delight of hearing you play, Miss Hasterling. Lady Margaret tells me you are quite talented.'

'I do enjoy the pianoforte. Do you play yourself, Mr Fullridge?'

'No, alas. I'm sausage-fingered, I'm afraid. I very much enjoy listening, though.'

Nodding towards their hostess, who was directing her guests towards the music room where a harp and a pianoforte stood ready, he continued, 'Ladies, shall we take our seats?'

Perhaps Markham—and Stratham—were not going to attend after all. Eliza told herself she felt only relief—and suppressed a curious lowering of the spirits she refused to call disappointment.

Fullridge maintained a light conversation while they selected their places, Eliza making sure her friend sat beside her. If she were going to entertain one of Maggie's prospects, she wanted her friend nearby to assist if necessary.

It was the second time she'd had a more extensive conversation with Fullridge. He was pleasing in appearance—tall, his posture erect, his face pleasant rather than handsome and only slightly lined, his brown hair stylishly brushed. His evening wear was impeccably tailored but classic, avoiding the nipped-in jackets and flaring trousers currently the height of gentleman's fashion. And he conversed easily, with a quiet charm and a self-confidence devoid of arrogance.

Was he a man she could contemplate marrying?

He seemed both honourable and amiable—but of course, he would be. Maggie would have had her mother, the Countess, comb her vast network of contacts to thoroughly screen any possible candidates before recommending them.

Was he honourable and amiable enough? A man she could respect and perhaps grow to love? Even if she felt none of the dizzying crescendo of excitement sitting beside him that came over her when Stratham was near?

She had to admit, before she'd experienced the awareness-inciting, hollow-in-the-pit-of-her-stomach, tingling-in-every-nerve arousal elicited by the Baron, she might have felt confident that a strong sensual attraction was not important in a long-term relationship, if affection and respect were present.

Now she felt that such a relationship would be...lacking, if she must live her whole life without it.

But no matter how much he attracted her, Stratham was not a possible choice, even if she managed to convince him she didn't have designs on his father. She must never forget George's harshly taught lesson—that Eliza Hasterling, with her small dowry and undistinguished pedigree, was not a suitable match for a viscount's heir. He might flirt and toy with her, but any serious attentions would be directed elsewhere.

Although once Stratham realised she wasn't trying to charm his father, he would likely drop the acquaintance in a heartbeat.

A touch to her shoulder startled her out of those ruminations. 'Miss Hasterling, I apologise for our late arrival!' Markham's voice announced. 'I'm sorry to have forfeited the chance to converse with you before the music begins.'

She turned to smile over her shoulder at the Viscount. 'I'm glad you have arrived before the performances start, so you do not miss any. And you, Lord Stratham,' she added when, with a shock that sent a jolt of awareness through her, she noticed the son walking up behind his father.

She put a hand on her stomach, trying to still the annoying avian acrobatics that had erupted within.

Stay calm, she scolded herself. *Conversing with Markham or Fullridge does not alarm you. And there's no requirement for you to spend any time with Stratham.*

Suppressing the nervousness, she continued, 'You'll remember the Countess, her daughter, my friend Lady Margaret, and Mr Fullridge.'

'Please, ladies, keep your seats,' Markham said. 'We shall find our own in a moment. Countess, what a delightful surprise to see you back in London! For far too long you've not graced us with your presence.'

'All my daughter's doing,' Lady Comeryn replied, giving Lady Margaret a fond smile. 'She insisted we come to London for the Season. It's wonderful to be here again.'

'I—and all of society—am very glad to welcome you back. But I see our hostess motioning the musicians to begin, so we must find our places.' He looked back down at Eliza. 'I hope I will have the pleasure of hearing you play?'

She felt herself flush, Stratham's steady gaze heating her like an open flame. 'I shall perform if called upon.'

'Perhaps you would also honour me by playing that duet we talked about?' Markham continued.

'Perhaps we can.'

'I, too, should very much like to hear you play,' Stratham added.

After bowing again, father and son went to claim a chair. Eliza found her gaze following them. Had Stratham added a slight emphasis on 'you', as in he'd prefer her to play—alone? Or that he doubted her musical ability, as he doubted her scholarship?

Or was the nervous agitation he caused once again making her only imagine that hint of disapproval?

She turned back to her companions. She might not be sure of Stratham's reaction, but she wasn't imagining the frown on Fullridge's face as he watched the Viscount and the Baron take their seats, reminding her of his expression the day the gentlemen had called on her sister.

Did Fullridge consider them competitors for her regard? Was his own regard that serious?

If it was, should she encourage him? She was by now certain she could like him—but could she like him well enough to marry him?

She would have to give the matter serious consideration, if he did continue to press his attentions, since no hitherto unknown, dashing young man had appeared in the last two days to capture her interest.

Though even if such a one should magically appear in the short space between now and the Season's end, with her modest appearance and lack of dowry and connections, she thought ruefully, he'd be unlikely to be interested in *her*.

She hadn't initially taken Maggie's Grand Plan seriously, but with time ticking away, she ought to. And settle in her own mind what she preferred for her future: the security of a stable but unexciting marriage to a kind provider, or refusal to settle for less than a genuine, heartfelt love—even if that meant remaining unwed.

The musicians' opening chord interrupted her reflections. She looked over to see a pair of young ladies beginning a popular song, accompanied by pianoforte and harp. Both instruments and voices being pleasing, she pushed the worries from her mind and gave herself over to the music.

* * *

At the first break, Lord Markham approached her party in the refreshment room. With impeccable manners, he didn't immediately single her out, but made general conversation with the group. His son, for once, did not hover at his father's elbow, instead making the rounds of the assembly, speaking with various acquaintances. But every time Eliza chanced a quick glance at him, he seemed to be looking at her. Once, she even accidentally met his gaze, triggering a wave of heat that sent a prickly awareness through her—and a flush of embarrassment, that he might think she'd been studying him as assiduously as he seemed to be studying her.

Even if it were true, she didn't want him to realise it.

At length, with the Countess engaging Fullridge in talk about the apple harvest on his estate and with Maggie chatting with another friend, Markham turned to smile on her. 'What do you intend to play when you are called upon?'

'Mr Neate's *Capriccio*, or perhaps a Haydn piece.'

'Excellent! I do admire Neate's compositions. Do you happen to know Schubert's *Sonata in C major* for four hands?' At her nod, he continued, 'Once you finish your solo performance, might you play it with me? Although I fear I'm somewhat out of practice. I've not played since…'

His words trailed off. From the sudden sadness of his expression, she knew immediately what he'd been going to say. In her desire to banish the grief painted on his face, she forgot her half-formed resolve to avoid reinforcing Stratham's suspicions by performing with his father. 'I'm sure you would be excellent, and yes, I would enjoy accompanying you in the Schubert,' she said impulsively. 'It's a lovely piece.'

He rewarded her with a smile that tempered his grief. 'Thank you! I shall enjoy that.'

Eliza stifled a sigh. She hoped the satisfaction of cheering Markham would be worth the potential disapproval their duet might arouse in his son.

Then a stern resolve rallied her. She wasn't setting her cap for the Viscount. It wasn't *enticement* for her to perform with Markham, especially if doing so helped ease the sadness of losing his wife.

If their playing together bothered Stratham, he could just get over it.

The intermission concluded, after the next group of musicians had performed, Mrs Chiverton looked to Eliza. 'Miss Hasterling, would you honour us now?'

Eliza nodded. 'It would be my pleasure.'

'Be brilliant,' Maggie whispered as she rose from her seat.

Fullridge rose, too. 'May I turn the pages for you?'

She was about to reply that she didn't need any assistance, being accustomed at home to turning the pages herself. But Fullridge gave her an engaging smile accompanied by such a look of entreaty, she couldn't make herself refuse. 'That would be helpful, thank you.'

As she walked to the pianoforte, she sneaked a glance at Stratham—and realised, with another tingling shock, that he was still watching her intently. As she took her place and prepared to play, she could almost feel his gaze on her back.

Her nerves fluttered, making her fingers tremble. Then a wave of anger displaced her unease. She didn't need to impress Stratham or fret about his opinion of her. *She* knew her intentions towards his father were innocent; she'd not let his scrutiny diminish her pleasure in playing—or make her nervous enough to falter and make mistakes. She would not allow him to spoil her enjoyment of the music she loved.

Her turbulent emotions eased as soon as she moved her hands in the familiar opening chords. Soon, she was caught up in the melodious beauty of the piece she knew so well, she hardly needed to glance at the pages Fullridge turned for her.

As the harmonies filled her ears and resonated in her chest, her worries about whether or not to take a husband for security alone faded. Even her sadness at perhaps giving up for ever the girlhood dream of finding a man whom she could love with all her being dissolved, replaced by the pure joy of the music. As she played the final chords, she felt wholly at peace.

It took her a few minutes to emerge from her abstraction and realise the company was clapping enthusiastically. Mrs Chiverton walked over to pat her shoulder. 'Marvellous, my dear, as always! Lord Markham has asked if he might play a duet with you. A request I second with enthusiasm—if you would indulge us.'

'You play like an angel,' said the gentleman himself, who'd approached behind his hostess. Looking down at her with appreciation, he added, 'I only hope my playing won't mar your superior performance.'

She gave him an encouraging smile. 'I am sure you will be just fine. Your fingers will remember the patterns as soon as you begin moving them over the keys.'

'I certainly hope so. Mr Fullridge, you may take a seat. I can turn the pages now, though I am sure the lady appreciated your assistance.'

Looking put out at being dismissed, Fullridge frowned. Wishing to avoid any potential dispute, Eliza said quickly, 'I did indeed appreciate your help. Perhaps I can call on you again later? For now, I should begin the duet. Other musicians are waiting to perform.'

Given no excuse to linger, Fullridge said, 'Perhaps you will take some refreshment with me later, Miss Hasterling. My Lord.' After a bow, he walked off.

'I hope the gentleman will not be too cross with me for purloining you,' Markham said.

'I'm sure he will recover,' Eliza said drily. Though Fullridge did seem interested in pursuing her, she'd not give him exclusive encouragement—yet. Not until she was quite certain that she could envisage him as a potential spouse.

As Markham took his place on the bench, Eliza appreciated his solid, comfortingly masculine presence beside her, as she had Fullridge's. But she felt none of the sizzling spark of connection the nearness of Markham's son engendered.

Damn and blast! Why did her foolish senses sing for a man who was out of her reach, one who seemed to disapprove of her into the bargain? She reminded herself again of her resolve to ignore him and turned her attention to the music.

At her nod, they began. As the piece progressed, she realised Markham was a competent rather than a brilliant pianist. But his enthusiasm and the love of music evident in every line of his body triumphed over mere technical brilliance, making his performance compelling. As the final notes faded, the audience erupted in applause.

'That was wonderful!' Eliza said, smiling up at Markham. 'I'd forgotten how much I enjoy duets in general, and this piece in particular! My sisters prefer singing to playing, you see, so I don't often get to perform the Schubert.'

'Playing with such an accomplished musician was a true delight,' Markham said, smiling back at her. 'I hope we can perform together again very soon.'

'I would like that,' Eliza said—and then felt, rather than saw, Stratham approach. He halted next to the piano bench, and though he stood a foot away, the connection humming between them felt almost as tangible as the smooth pianoforte keys beneath her fingers.

A tingling warmth spread through her body, from the top of her head to the tip of her toes. Although, she thought acidly, after a stolen glance at Stratham's sober face, *that* melody of attraction was most assuredly a solo on her part, not a duet.

'Did you enjoy the Schubert, Son?' Markham asked.

'It's always a pleasure to hear you perform, Father. Miss Hasterling, your technique is impressive. All young ladies play, of course, but you have a real talent.'

Eliza wasn't sure whether to be gratified by his praise or annoyed. Once again, he'd seemed to have doubted her claim of proficiency and been surprised to have it proven. 'Thank you,' she said at last.

'Might I prevail upon you to play Beethoven's *Sonata in D Major*—with me? It's one of my favourites.'

The request drew an approving nod from Markham. 'You should play with Stratham, my dear. He is more talented than I, his skill inherited from his dear mama, who was an excellent musician.'

Play…with Stratham? Sit but a few inches away from him on the piano bench? It had been hard enough to shut out thoughts of him watching her play; how could she possibly concentrate on the music with him right beside her, her pesky nerves vibrating as if she were a harp string he could pluck at will?

'I've already performed twice,' she temporised. 'I should give others a chance.'

'But I've not performed yet. You'd be helping me. Think of it as…a substitute means of turning pages,' Stratham coaxed.

If she were turning pages, she could at least stand a few feet away, rather than sit right beside him. Before she could marshal her muddled thoughts to offer further objections, Markham said, 'Won't you indulge me by agreeing? I do so love the piece! I haven't heard it played for…some time.'

Eliza looked over to see his face once again shadowed by melancholy. Was he remembering his wife performing the Beethoven with his son?

Could she put aside her discomfort at being near Stratham long enough to create a new memory for Markham that might displace the sad ones of his loss?

Her heart wrung in sympathy, she couldn't refuse. No matter how rattled Stratham's presence on the piano bench might make her.

'If it will please you, of course, I must agree,' she capitulated.

'Thank you, my dear,' he murmured, pressing her hand briefly before rising from the bench to clap Stratham on the shoulder. 'You must live up to my praise of your talent, Son.'

'I will endeavour to do so, Father,' Stratham said as he took his seat.

Though she didn't even glance at him, a ripple of sensation washed through her, as if her sensitised nerves could feel the very air he displaced when he sat beside her.

Eliza gritted her teeth. She would *not* let Stratham distract her and ruin her performance of the music his father had requested. No matter how difficult it might be to ignore the response he seemed to draw so easily from her.

Remember what attraction led to with George, she warned herself as she tried to still the tension humming through her body. Stiffening her limbs in defence, she repeated silently, *Focus on the music... Focus on the music...*

Chapter Six

Gazing with growing dismay at the look of…enchantment that came over his father's face while he played the duet with Miss Hasterling, Giles decided he had to do *something*. His father hadn't worn such a rapturous expression since he'd last performed with his wife.

Miss Hasterling was not only a competent musician, she'd succeeded in breaking through the sadness of the Viscount's memories—until tonight, he'd avoided listening to anyone perform, much less expressed any inclination to play himself. Tapping into the love his father had for music seemed to have deepened the Viscount's attraction to the lady.

What if, when the duet ended, his delighted father escorted Miss Hasterling to her seat and remained beside her the rest of evening? Paying her attentions so marked that everyone present would notice them? Raising expectations in society that he had definite interest in the lady? Raising her expectations as well, and those of her family.

Raising expectations the Viscount might then feel obligated to satisfy.

Giles couldn't let the magic of the music lull his father into a making a move that would prematurely obligate him to the lady. For even if the Viscount later realised that, under the spell of melancholy and melody, he'd treated her with an ill-advised partiality, if he felt he'd given Miss Hasterling and society the impression that his intentions were serious, he would not withdraw and expose her to criticism. No matter how much he might later regret his rashness.

The only action Giles could think of to prevent that was to keep Miss Hasterling at the keyboard—though it meant he'd have to share it with her.

Not that sitting beside her would be a hardship. She might not be an accredited Beauty, but he was finding her subtle attractiveness more and more appealing. If Lucinda was like the dazzling spectacle of a multi-coloured sunset streaking the sky with vivid colour, Miss Hasterling was more like the gentle glow of a sun-dappled early morning, the misty air softening the landscape's edges and cloaking everything in soft, muted hues.

She was…soothing. Perhaps that calm was part of what appealed to his father. And if the attraction lasted, he would be the first to approve. But it was too soon to have the Viscount feel honour-bound to single out a woman he knew so slightly.

Before the last chords faded, Giles was on his feet approaching the piano bench, complimenting the performers and then begging the honour of playing with Miss Hasterling himself.

In any event, though once again she looked reluctant to agree, she evidently couldn't find a good enough excuse to wriggle out of it, especially with his father pressing her to play.

Giles felt a momentary pang of conscience as he took his seat. He'd more or less forced Miss Hasterling into this, giving her little chance to demur if she truly didn't wish to perform the piece. As his father took a seat in the audience, he said softly, 'Are you agreeable to playing the Beethoven? It is rather difficult.'

'Are you worried my skill is not up to the task?' she asked tartly. 'I shall endeavour not to embarrass you.'

So the gentle kitten had claws, he thought, amused by her unexpected feistiness. 'I didn't intend to coerce you into playing the piece, if you don't feel comfortable performing it. We could play something else.'

'I think I can manage,' she said, still avoiding looking at him directly. 'If you can.'

Giles suppressed a grin. Was she throwing down the gauntlet? He'd have to show her he was up to the task. 'By all means. I should probably warm up, if you will allow me a few minutes. I've not played in some time.'

'Certainly.' She gestured towards the keyboard. 'Make whatever preparations you wish.'

'Thank you.' Turning towards the assembly, he raised his voice to say, 'Miss Hasterling has agreed to play the Beethoven *Sonata in D* with me. So as not to ruin her performance, I shall need to limber my wrists before we begin, if the company will indulge me.'

Mrs Chiverton, who had approached the bench after the end of the duet, smiled down at him. 'I think I can speak for the assembly in saying that, for the pleasure of hearing Beethoven, we are quite willing to wait. Please, take all the time you need.'

Giles played a few scales and then some intervals, stretching out his hands so he would be able to reach the chords needed to play the Beethoven. Though he was concentrating on the music, he found himself very conscious of Miss Hasterling beside him.

Her subtle lavender scent. Her dark brown hair, the

curls pinned atop her head glinting in the candlelight. Her figure, though slim, showing in silhouette a pleasing fullness in the bust he hadn't noticed before, perhaps because her modest necklines didn't draw attention to her attributes. Her face also in silhouette, outlining the soft round of cheeks and lush plumpness of her lips.

He felt his body stir, her physical presence weaving a gossamer web of attraction that once again aroused his senses. Though she sat completely still and silent, a barely perceptible tension in her figure seemed to mirror the awareness in his chest...the whisper of sensual connection simmering between them. Was she as aware of it as he was?

The idea sent a bolt of alarm and confusion through him, making his hands jerk so that he fumbled over the chord. She drew in a sharp breath as he righted his fingers with a murmured apology.

Admonishing himself to concentrate, he had to concede his father would be able to admire more than just the kindness and compassion he seemed to think she possessed. And he must ignore this newly noted attractiveness, lest he become so distracted he embarrass himself by performing badly.

He redoubled his concentration on the music, playing until he felt his fingers and wrists were relaxed and limbered. Turning to her, he said, 'Shall we begin?'

She started, as if pulled from abstraction, then darted a look at him. As their gazes caught, Giles saw in her eyes the same reluctant attraction he felt.

So he'd not been imagining that subtle tension in her body—or the fact that it indicated she too was aware of the pull between them.

As he pushed away the disturbing implications of that fact, she said, 'I'm ready when you are.'

Shaken more than he wanted to be, he nodded and focused back on the score. 'Then let us start.'

As they played, Giles forced his concentration to remain on the music, which was indeed difficult enough to require full attention. Just below the level of consciousness, though, he remained aware of the attraction buzzing between them.

He supposed he should be pleased to discover a woman other than Lucinda could attract him. Be happy that the spell she'd cast over him for so long might finally be weakening.

As the piece progressed, the intricate melody began to relax him. His fingers recaptured the familiar patterns while the music's beauty filled him with a rising euphoria. In ability, they were well matched, and as the piece drew to a close, he knew without being immodest that their joint performance was outstanding.

The enthusiastic applause that greeted the final chords confirmed his assessment.

Under cover of the clapping, Giles turned to Miss Hasterling. 'Thank you for playing with me. It has been a delight,' he said, somewhat surprised to realise he meant every word.

'Your father told me your family often used to play together. But then your mother...' Her voice trailed off. 'I'm so sorry for your loss.'

The ache of that loss, muted but always present, intensified, closing his throat and bringing the burn of tears. After struggling to recover his voice, he said, 'I hadn't realised until tonight quite how much I've missed playing.'

'Perhaps it's time for you to begin again.' Gesturing to the crowd with a smile, she added, 'Your audience certainly enjoyed it. Especially your father.'

It wasn't quite the expansive Madonna smile she'd gifted Fullridge, but her expression held more warmth than she previously accorded him. He felt himself… buoyed by it.

'Perhaps we can play again together.'

Was that a look of alarm in her eyes? Before he could decide, the expression vanished. 'Perhaps,' she said non-committally. 'But now we must cede our place.'

Suddenly he wished he could compel her to linger, so he might experience more of the odd effect she was causing, at once arousing and strangely soothing. But he had of necessity to rise from the bench as she did.

As they walked away, Giles murmured, 'May I escort you back to your party?'

She turned to him, raising an eyebrow. 'Though I'm unlikely to get lost between here and the third row of chairs, you may accompany me if you wish,' she said, her tone amused.

That reply gave him the first evidence that she possessed a sense of humour, tart but gentle. The image of a kitten with claws recurred. Although this was more the kneading of a purring kitten than a sharp slash of a paw designed to draw blood.

Giles walked her to re-join her friends, conscious now of an unmistakable sensual connection between them. Had it been there from the first, and he too focused on the threat to his father to notice? Or had it been too muted for him to note until it slowly, gradually strengthened?

The feel of it was more the soft background murmur of a brook as one walked through the woods than the crash of ocean waves smashing upon the seashore, as his immediate, overpowering attraction to Lucinda had been.

That attraction was now dissipated by heartache and

his realisation that the relationship could never become what he'd wanted.

Muted attraction would be easier to walk away from, he imagined. Not that he intended to become close enough to Miss Hasterling that he needed to walk away. Once he established the truth about the lady's character, assuming it was favourable, he would bow out and leave her to his father.

Somehow, that conclusion didn't seem as satisfying as it once had.

Shaking off that thought, he had to admit that, thus far, she seemed to be exactly what she appeared. But smitten as his father had looked after they played together, he would continue his investigations a bit longer, just to be sure.

By now, they'd reached the chairs where Lady Margaret, the Countess, and the gentleman who'd turned pages for her—Fullridge, if he remembered correctly—awaited her. Miss Hasterling curtsied, thanked him for performing with her and took her seat, giving him no excuse to linger.

With more reluctance than he'd expected, he bowed and walked back to his father.

'Excellent performance, Son,' Markham said. 'You have your mother's touch. Of course, it helps to have a fine co-performer. What a joy it was to hear that music again! To listen to it and to play it.'

'Do you intend to seek a repetition?' he asked, his father's enthusiasm setting him once again on guard.

The Viscount nodded. 'I would like to perform with Miss Hasterling again. Although the tenor of our next meeting will be literary. I shall bring along my copy of Petrarch when I call. I'm eager to learn which verses she particularly enjoys.'

Was there any way he could invite himself along? Giles couldn't immediately think of one that wouldn't make his desire to chaperon far too obvious. Unfortunately, one didn't need to bring flowers to a female with whom one had performed during a musicale.

'I hope her expertise with Petrarch is as exemplary as her ability on pianoforte,' he said after a moment.

'I will enjoy discussing literature again,' the Viscount said. 'But we must hush. The next performer is beginning.'

'I'm going for a glass of wine,' Giles murmured. Though he was glad to see his father's spirits so much improved, he couldn't quite yet overcome his concern about the possibility of the Viscount being prematurely carried away by the charms of Miss Hasterling.

Charms for which he was beginning to have a much greater appreciation.

More interested in assessing the evening's events than listening to the performances, Giles wandered into the refreshment room. With the music ongoing, the sole other occupants of the room were two older matrons, feathered headdresses bobbing as they leaned together, obviously gossiping.

Giles took a glass of wine from a side table near the entrance. Though not at all interested in their exchange, as the ladies raised their voices to be heard over the music, he couldn't help but overhear them.

'Her looks are passable,' the first matron was saying.

'Yes, and quite talented. A shame there's no money to make up for her lack of elevated connections.'

The other matron tittered. 'Lady Margaret is trying to help her corral an elderly admirer.'

'And none too soon. The family can't afford another

Season, I've heard. She must be desperate to make a
match as soon as possible.'

'I thought Markham looked interested after their
duet together.'

'That would be a coup! She should reel him in as
soon as possible!'

'Yes. Before he fully recovers from his wife's death
and realises she is far beneath his consideration.'

At a sudden lull in the music, both looked towards the
door—and saw Giles. Trying not to grimace, he bowed.
'Ladies.'

The two matrons curtsied. In the next moment, their
gazes falling to the wine glass he held, they must have
realised he'd been in the room long enough to overhear them. Looking guilty, both put down their own
glasses and hurried out, murmuring a farewell as they
passed him.

Giles's pleasant expression faded to a frown after their
speedy exit. *Desperate? Reel him in before he recovers?*

He'd already assumed that if her financial difficul-
ties were pressing, Miss Hasterling would need to wed
soon—and nabbing a wealthy viscount *would* be a coup.
Was that her intention? Or had he only overheard a bit
of malicious gossip?

Sighing, Giles downed his wine. He didn't *think* the
lady was mercenary enough to focus exclusively on
the wealthiest prospect. But he shouldn't relax his vig-
ilance just yet.

Though he admitted, keeping tabs on Miss Hasterling no longer seemed quite such an imposition.

The following morning, his head aching from his
after-midnight revels, Giles entered the breakfast room
and halted, surprised to find his father still there. They'd

parted company after the musicale, Giles going on to his club where he'd been promised to friends for a late evening of cards, an engagement his father had declined to join. Since they'd not ended the contest until the wee hours of the morning, he was coming down much later than he would have expected to encounter the Viscount still at table.

His father took one look at him and chucked. 'I hope you won to compensate for the headache I see you're nursing.'

'I did,' he confirmed, grimacing as his father set down the coffee pot with an over-loud clank. 'Though if after Bunting's best efforts, I still look rough enough for you to notice, I should give him the sack.'

'Spare poor Bunting. I've spent enough evenings like last night to recognise the signs. Winning always seems to require an immoderate quantity of brandy.'

'I'm not sure the blunt I won was worth turning my head into the anvil the devil's minions are currently hammering on.'

Although in truth, he couldn't blame his state this morning solely on the challenge of matching his friends during a night of rivalry and revelry. After the musicale, he'd been unsettled by a mix of unexpected emotions—increased curiosity about Miss Hasterling, sharpening desire and a surprisingly strong pleasure in her company that complicated his initially simple goal of ascertaining her true intentions towards his father. Layered on top of those were his lingering grief over the long, fruitless relationship with Lucinda and the spectre of the break with her he felt in his bones must come but dreaded.

'Shall we move on to a more pleasant topic?' his father said as Giles dropped into a chair and gulped down some scalding coffee. 'First, thank you again for playing last night. It truly was a pleasure to listen to you.'

'A pleasure to listen to you perform as well. An even greater pleasure, to discover you were *willing* to do so.'

His father was silent a moment before uttering a long, slow sigh. 'It doesn't get…much easier. But wallowing in grief won't change things. One can only move forward. And I admit, during the time I was playing, grief receded and the music touched a vein of joy I've not felt in months.' He smiled softly. 'I think your mama would have approved.'

Giles swallowed hard against the emotion swelling in his chest. 'I know she would have,' he said when he could speak.

'You seemed to enjoy performing with the lady as well.'

Was that why his father had waited for him—to quiz him about his time with Miss Hasterling? His unsettled feelings about the lady putting him instantly on his guard, Giles said carefully, 'It is energising to play with someone so accomplished.'

His father waited, but Giles did not elaborate. He wasn't ready to admit, even to himself, the confusion of emotions she'd engendered.

The silence stretched between them until his father said, 'I know you won't appreciate my saying anything, but I feel I must, since it touches on my own intentions. I'm encouraged to see you engage with…a different lady. One who is not only eligible, but who from everything I've observed appears to possess the qualities of sweetness, compassion, humour and intelligence I believe so essential in a companion. You did enjoy her company, didn't you?'

He looked up sharply at his father, immediately regretting the swift movement that intensified the pounding in his head. 'Yes, she was pleasant company.'

And more, he thought. *That sizzle of attraction made me quite happy to remain beside her. The glimpse of that feisty spirit beneath the sweet demeanour teased me to want to know her better.*

'Would you be interested in…pursuing her?'

His father's unexpected question sent another unpleasantly sharp shock through his head. Would he want to?

From the treacle-thickness of his morning-after brain, a bubble of excitement arose. Succeeding excitement was the recognition that if it prevented his father from making any premature moves in her direction, pursuing Miss Hasterling might be a wise course. Especially if he were doing so at his father's behest, guaranteeing that his sire wouldn't feel like Giles was trying to cut him out.

Then his initial excitement faded. Though he wished to delay his father's courtship, in paying the lady attention himself, it would be *Giles* raising expectations that he had no intention of fulfilling.

To actively pursue and then drop Miss Hasterling would be the dishonourable act of rogue. No matter what face he later put upon it to the world, society always concluded a gentleman's withdrawal was due to some fault he'd discovered in the lady. Inaccurate as that assessment might be, the conclusion would further reduce Miss Hasterling's chances of making an eligible match, chances her modest dowry and lack of elevated family connections had already made small.

Even to protect his father, he couldn't do that.

'I find her…intriguing, but as I've said, I'm not yet ready to settle down with any woman.'

'It wouldn't hurt to explore the possibilities,' his father countered. 'I admit, I'm eager to have you marry and set up your nursery. You are my heir, after all. More than that, I would have you find the same contentment I found with your dear mama. Miss Hasterling may not be the lady to provide that—but then again, she might be. You admit she's piqued your interest. Why not become better acquainted, and see what happens?'

The Viscount raised a hand to forestall Giles's protest. 'I understand you would be reluctant to single her out in case you should later decide you do not suit, as breaking off the relationship would harm Miss Hasterling's reputation. But if you should conclude that you don't want to proceed, I promise to step back in and provide the full support of the family's rank and position on her behalf, to make sure neither her character nor her reputation suffer any damage. Besides, as you know, I find the lady appealing myself.'

Giles stared at his father. 'You are saying…you would defer your pursuit of the lady and to allow me to step in?'

'I would defer it…for you. It's been…difficult, watching you invest years in a relationship, a person, I felt would never provide what you needed and deserved. I held my tongue, sure you wouldn't appreciate my interference—and frankly, knowing you were too bewitched to listen to advice. But losing your mother gives me some idea of the pain a broken relationship causes. Even if Miss Hasterling is not the one to mend all the fractured places, if she coaxes you to look elsewhere and begin healing, it is well worth ceding my place. I would give much to see you happy.'

'Thank you,' he murmured, feeling somewhat guilty for wanting to delay that for his father by putting a spoke in his wheel with Miss Hasterling. Then he reminded himself that he wanted recovery and contentment for his father, too, by having him eventually settle with a companion who would be devoted to the Viscount and value him for himself.

'Well, what do you think, Son? Will you make a try for Miss Hasterling?'

His father had just handed him a golden opportunity to achieve all his aims—without harming a lady who was probably innocent of any selfish scheming.

How could he refuse?

That niggle of excitement surfaced again at the idea of pursuing Miss Hasterling for himself. Squelching it, he reminded himself he would be doing this for his father, getting to know her better so he might make sure her character was sterling enough to deserve Markham's regard.

Or his, a little voice whispered.

Silencing it, he said, 'Yes, I'll accept your bargain. But only if you promise you won't set your expectations too high. I may finally agree with you about that…other matter, but I'm not ready to turn about and seriously pursue another lady.'

'Fair enough,' his father agreed. 'Even if nothing develops between you and Miss Hasterling, that change alone is worth celebrating! So, I was to call on her in two days, to discuss Petrarch. You can go in my stead.'

'With Miss Hasterling expecting you, how do I explain your absence?'

'Perhaps I'll go to Stratham Hall. You can tell her I had to return to take care of some unexpected estate matter—not a prevarication, since there is always some estate matter needing attention! I could give you several weeks to explore a relationship, then return and we can evaluate where we are.'

'Are you sure you want to do this? I truly don't want to harm her, and after a time away, you might change your mind about being willing to step in. I don't wish you to obligate yourself to do something you later come to regret.'

'I've enough experience of life to know my own mind, and I've observed enough about Miss Hasterling to know I would be happy to step back in. Besides, my admiration and continued attendance upon her would be sufficient to encourage other suitors, even if I did not court her myself. Speaking of courtship, can you begin this endeavour with an open mind...not always comparing her to a certain other woman? I would have you judge her fairly, for herself alone.'

Could he honestly pledge to do that? Comparisons would be inevitable, but he could promise to view her on own merits. 'I can do that.'

'Excellent,' the Viscount said with a smile. 'I'll leave you to nurse your coffee and your head. And make my plans to return to Stratham.'

Clapping him on the shoulder, his father rose and walked out. Giles went back to sipping his coffee, occasionally rubbing his aching temples.

Was he wise to have agreed to this scheme? Or, when his head stopped aching and he could think clearly, would he come to regret it? He was heading towards believing Miss Hasterling innocent of scheming, but he hadn't quite acquitted her yet. Could he submerge his remaining suspicions and appear only gracious and admiring?

But before he could begin even a mock courtship, he would have to finally break with Lucinda.

Chapter Seven

In the afternoon two days later, Eliza sat with her sister in Lady Dunbarton's drawing room. This being their usual at-home day, they had been entertaining acquaintances who dropped by to pay their respects and friends eager to exchange a bit of gossip. As the afternoon wore on, Eliza found her nerves stretching tighter and tighter.

Not because of her anticipated meeting with Lord Markham, who had promised to call to discuss Petrarch. She looked forward to that interlude with every expectation of enjoyment. She'd loved the sessions exploring with her father the sharp, sweet, often melancholy verses. She hoped the Viscount might have a translation that showed the verses from a different perspective.

Even if he might be evaluating her as a potential bride, a possibility she thought unlikely, the prospect didn't alarm her…too much. From the first, she'd felt she could relax and be herself around him. And since his title made him, in Lady Margaret's opinion, undesirable as a potential husband, she didn't have to worry about trying to entice him to meet Maggie's expectations, as she frankly did whenever she spent time with Mr Fullridge.

No, what had her stomach tied in knots was worrying over whether Stratham might decide to accompany his father.

Not that he had any excuse to trail his father this time. He'd already allowed he wasn't a scholar, so a literary conversation couldn't be of much interest to him.

A flare of annoyance flamed up. She would be truly irritated if he *did* appear, marring what should be the pure enjoyment of discussing Petrarch. Complicating everything by inciting that response he seemed able to pull from her by his simple presence, even if all he did was glower at her.

Although the look he'd given her after they played that duet might have been heated...but inexperienced as she was, she was pretty sure it hadn't been hostile.

It seemed unbelievable that he might actually be *attracted* to her...despite the intensity of his gaze and breath-suspending, tingling surge of energy that arced between them.

Could he be attracted to her?

She couldn't help feeling some feminine satisfaction if he were, though the possibility was surely remote. Stratham was just as desirable a marital prospect—even a greater one—than his father, being younger, handsome, already wealthy in his own right as well as heir to a viscount. Were he ready to wed, he might have his pick from any of number of well-born and well-dowered Diamonds.

And as she'd learned to her bitter humiliation, Miss Eliza Hasterling was neither well dowered nor well born enough to be in the running.

Not that she wanted to be, of course.

So why would he pursue that...something between them? Unlike young George, he was doubtless confident of his ability to charm and had no need to practise it. Or was he callous enough to try to intrigue a female just for sport?

Despite Maggie's negative opinion of aristocrats, she couldn't believe that of him.

Nor was there any *need* for him to accompany the Viscount. Surely by now he had figured out that she wasn't attempting to entrap his father.

A jab to her knee jolted her out of those thoughts. Looking up to see her sister give her an exasperated look, she realised Lady Dunbarton must have asked her a question several times without receiving an answer.

Summoning a guilty smile, she said, 'Sorry, I was wool-gathering. What did you say?'

'Mrs Anderson complimented you on your superior musicianship at Mrs Chiverton's musicale,' Lady Dunbarton said, giving her another little frown that seemed to be…a warning?

'Thank you,' Eliza said automatically. As the comment registered, though, she creased her brow in confusion. 'Forgive me, Mrs Anderson, but I don't recall you being present. You must excuse me for not greeting you.'

'Oh, I wasn't present. My friend, Lady Etherbert, was, and gave quite a glowing account of your performance.' She paused, raking Eliza with an appraising glance before adding, 'She praised both your duet partners as well. Lord Markham and Lord Stratham, I believe? Clever of you to have taken advantage of your skill to monopolise their attention.'

The lady continued to pin her with an almost accusatory look, making Eliza feel like a butterfly in a collector's display box viewed by an observer who found the specimen distasteful.

So that had been the reason for her sister's warning glance.

She hadn't until this moment considered that the attention shown her by the Viscount and the Baron had not just unsettled and confused *her*. For many in society, having a wealthy viscount and his highly eligible son show her such partiality would be an affront—viewed as an attempt by a female of little importance to try to steal for herself attentions that should more properly be given to females of higher birth and status.

Like viscount's daughter Georgiana Etherbert, the daughter of Mrs Anderson's wealthy friend Lady Etherbert.

Ever the peacemaker, before Eliza could figure out what to reply that complimented the abilities of the gentlemen while minimising the importance she—and the rest of society—should attach to their choosing *her* as a duet partner, the butler appeared to usher in another visitor.

Shock rippled through her as she heard him announce Lord Stratham. Followed by a second shock when the Baron entered the room, a volume tucked under his arm…alone.

Where was Lord Markham?

Realising Mrs Anderson had turned from the visitor to stare at her, Eliza hoped the blush she felt suffusing her face wasn't too vivid. Tearing her gaze from Stratham, she tried to school her expression into one of polite interest. One that wouldn't reveal the turmoil roiling in her stomach and the agitation that shot sparks to every nerve.

'Good afternoon, ladies,' Stratham said as he walked over, then halted beside the sofa to offer them a bow. 'It's unfortunate you were not able to witness Miss Hasterling's performance, Mrs Anderson. What a treat it was! Though the musicale was quite enjoyable, your presence was missed. One must always regret losing an opportunity to chat with a lady as witty as she is lovely.'

Eliza repressed a smile. Her initial embarrassment that Stratham had obviously overheard Mrs Anderson's remarks—and that lady's less than subtle innuendo—faded as the Baron emptied a butter boat of compliments on the woman, diverting her from directing towards Eliza a disapproval she was more accustomed to encountering from him. Though she could hardly blame the preening woman for losing track of the conversation. She knew all too well how distractingly charming Stratham could be.

'I'm sure it was my loss, to have missed the opportunity to hear you and your father perform,' Mrs Anderson replied. 'As I recall, you are both excellent.'

'Perhaps you might do us the honour on another occasion,' Stratham said smoothly.

Now Eliza had to stifle a laugh. It was well known that Mrs Anderson had no musical talent whatsoever, the main reason she had not attended Mrs Chiverton's event, as she was wise enough not to expose her deficiency by attempting to perform.

'I would never presume to puff myself off by playing in public,' she said, casting a darkling look at Eliza, 'but surely would enjoy listening to you. When a handsome gentleman is also charming and talented, it's no wonder Miss Etherbert, my dear friend's daughter, sings your praises so highly!'

'How kind of the young lady. I'd hoped to continue the discussion I began at the pianoforte with Miss Hasterling about the harmonic patterns in Beethoven's sonatas. If you would indulge me?'

'I'm afraid I'd add nothing to the conversation,' Lady

Dunbarton said with a chuckle. 'Eliza received all the musical talent in our family.'

'I should take my leave,' Mrs Anderson said, rising to curtsy to them. Her sister's guest hastened out, probably anxious, Eliza thought with an inward grin, to spread around the *ton* the shocking news that Lord Stratham had paid a call upon the lowly Miss Hasterling. Inexplicable!

And alarming, the succeeding thought stifled her mirth. Not just because it ruffled society's feathers about which young ladies were most deserving of attention.

What did the Baron mean by calling on her—and without his father?

One immediate explanation causing her sudden concern, Eliza said anxiously, 'I hope Lord Markham is well.'

Stratham raised an eyebrow, as if surprised by the enquiry. 'He is in excellent health.'

'I am relieved to hear it.'

'Ah, yes, you were expecting Petrarch.' With a wry grimace, he looked down at the book under his arm. 'Mrs Anderson's comments about music so distracted me, I almost forgot my purpose in coming.'

At the mention of that lady, Eliza could no longer suppress a chuckle. 'You are the most complete hand! Not to disparage Mrs Anderson *too* much, but it's common knowledge that she possesses little conversation beyond gossip. To describe her as "as witty as she is lovely" was overdoing it a bit!'

He grinned. 'Not at all. True, I said one must regret not spending time with a lady as witty as she is lovely— an indisputable fact. But I never said *Mrs Anderson* was such a lady.'

Eliza's eyes widened. 'Only let her infer it. What a clever trickster you are, Sir!'

'How so? Had it been the two of us conversing, would *you* have assumed I referred to you?'

'Well, no, I would have assumed you were making a general observation—' She broke off.

'I rest my case. Father had planned to bring the Petrarch himself, but was unexpectedly summoned back to Stratham Hall to deal with some estate business. He asked that I come by to explain his absence and offer you his copy of the *Canzoniere*. He imagined that the volume you read is probably in your father's library and wanted you to have this to refresh your memory before he returns to make that postponed visit. You were to discuss the poems, I believe?' He smiled. 'So you might display your superior abilities in Latin?'

Was he...*teasing* her? This time, his tone sounded more amused than accusing. Not quite sure how to respond to a friendly overture, she said, 'You must not have glanced into the volume. Most of Petrarch's writings are in Latin, but the love poems were composed in the Italian vulgate of his day.'

Stratham chuckled. 'I'm not sure I'd know the difference. If I may?' He waved to the now-unoccupied seat on the sofa beside her.

'Of—of course,' Eliza stuttered, her nerves tingling already at the prospect of his proximity. She had to hold in a deep breath to keep from sighing as she felt, more than saw, him sit beside her...as if every nerve on that side of her body were calibrating the distance separating them...and burning to have him slide closer.

'Dialectic Italian remained structurally quite close to Latin for a considerable time, did it not?' he said, jolting her out of that intense physical awareness.

'So my father says,' she replied, forcing her mind back to conversation. She might be disappointed that her discussion with the Viscount would be delayed, but she was also relieved that she would not have to balance being polite to the father while resisting the appeal of the disapproving son.

Though for whatever reason, today he didn't seem quite so disapproving.

Thrusting from her mind the puzzle of why that might be so, as her sister escorted a newly arrived guest to join her on the other sofa, Eliza continued, 'Are you a fancier of Petrarch, too?'

'No, as I admitted earlier, I'm not much of a scholar. I prefer vigorous activity out in the fresh air. But my father is such an enthusiast, I am curious which of the poems you like, and why.'

She blinked up at him, uncertain. 'You've accomplished your errand and can take your leave. You needn't linger and chat out of politeness.'

As I can't imagine why a gentleman who prefers vigorous outdoor pursuits would be interested in my opinion of three-hundred-year-old love poems.

'I'm not just being polite. I find your interest in Petrarch…curious.'

That prompted another laugh. 'You are not alone in thinking me "curious"! My sisters, even my mother, certainly do. Of all the females in the household, my father found me most like him in tastes and interests. As I think I mentioned, my only brother is quite a bit younger. When I was growing up, as Father hadn't yet had a son, I sort of fell into the place of one. I loved spending time in the library with him, studying and reading! Or engaging in other masculine pursuits.'

Stratham raised his eyebrows. 'Other masculine pursuits? Such as?'

'Riding. Driving. Hunting and pistol shooting. The

latter more for protection. A vicar often rides out late or tarries overnight keeping vigil with the sick or dying, and we have only a handful of maids and one elderly manservant living in. Father felt more comfortable knowing one of us could scare off an intruder, if necessary.'

'How accurately could you scare off an intruder?' Stratham asked, looking amused.

'Accurately enough. What use would I be if I were more likely to blow off my foot than discourage a would-be thief?' Eliza sighed. 'Now you will be thinking me unwomanly as well as a bluestocking. Whisper that abroad, and my reputation will be well and truly ruined!'

Chuckling, Stratham put a finger to his lips. 'Your secrets are safe with me. So, your father shared his love of literature. Why fancy Petrarch, in particular?'

'Partly for the sweet, sad beauty of the poems themselves. Partly because the great scholar, who in his philosophical writings seems confident and almost all knowing, reveals himself in the poems to be as uncertain and vulnerable as any flawed mortal. How romantic, to fall in love at first sight with his great muse, Laura! To cherish her through the years, even though they could never be together.'

She paused, but when he nodded encouragement, continued, 'She was already married, you see, and he was a priest, not able to marry even if she had been free, for in those days, once committed to the church, one could not leave.' She sighed. 'I suppose we all yearn to inspire a love like that. My parents share one—theirs quietly domestic and not star-crossed, but equally committed.' She looked up at Stratham. 'I suspect your parents did as well.'

As she had narrated her account, the amusement on Stratham's face had faded and he nodded soberly. 'Perhaps that is what Father finds so appealing about Petrarch.'

'Since being cast into the Marriage Mart, I've come to further appreciate Petrarch's predicament,' she added, perhaps too frankly. 'How the desire for incomparable love endures, even when it becomes more and more evident that one will never possess it.'

'Are you giving up on finding it?' Stratham asked, studying her closely.

Meaning was she ready to settle for simply luring some man into marriage? Any man, any marriage, so as not to end up a spinster?

Not sure of the answer to that yet herself, she said, 'Petrarch never did. He wrote poems to his Laura for over forty years, even after her death.'

'Is it fidelity or foolishness to hang on to a love that can never be?' Stratham said softly, almost to himself. Somehow, she didn't think he expected an answer.

It was foolishness to allow herself a partiality that could never bear fruit.

In a lighter tone, she continued, 'In any event, the first translations made in Henry VIII's day established the pattern of the ten-syllable line for verse. Which later became the classic English poetic style, as well providing some of its most common themes. Love that is desired but painful. The soul that fluctuates from yearning for it to wishing to be spared its torments.'

'Classic themes indeed,' the Baron said with such a trace of sadness, Eliza couldn't help thinking he might have been pierced by a misplaced Cupid's dart himself at some time. Though she couldn't imagine him falling for a woman who wouldn't reciprocate his regard.

'So...tell me your favourite poem,' he commanded, putting an end to her speculation. 'What struck you most and still stays with you.'

'A single favourite? My, that is a daunting task.'

'Perhaps. But none the less, choose one,' he prompted.

Frowning, she took the volume and flipped through the pages. 'Very well. This encapsulates all the yearning and regret of hopeless love:

"I look, think, burn, weep;
and she who destroys me
Is always before my eyes to my sweet distress... War
is my state, filled with grief and anger,
And only in thinking of her do I find peace.
So from one pure living fountain
Flow the sweet and bitter which I drink:
One hand alone heals me and pierces me.
And so that my ordeal may not reach haven I am
born and die a thousand times each day."'

As she closed the volume, Stratham stared, not so much at, as beyond her. 'Why would one ever seek to love, only to end up in such a state?'

For an instant, she saw in his eyes an anguish that shocked her. The simmering tension between them taking on a poignant ache, she yearned to reach out and touch his face. To offer comfort.

Fortunately, before she could move, he shook his head, as if to dislodge from his mind whatever painful thought had invaded it.

'Keep the Petrarch for my father's return,' he said, placing the book on the side table. 'But I would offer one other favour in compensation for disappointing you of your serious discussion of the poet. I believe you mentioned you enjoyed riding. Would you accompany me to the park some morning?'

Whatever wound the love poems had pricked, he no longer wanted to discuss them. Stumbling to adjust to the sudden change of topic, she said, 'Y-yes, I love riding. But as I told you, I did not bring a horse to London.'

'We brought my mother's mare Ginger to the city with us, intending to sell her at Tattersall's, as my sisters have no need of another horse. A sweet goer with beautiful paces, she's still young and is too excellent a beast to be left idle.' He sighed. 'She's well looked after by my grooms, but I haven't quite been able to make myself part with her yet, so she is still in the stables and always enjoys exercise. You would be doing me a favour if you'd agree to ride her.'

He hadn't been able to sell the animal who'd been so great a part of his mother's life, Eliza filled in the unspoken details. She'd been about to refuse—heaven knew, much as she loved riding, she didn't need to tempt herself by spending any more time in the dangerously attractive Baron's company. But the melancholy on his face, coming so soon after that glimpse of pain she'd seen in his eyes upon hearing the verses about tortured love, elicited a sympathy she couldn't quite suppress.

What harm would it do to grant the request, especially if it brightened those now-shadowed eyes? She'd be seated on horseback, safely distanced from him, riding barely close enough to converse. She could trot ahead and not converse at all, if that made her easier.

'I'd be honoured,' she said at last, capitulating.

'Excellent! I would be available morning after next, if that would be convenient.'

She nodded. 'I will not be engaged that morning.'

'Shall I bring Ginger by around eight? It's more enjoyable to ride early before the park fills with visitors. We could even gallop, if it's not too crowded.'

'I would like that very much.' To ride again—and even gallop? That truly would be a joy worth risking the intoxicating allure of his company. Especially intoxicating, when he seemed to be pleased by her company, rather than disapproving.

He rose, smiling. 'I shall see you then.' He gave her a quick bow, then walked over to take his leave of her sister, still entertaining another caller.

Eliza watched him walk out, letting herself enjoy the handsome, compelling masculine picture he presented. To ride—and share his company! That was indeed recompense for losing the chance to discuss poetry with the Viscount.

As her sensitised nerves slowly calmed after his departure, she told herself she was wise enough not to make any more of his offer than a gentleman's attempt to ease the disappointment his father had caused a lady.

Chapter Eight

In the early evening the following day, Giles stepped down from the hackney in front of a handsome town house on Hill Street. He gazed up at the familiar façade, an ache in his chest as the words of the Petrarch sonnet echoed in his head.

I look, think, burn, weep;
and she who destroys me
Is always before my eyes to my sweet distress...
So from one pure living fountain
Flow the sweet and bitter which I drink:
One hand alone heals me and pierces me.

Miss Hasterling could not have known how deeply those words had cut into his heart and burned into his memory upon first hearing, for the poet could have written them just for him. But unlike Petrarch, he was resolved to finally free himself from a hopeless passion. Even if, as Miss Hasterling seemed to fear for herself, he never found that great, fulfilling love for which all humans yearn.

Clutching the jeweller's box, he walked up the front steps.

The butler admitted him with a smile. 'Evening, Your Lordship! So good to see you again. We've been missing you.'

Another time, he would have returned the smile and replied he'd missed them, too. And though he had, that longing was overlaid by the knowledge that he'd reached the point where staying away hurt less than coming here. It was time to end the '*sweet distress*' once and for all.

'I can find my way up,' he said, handing the man his hat and cane.

'Shall I send up a light supper?' the butler asked.

'Not for me; I can't stay long.'

Too well trained to show any surprise at this change of routine, the butler simply bowed. 'As you wish, my lord.'

Once upstairs, Giles paused on the threshold of Lucinda's room, where he had stood before entering so many times before, silently gazing on her beauty as she sat at her dressing table, her maid brushing out her long golden hair. It being early evening, she would have only recently arisen from bed; she'd be discussing with her dresser which gown and jewels to wear for whatever evening activity she had planned. Or if she were expecting him, she'd be arrayed, as she was now, in a silk dressing gown that outlined a voluptuous figure, reminding him instantly of the pleasure she could give him.

This time, he felt a familiar admiration for her beauty, but to his relief, only a bearable stab of grief. Not the welling up of fierce emotion he'd feared, a revival of the strangling attachment that had yoked him to her for so long.

The maid noticed him first and nodded. Lucinda looked back, surprise turning to an expression of delight. 'Giles! So you've come at last! You may go, Greenfield,' she said, waving to the maid, who surrendered the hairbrush and slipped out.

'Would you like to finish?' Lucinda asked, offering him the brush.

How many times had their nights begun like that? Him wielding the brush in long slow strokes through the gold of her hair while her perfume filled his nostrils... waiting, breath suspended in anticipation, until she reached behind her and began caressing him through his trousers, then opening the buttons of his trouser flap, slowly, teasingly, one at a time, until he was mad with desire for her...

'It looks tidy enough,' he said, keeping his hands at his sides.

She accepted the rebuff with only a brief frown. 'Join me by fire, then? Or shall we proceed right to bed? It has been quite some time, after all.' She stood and walked to him in a sultry sway of hips, then rose on tiptoe to kiss him.

He turned his head so her lips connected with his cheek. 'The sofa for now.'

She frowned again, but linked her fingers with his when he allowed her to take his arm. He saw her note with a satisfied little smile the box in his other hand.

'Wine?' she asked as she led him to a seat by the fire, then poured two glasses from a decanter on the sideboard. 'I'll have Wilson bring supper later.'

'I already informed him I can't stay.'

With a moue of displeasure, she presented him a glass. 'I see you're going to punish me. But not too much.' She tapped the box. 'You've finally forgiven me, haven't you?'

He smiled faintly. 'You are forgiven.'

'I'm so glad! Oh, I know I'm…naughty sometimes, but I just can't help myself! And I'm always so sorry afterwards! May I?'

He handed her the box. After taking the chair beside his, she opened it, then gave a gasp of pleasure as she slipped out the diamond and sapphire creation. 'You know how much I love diamonds! With sapphires, for my eyes, of course?'

He nodded, a dull thud of ache and loss beating in his chest. But he refrained from adding, as he usually did, *No jewel could compare with the brilliance of your eyes.*

She waited for a moment, but when he remained silent, did not call him out over the omission. Slipping on the bracelet, she rotated her wrist to admire the jewels sparkling in the firelight.

She turned back to give him a brilliant smile. 'You know I *try* to be good. This will help remind me.'

Bracing himself, Giles said quietly, 'It's not a reminder. It's a goodbye, Lucinda.'

She glanced up sharply. 'You are still angry.'

'No, I'm not,' he said—and realised, after so many episodes of jealousy, fury and angst, this time it was true. 'I've just finally come to accept that we don't want the same things. I don't think we ever will.'

'I know you're not as absorbed in politics and the Court as I am, but are we so unhappy as we are?'

'I am,' he said bluntly. 'I've been unhappy for some time. As I think you know. The future that excites me is not in government, but in managing the estate. Granted, at first I took over for Father by necessity. But then I found… I liked the work. Performing tasks that actually accomplish something, like producing crops and assisting tenants.'

'But you *love* London! You'll be bored to flinders

tucked away in Hampshire, once the novelty of running the estate yourself wears off.'

'I don't think so. I've been tending Stratham for a year now. Yes, I enjoy the theatres and clubs of London, but not the part that fascinates you. The clash and clamour of political parties. The interminable dinners discussing strategy. The intrigues at Court.'

She shrugged. 'Such as they are. Court has been rather tame under Sailor Billy.'

'There are still intrigues surrounding the Duchess of Kent, the tug of war over young Victoria between her mother and the King, who loathes the woman. You'll want to help Melbourne prepare.'

'It is exciting to think about a new reign soon to begin!'

'Yes, it will be exciting. And there will be no lack of courtiers eager to take my place.'

Her smile faded. 'That might be so. But none of them would be you.'

Giles shrugged. 'You'll adjust. Don't think I don't treasure…some memories. But it's time for you to go on with your preferred life, for me to fully assume the responsibilities of mine. We've drifted long enough.'

Rising from his chair, he kissed her fingers. 'Goodbye, Lucinda. God keep you.'

She wrapped those fingers around his hand, refusing to release it. 'You know you don't mean it. You've been angry before, but you always come back. You'll regret these hasty words…once you lie awake in your cold, lonely bed.'

She rose as well, draping herself against him. He felt the soft mounds of her breasts pressed against his chest, her belly rubbing against his breeches.

Even now, he felt his body stir. Just as she had drawn him back the other times he'd tried to end it, his head telling him leaving was for the best while the body on fire for the pleasure she promised warred against that resolve until he succumbed.

Not this time.

He truly hadn't been angry at first, but fury erupted now, that she would try once again to use against him the desire she could rouse so easily, even after he'd announced his decision.

He tugged loose the arms she'd flung around his neck and pushed her away. 'Maybe I will regret it. If so, I'll just have to deal with it. As I've dealt with all the rest these last few years.'

As he turned towards the door, her eyes widened in alarm. He saw in them the exact moment she realised that this time, he truly was going to leave her.

After a frozen instant, she paced after him. 'Fine, then; go back to your bucolic acres. You'll miss me soon enough, as you have every other time you've rusticated in the country. And when you do return, don't be so sure I'll take you back! As you pointed out, there are plenty of others eager to take your place. To think, all those months you were playing country gentleman at Stratham, I've been so loyal!'

He paused, turning to face her. 'Have you?' he asked, raising his eyebrows.

She coloured slightly. 'You knew you always owned my heart.'

Even if you let out your body, he thought, but bit his tongue before the words escaped. Ending was hard enough; he'd not let it turn ugly. 'I wish you joy of them.'

With a final bow from the doorway, he walked out.

'Giles?' she called after him, wonderingly. And then 'Giles!' an angry shout. As he closed the door, he heard a clatter as the bracelet she'd pitched at him struck it.

Numbly he walked down the stairs, collected his hat and cane, and proceeded outside, waiting for the pain to begin. He'd taken a hackney rather than drive himself so he might walk home, knowing from past experience that he would need time alone before he could face anyone.

Before, when he left after they'd quarrelled, he'd felt literally like knives were slicing into his gut at the possibility that the relationship might be ending. Then, after several hours of anguished pacing, he'd find himself back on Bond Street, looking for a gaudy trinket that might mend the breach and bring them back together again.

Pain assailed him now, but muted by a sense of sad inevitability. Every word he'd said to her had been true, not spoken in anger or hurt. She thrived in the elevated atmosphere of the Court, in the bustle of London and the gossip of society, surrounded by approval and admiration. She was no more able to give up that universal acclaim to bask in the love of one single man than she was to leave London to live in the wilds of the country.

She'd never be happy as a landowner's wife tending her stillroom and garden, overseeing the housekeeping, calling on neighbouring gentry and bringing soup to tenants' sick children. While he spent his days away from her, riding his acres, supervising lambing and calving and the harvesting of watercress, consulting with tenants on refurbishing cottage roofs or buying new ploughs and seed for the next growing season.

They were stars on different courses. It had taken his mother's loss, his father's grief—and perhaps exposure to a feisty, prosaic and practical, Petrarch-quoting young lady to make him finally accept that.

What did it mean for his relationship with that practical, prosaic young lady? He didn't know, but in the ashes of his burned-out love there was slowly rising a faint, feeble phoenix of desire to explore a new path and see where it led.

Chapter Nine

Early the following morning, dressed in her riding habit, Eliza paced the morning room as she waited for Stratham to collect her. She told herself most of her giddy excitement was the anticipation of exploring the paces of a new mount and the tantalising possibility of a gallop. Stratham was simply performing a favour for his father, after all. He hadn't invited her to ride on his own behalf.

Or had he?

Certainly there was *something* between them. A current of sensual attraction drawing them together, quite strongly on her part, even when they played at the musicale, while she still sensed his undercurrent of suspicion. They had both delighted at playing with a superior partner; judging by the expression of unalloyed pleasure she noted on his face, for a time, even his doubts had been suspended.

Maybe that shared love of music had softened him. He'd seemed more accepting when he called two days ago. That subtle but perceptible hint of disapproval had been absent; he'd seemed to find her amusing, and her company…congenial.

Which was a fortunate development. It would be easier to remain friends with his father, whose company she genuinely enjoyed, if she were not plagued by trying to dispel the suspicions of the son. And if he were no longer suspicious, he could remove his tempting presence from their meetings, allowing her to relax in the Viscount's company…and squelch for good the daydreams during which she found herself embroidering upon that magical musical interlude with Stratham.

Imagining there might be something more between them was a silly fantasy born out of that persistent sensual pull, she told herself firmly. A hope life and her own experience should convince her was as real as a desert mirage. Stratham might agree to perform on the pianoforte with her, but that's the only duet he intended to play.

Instead of fruitless daydreams, she should be hinting for *Fullridge* to go riding with her. Or at least view with anticipation knowing that he would be present at the dinner to which Maggie and the Countess had invited her. She needed to spend more time with that gentleman so she could decide whether to encourage him further or eliminate him from consideration.

With Markham now out of London—and never a realistic contender to begin with—Fullridge was, after all, her only viable candidate as a potential husband. If she could not embrace the idea of becoming a loving and faithful wife to him, the alternative was almost certainly spinsterhood.

She loved her family and would happily offer them a lifetime of service. And yet…

She never used to think of herself as indecisive. But now, facing a decision that would literally determine the course of the rest of her life, she found herself completely unable to make a choice.

Thus, the need to spend more time with Fullridge and the sooner, the better.

With the pressure of such a weighty decision looming, she should view this ride as a momentary escape and a pleasant diversion. And if it also happened to be overlaid by the titillation of an impossible but none the less exciting sizzle of sensual attraction, she should simply enjoy the moment.

Still, she jumped when the butler walked in to announce Lord Stratham.

She placed a hand on her chest to quell her heart's fluttering as she waited for him to enter. It would certainly be helpful for a maiden's composure, she thought wryly as she watched him walk in, if he weren't *quite* so handsome, his tall, lean form not *quite* so worthy of admiration, and the energy he exuded not *quite* so compelling.

'I see you are ready to leave,' he said, inspecting her riding habit with approval. 'Shall we go at once? The sooner we arrive, the more likely the park will be empty enough for us to fully enjoy the ride.'

'Yes, let's go. I'm eager for that gallop.'

He raised an eyebrow. 'I make no promises about a gallop—yet. After you.' He motioned for her to precede him.

Eliza hastened down the entry stairs and out to the street, where Stratham's groom held three horses on short tethers. With a cry of delight, she strode over to the ginger-coloured mare with dark mane and socks. 'She is lovely, just as you promised!' Greeting the horse, she let the mare sniff her, then stroked her neck.

'Her paces are just as lovely,' Stratham said, smiling at her enthusiasm. 'I brought Paxton, my groom.' He gestured towards the man holding the reins of the three horses, who inclined his head to her nod. 'He will lead Ginger to the park while you grow accustomed to her.'

Though delighted about the outing, her sister had objected to having Stratham's groom accompany them, insisting a Dunbarton groom would make a more proper chaperon. Eliza countered that it made more sense to take a groom who was familiar with the horse she was to ride. Besides, her sister couldn't really fear that Stratham had nefarious designs on her person.

Standing in Stratham's presence, she chuckled now, remembering that exchange. The notion that he might harbour a secret desire to spirit her away for illicit love-making seemed even more ludicrous. But she was also guiltily glad his groom attended them, for Stratham would probably feel obligated to assist her to mount rather than turn her over to a stranger.

'If you're sufficiently acquainted, I'll help you up,' he said, confirming her guess. Shivery anticipation tingling through her, she nodded, meaning to enjoy every second.

And ah, yes, she relished the burn of his fingers at her waist, her hand, as he helped her into the side saddle! She even thanked the mare, who sidled a bit, requiring Stratham to maintain his hold on her longer than would otherwise have been proper.

Could she ever feel half this giddy excitement at the touch of Fullridge's hands? Just half; she could live with half and be thankful. But could she marry and live as wife to a husband and do without such delicious sweetness completely?

Savouring the still-tingling aftermath of Stratham's touch as she took the reins, she was beginning to believe that she couldn't honestly pledge honour and fidelity to a husband unless the relationship promised some level of sensual satisfaction.

Forcing her attention back to riding, she considered refusing to let the groom lead her mare. The horse had already shown herself responsive, making Eliza sure she could control her mount with ease. But realising it would be prudent in case of some unexpected incident to have another hand on the reins, she made herself submit, eager to reach the park, prove her riding skill and claim the treat of a gallop Stratham had dangled.

The congestion of vehicles and pedestrians in the streets meant it wasn't always possible for Stratham to ride beside her, but she noted he kept a close watch on her. 'Checking to make sure I don't fall off?' she asked when they were once again side by side. 'I promise you, I shall not.'

'Your sister entrusted you to my care, making me responsible for your safety,' he replied. 'So yes, I'll watch to make sure you are secure in the saddle. Which, I concede, you seem to be.'

'So we may have that gallop, once we reach the park?'

He shook his head at her, looking amused. 'Perhaps. If the park isn't crowded. And after I observe how well you walk, then trot, then canter on Ginger.'

Eliza gave an exaggerated sigh. 'He mistrusts us, Ginger,' she said into the horse's ear. 'We must show him the error of his ways by beating his tall black beast when we gallop.'

When the mare nickered, as if in response, Eliza laughed. 'See? Ginger agrees with me.'

Stratham only shook his head at her, smiling.

After reaching Hyde Park without incident and waiting, her excitement rising, for the groom to release the reins, Eliza realised how much she'd missed riding. Wherever she ended up, either married or living with family, she must always have horses available, she thought, and grinned to herself.

There, she'd made one decision—even if it was an easy one!

As was her decision that she must have sensual fulfilment? How could she achieve that, if she did not marry? By chancing an illicit liaison…with someone as compelling as Stratham?

A bolt of sensation heated her skin. Shaking her head to rid herself of that erotic speculation, she chided herself to concentrate on the immediate pleasures of this ride. Turning to Stratham, she said, 'Shall we begin my test?'

He nodded for the groom to release the check rein. 'We'll start with a walk.'

They did, and she'd been right: the mare was beautifully behaved, answering her rider's signals at once and seeming as eager as Eliza to proceed to at a faster pace. Finally, after an extended canter, Stratham signalled her to pull up the horse before a long, empty stretch of Rotten Row.

'No strolling dandies, no tooling carriages, no nursemaids pushing babies or dairymaids tending cattle,' Eliza said, indicating the road ahead. 'Can we gallop at last?'

'To the curve of the carriageway, then?'

She nodded agreement, and with a click of her heels, the mare sped off. Delight filled her as the mare's even pace ate up the ground, the wind whipping tendrils of hair from her braids and tugging at her hat. She hadn't really expected to keep up with Stratham's rangy gelding, but after thundering down the path, she pulled the little mare up less than a length behind Stratham.

'Wonderful!' she cried, patting the mare's neck. 'I

believe this little lady enjoyed the gallop as much as I did.'

'She does like a run. And you're as skilled at riding as you are on pianoforte,' Stratham admitted. 'Like my mother was.' Sadness passed over his face briefly before he smiled again. 'It seems fitting for you to be riding Ginger.'

'I'm very grateful you've loaned her to me. I'd be happy to exercise her for as long as you keep her.'

'You'd both be happy then, wouldn't you, Ginger?' he said, leaning over to give the horse a pat. 'Shall we have a walk and cool them down?'

'Can we have another gallop before we leave the park?'

Stratham looked around at the quantity of visitors strolling the pathways and the number of carriages now driving along. 'It's already more crowded. We could chance a canter, perhaps.'

'Not as good as a gallop, but it will have to do.'

As the two horses started off at a walk—and riding a safe distance from him—Eliza felt as comfortable as she ever had in Stratham's company. Revelling in riding a splendid mount under a warm sun and feeling towards Stratham just a manageable sizzle of attraction, Eliza let herself simply savour the experience.

As a smart equipage tooled towards them, Eliza pointed to it. 'That's similar to your phaeton, isn't it?'

After glancing at it, Stratham nodded. 'Yes, my highperch phaeton is very like. The vehicle's body is ebony rather than green, but it might have been built by the same carriage maker.'

Eliza watched it pass with a sigh. 'I should love to try driving it some time.'

Stratham gave her a look. 'You're joking, of course.'

'Not at all. I haven't done any driving since coming

to London, but I often drove my sisters or my mother at home. After all, Father was frequently away on parish business and wasn't available every time someone wanted to go into the village or visit friends.'

Stratham didn't dispute her claim, but a lift of his eyebrows indicated he wasn't convinced. His scepticism irking her, she said, 'Do you doubt my word? I'm not boasting; I only tell the truth. I'd never pretend to be something I'm not.'

'Unlike Mrs Anderson, who pretended to be a connoisseur of music but really only wanted to promote the interests of her friend's marriageable daughter?'

'She's doubtless fond of her friend's daughter, so it's only natural she would want to put her forward. Especially to such an eligible gentleman.'

He gave her a quizzical look. 'You defend her even after she tried to disparage you? Yes, I heard the remark about you taking advantage of your skill to "monopolise" my father's attention. And mine.'

'Perhaps she just didn't express herself well. Many people don't.'

Looking exasperated, he shook his head. 'Are you truly naive enough to believe that?'

'I always wish to give someone the benefit of the doubt.'

'Then you are bound to often be disappointed.'

'What a cynical view! Of course, I know some people *intend* to be disparaging, tearing down others to make themselves look better. But being realistic about human frailty doesn't mean I can't also hope for the best. And by expecting the best, perhaps encourage someone to do better than they might otherwise. No one has incentive to improve if everyone expects the worst of him. The world may not be as good as one would prefer, but one can always find something worthy of admiration. The brilliance of a sunset. A child's joyful laughter. An unexpected act of kindness. Beauty is there to be seen, too, if one looks for it.'

Stratham gazed at her wonderingly, as if trying to decide if she truly meant what she said. 'You really believe that?' he asked at last.

'I do. What good does it do if I look at my fellow man only with suspicion and cynicism? As I said, by encouraging the best in others, sometimes one gets it. If that happens, one can celebrate. If not, one can hope for better the next time.'

Stratham shook his head. 'I can't decide if you are hopelessly naive—or incredibly good.'

Eliza laughed. 'I'm neither. I just don't want to spend my life under a dark cloud, always suspicious, quick to take offence and looking for the worst. Where is the joy in that? Life sends enough blows to weather without ignoring such hope and beauty and solace as it does provide.'

He studied her for a moment. 'I hope you never encounter a disaster that shakes that optimistic view.'

'Optimism comes from within, not from outside. One must "rejoice in all circumstances", after all.'

'A suitable Biblical quote for a clergyman's daughter, but easier said than done,' he declared, his horse suddenly sidling as if to underline his point. 'You see, Midnight agrees.'

Eliza laughed. 'He's only shying because a leaf has caught under the far edge of the saddle blanket,' she observed, pointing to it. 'It must have stuck to his sweaty skin after our gallop. It flutters each time the breeze blows, which must disturb him, since he can feel but not see it. Let me ride closer and remove it.'

'No, I'll do it. If he's anxious, he may kick out if Ginger gets too close.' Pulling up his mount, Stratham swung down from saddle, soon discovering and pulling free the offending leaf.

'How small a thing can sometimes overset us,' he observed as he tossed it away.

'Sometimes a small detail isn't so small.' Deciding to take advantage of the camaraderie of the ride to ask the question that had troubled her from the first, Eliza continued, 'You accuse me of being overly sanguine, but I assure you, I view life and people with a realistic eye. So, much as I appreciate this invitation to ride, I must ask…have you begun calling on me only to forestall your father from seeking my company?'

She saw at once that Stratham hadn't anticipated she would ask such a blunt question. But the mere fact that he looked dismayed, unable to come up with a quick, convincing denial, told her that must be the truth.

So much for thinking the best of everyone. She'd been so hopeful that, even if he'd initially been suspicious, he now recognised her true character. She was more disappointed—and, frankly, hurt—than she'd anticipated to discover she was mistaken.

'Do you truly think I'm trying to entrap the Viscount into offering for me? Cynical indeed, my lord! I grant you, females have so little control over their lives, the need to marry well is so important, you have some justification for entertaining that suspicion. But after we've become better acquainted, to know that you still convict *me* of entertaining such motives? I resent that immensely!'

'You said yourself that females need to marry well,' Stratham countered. 'How could I not find it suspicious that my father suddenly became so familiar with a female previously unknown to us? By the way, how, exactly, did you insinuate yourself into his good graces with such speed?'

'Insinuate myself—!' she echoed, incensed. 'The story behind our acquaintance is your father's to tell, if he chooses to. Speak to him.'

'Or is that only a convenient way of avoiding an answer? Which is even more suspicious.'

Over the years, she'd done a much better job of controlling her temper, but at his continued insinuations, fury erupted. 'If you want to accuse someone of being devious, maybe you should look to yourself! I've done nothing but be pleasant and obliging to your father. Whereas, with your courteous words and flattering invitation, you deliberately set out to deceive me about *your* intentions!'

'Only because deception was warranted,' he snapped back, looking as angry as she felt.

If she had been closer and not on horseback, she might have forgotten herself enough to slap him, so incensed was she. Whatever attraction she'd previously felt had withered in its heat, leaving only a desire to quit his obnoxious presence.

'I think we've said quite enough,' she fumed. 'You gentlemen seem to think only *you* have honour, but females do too, and you have disparaged mine. I shall bid you goodbye before this conversation disintegrates any further.' With that, she spurred her horse and took off at a gallop.

The fury of the wind catching at her hair and battering her hat matched her mood, so angry she couldn't even enjoy the gallop as she guided the mare around carriages, walkers and riders. Embarrassment deepening her hurt, she castigated herself for the stupidity of even considering Stratham had sought out her company because he'd felt some connection between them.

A mutual attraction and a developing camaraderie? What a fool she'd been—naive indeed! Had the past truly taught her nothing? Stratham had asked her to dance, sent her flowers, played the duet, and asked her to ride only to prevent her from supposedly trying to trap the Viscount into an advantageous marriage.

Insufferable, egotistical, condescending…her brain threw out adjective after pejorative adjective as she sped out of the park, pushing the mare as fast as she dared along the busy streets back to her sister's house. She avoided the most direct route, slipping down mews and backtracking to lessen the likelihood of Stratham catching up to her. She couldn't, wouldn't endure speaking with him right now.

She'd have one of the Dunbarton grooms return Ginger to the Viscount's stables. Then take a long, brisk walk in the town house garden before she would be able to return inside and risk encountering her sister.

As her anger faded, disappointment and dejection grew. She tried to look at every situation in the best light, as she'd told Stratham, but right now she was struggling to find a positive way to view these circumstances— and him. She supposed it was admirable that he wanted to protect his father. Although regrettable that he held such a cynical view of females, apparently believing them incapable of honesty when it came to seeking to better their position through marriage. But changing that sour view was not her problem.

She wouldn't have to worry any longer about the allure of his presence. It was unlikely that she'd see him again. Nor the Viscount, probably, once Stratham reported on their bitter exchange.

Just as well. She'd send back the Viscount's copy of Petrarch with a note expressing her thanks. Both the Viscount and the Baron were above her touch, after all. She'd give herself a short time to recover from her hurt and disillusion, a disappointment made keener by recalling the joyous excitement on the face of Lady Laura during the several afternoons she and Maggie had assisted their friend with her wedding preparations.

Not everyone could be fortunate enough to unexpectedly discover a forever love like that shared by Laura and her betrothed. Some must settle for the practical and prosaic—as she would by banishing Stratham from her mind and bending all her efforts to resolving the dilemma of her future, either accepting Fullridge's suit or the alternative of remaining unwed.

She was too dispirited at the moment to ponder either option.

By the time she reached the Dunbarton mews, she'd gone from furious to resigned to regretful. She should have lodged a strong but courteous objection to Stratham's suspicions, informed him that in light of them, she preferred to return home, and allowed him—or at least the groom—to escort her, rather than haring off impetuously through the city streets. Nor should she have made such sharp remarks to Stratham, even though she'd felt wronged—and once again, humiliated.

After she turned the mare over to a groom with instructions to rub her down and then return her to her owner, she slipped into the garden. As she paced, she considered ruefully how she'd thought—erroneously, it appeared—to have overcome the 'boyish impetuosity' of youth even her gentle mother had deplored. It was lowering to consider that perhaps she was habitually courteous and kind only because she was never provoked to be otherwise. When stung by Stratham's unfair accusations, she'd lost both courtesy and her temper.

Perhaps Stratham wasn't the only one whose character needed work.

She dreaded returning to the house, where her sister would undoubtedly greet her with a volley of questions about their ride. What was she to reply?

It would take a few more circuits along the garden paths until she was calm enough to mendaciously tell her sister that the ride had been pleasant, but she did not think it would be repeated. That with the Viscount gone to tend to estate matters, she didn't expect either Markham or his son to call again.

Which was a good thing. She should have known better than to have entertained the ridiculous notion that Stratham might be attracted to her. And if her eyes persisted in tearing up and she had to resist a strong desire to weep, that was her own fault. She should have learned her lesson years ago.

As she had then, she would weather this storm and emerge from it calm again, she told herself, swiping away a tear. She would view her future dispassionately, realistically. And never, *ever*, be so foolish again.

Chapter Ten

Some time later, Giles sat in his chamber, pouring himself some wine and reviewing the events of the last few hours.

He was finally calmer after running through a gamut of emotions after his sharp exchange with Miss Hasterling. He should have anticipated that sooner or later, she would quiz him about his motives in seeking her out. Especially now that he knew she felt too that flash of desire whenever they were together. But not having prepared a convincing response, he'd been caught flat-footed, gaping like fish thrown up on the bank. Not surprisingly, Miss Hasterling had taken offence and denied there was any truth to his suspicions.

Females have honour, too, and you have disparaged mine, she'd said hotly.

He'd thought of her as a kitten, but on this occasion, she'd been more like a tigress, her eyes sparking with fury.

Dismay, chagrin and the lowering suspicion that she might be justified in her outrage had already begun tempering his initial anger when Ginger suddenly galloped off. All other emotion was swept away in the terror that, by provoking her into inattention while they argued, he'd allowed the mare to run away with her.

By the time he was able to remount and tear off after them, the horse was already approaching the park gates.

But by then, as he watched her gallop ahead of him, skilfully veering around carriages and pedestrians, he realised she was in full control of her mount. Fear faded, replaced again by anger—and shame. Both emotions increased as he had to slow his pace as he neared the gate to manoeuvre around the incoming carriages and riders. He didn't manage to catch up to her before she exited the park, and by the time he reached the city street, she had vanished.

He paused there, wondering which way she would go. Deciding she would first return the horse to the Markham stables, he rode to King Street. When there was no sign of them there, he doubled back towards Lady Dunbarton's. He arrived at the mews behind her sister's house in a cold sweat of dread, for skilful or not, a rider could easily suffer an accident on the congested London streets.

A quick peek inside showed Ginger was not in the Dunbarton stables, either. Abandoning his horse, he sped on foot to the front entrance, determined to gain admittance despite his dishevelled appearance, driven to know whether Miss Hasterling had arrived home safely. The butler looked him up and down, but being a viscount's heir conferred some privileges, and despite his muddy riding clothes, he was shown in.

A measure of relief eased his concern when the servant said he would enquire whether the lady would receive him—if she had been injured during her ride or not yet returned, his request would certainly have generated a more agitated response. When the servant returned to inform him Miss Hasterling was not receiving and he asked if the man was certain, the butler replied frostily that he'd had his instructions from the young lady herself. Only then had he been able to relax, knowing by that sharp reply that she was indeed home and unharmed. Nor was he surprised, after their angry exchange, that she was not inclined to receive him.

Relieved of his anxiety and much of his anger, he returned home to find Ginger brushed down and contentedly munching hay, looking none the worse for her dash through the streets. With the episode at an end, there was nothing to do but make himself presentable and ponder what to do next.

As he sipped the wine, he contemplated the debacle from every angle. He still wasn't ashamed of having entertained suspicions—at least initially. The shame began as he realised that, deep down, by the time of their ride today, he'd already become convinced Miss Hasterling was exactly what she appeared to be. Rather than getting angry at her anger, he should have acknowledged that and apologised for doubting her.

He still didn't know how she had suddenly become so familiar with his father—the Viscount's story to tell, she claimed—but he'd uncovered no evidence that she had been trying to trick or otherwise unfairly influence his father.

A man's word was his bond; she obviously felt that true for her as well, and in doubting her, he'd denigrated her character. He had to admit that had anyone accused *him* of underhanded actions and disbelieved his denial, he would have been just as angry.

He gave a rueful laugh. His father, who had not yet left for Stratham Hall, might safely remain in town, since it was unlikely Miss Hasterling would be interested in seeing any more of *him*.

Whether she was or not, he owed her an apology for

misjudging her—and, as she'd proclaimed, impugning her honour. But when he thought about penning a note and ending their association, something within resisted.

Miss Hasterling had occupied much of his thoughts and attentions recently—had it only been ten days since their first encounter? Giles was surprised and a bit alarmed to discover how dismayed he felt at the prospect of terminating their association. As their acquaintance continued, he'd become increasingly convinced she was exactly the compassionate, clever and empathetic female his father had recommended as the best sort of feminine companion.

She'd shown she shared a talent for the music he loved and a horsemanship that matched his own skill. She possessed both an engaging sense of humour and a strong sense of honour. He recalled her comments about looking for the best in her fellow man, focusing on the beauty and kindness in the world rather than its cruelties and shortcomings. It was energising and up-lifting to be in the company of someone who chose to emphasise the positive.

And she was lovely. Not in the dazzling, comet-streaking-through-the-night-sky way of a Lucinda, but in the quiet, comforting way that a hot fire draws one to the hearth on a cold evening. Conjuring up her image, he felt again that slow simmer of attraction. A comet was brilliant, but distant and ephemeral. A warm hearth comforted for a lifetime.

In short, she was a unique and interesting woman he wanted to know better. Not to keep her from working her wiles on his father, but for his own sake.

But if he wanted to have a chance to know her better, he was going to have to come up with an apology humble and convincing enough to persuade her to see him again.

He half rose from his chair, his immediate thought to run to Bond Street. But no, he realised, resuming his seat, this was not Lucinda, to be placated with an expensive trinket. Costly jewellery would be an inappropriate gift for an unmarried lady anyway. Right now, she'd probably throw it back in his teeth even if it weren't.

What could he send to prove he was truly regretful?

Always before when he'd been anxious for reconciliation, he'd not been the party who'd caused the breach. That he was now gave his need to make things right a new, more urgent edge.

Flowers were always acceptable, or books. Perhaps he could look at Hatchard's for other volumes of Petrarch? In the meantime, he would order a bouquet that exemplified remorse and send it with a note.

He hoped, after her avowal to look for the best in life and encourage improvement in others, she would accept his apology and let them begin again. Though he had no idea where a relationship might take them, with his father's promise to support her later if he ceased his pursuit, he had an ever-deepening desire to find out.

This time, for himself alone.

The following morning, Eliza sat in the breakfast room staring at the enormous bouquet that had just been delivered, the unopened note accompanying it in her hand.

'Gorgeous!' Lady Dunbarton proclaimed as she walked in. 'Someone is very impressed! Who is it from?'

'I don't know,' she said numbly.

'Well, open the card, goose!' her sister said, laughing. Eliza wasn't sure she wanted to. It was unlikely to have come from Fullridge, whom she hadn't seen since the musicale. After their acrimonious parting, why would Stratham send one?

But as she looked more closely at the blossoms selected, she began to suspect it might be from the Baron after all. Which was unfortunate, because she didn't need the temptation to forgive him that such an elaborate tribute seemed to urge.

The large selection of flowers had a common theme—especially when one noted the greenery which set them off. Sweet woodruff, representing humility, bluebells for humility as well, and an assortment of white blooms denoting purity, along with daffodils indicating sincere regard, daisies for innocence, and iris that added notes of faith, trust, wisdom, hope and valour. Was that recalling her claim to look for the best in people? The sender had even managed to locate some early white roses… which signified a request for new beginnings.

With all the messages the flower choice conveyed, she hardly needed to read the note.

But trapped under her sister's gaze, she couldn't avoid it. She'd fobbed Maria off yesterday, proud of the calm tone she'd managed while describing a 'pleasant' ride during which the Baron had advised her of his father's departure, and her conclusion that they would not be seeing either gentleman again soon. It was only reasonable that her sister would want to know if this bouquet represented the advance of some other courtship. Maria wanted the best for her, and with the Season soon to end, was increasingly worried that Eliza would finish it unwed.

She pulled the single sheet from the envelope, a surge of troubled emotions filling her. That unease deepened as she noted Stratham's rather than Markham's crest on the stationery.

My dear Miss Hasterling,
Please accept this humble tribute as my sincere apology for my boorish behaviour yesterday. I had no excuse to be angry, while you had every reason. You rightly pointed out that had anyone questioned my veracity, thereby impugning my honour, I would have been incensed.

I confess I did entertain suspicions about your motives in regard to my father upon our first acquaintance, but our subsequent association had already done much to dispel them. I should have accepted your word as the final reason to dismiss them entirely.

Please forgive me for not doing so. I regret my conduct and beg that you will harness that sterling character that seeks to find the best in your fellow man and give me an opportunity to begin again. I pledge to do better.
Yours sincerely,
Stratham

'Well, what did it say?' her sister demanded. 'Who is it from?'

'From… King Street,' she said, not wanting to lie outright.

'King Street?' her sister echoed. 'It took you that long to read an address?'

'I was admiring the crest and trying to determine its symbolism,' she said lamely. 'Stratham told me his father would be out of town for some time. Perhaps he wished to send a parting tribute.' None of that was strictly a falsehood, she told herself.

Lady Dunbarton's sceptical expression said she didn't believe her, but thankfully she didn't press Eliza further. 'That was kind of the gentleman. You must return a note of thanks.'

Eliza nodded to her sister, but what she really wanted to do was send the whole bouquet back. Unfortunately, there was no way to refuse the flowers without giving her sister an explanation she would rather avoid.

After almost shouting her down in the park, how dare Stratham now sound so…reasonable? So apologetic? Conceding he had insulted her, admitting he now believed she'd not tried to cast out lures to his father? Making it difficult to impossible for her not to forgive him.

In spite of her attempt to always look for the best in her fellow man—how aggravating of Stratham to use that aspiration against her!—she'd rather try to squelch any sympathy and maintain her anger. Only anger could buttress her against the insidious allure of his charm and that pesky, persistent sensual attraction that pulled her to him like iron filings to a magnet.

'I'll go write that note,' she said, anxious to quit her sister's scrutiny.

The note she sent back, she thought as she walked to her chamber, would not be the simple thanks her sister recommended. She would be courteous but firm, telling Stratham she didn't need expensive bribes to leave his father alone, as she had no intention of 'luring' him. Since their whole acquaintance had been based on that erroneous assumption, now that he accepted his suspicions were groundless, there was no further need for them to associate.

Not if she was to clear her mind and concentrate on

attainable ways to settle her future, she thought. She couldn't afford to squander any more of the Season in his titillating, exciting, but ultimately pointless company. She needed a husband, not a duet partner or a riding companion who inspired her with impossible erotic yearnings.

Would he call again after he received her note? The problem with not confiding in her sister was she'd given her sponsor no reason not to admit Stratham if he did visit. Prowling the town house garden wouldn't distance her far enough from her sister's expectation that she receive him if he showed up at Brook Street.

As she finished the note, a potential haven occurred. In storms past, she'd taken refuge in her father's library, escaping the heartache of the present by immersing herself in the past. That library wasn't available, but she had nearby an even better resource, one where she and her father had spent pleasant hours on previous trips to London. The King's Library at the British Museum housed King George IV's donation of over sixty-five thousand volumes, including works of history, theology, geography and classical French, Italian and British literature from the earliest printed books to those of the present day.

A sense of calm descended, sweetened by a touch of anticipation. She hadn't made time to visit the Library during this year's sojourn in the City, so spending an afternoon there would be a genuine pleasure. It wasn't a long-term solution, should Stratham persist in his attempts at a reconciliation, but it would work for today.

Though she would avoid reading any Petrarch.

An hour later, Eliza halted before the imposing Greek portico of the East Wing of the British Museum, letting its classic beauty settle over her, calming and inspiring despite the noise and dust created by the ongoing construction of the matching wings behind her.

She spared a rueful glance at her maid, wishing she could have had her father accompany her instead. Her sister, rightfully, wouldn't allow her to traipse about London without a companion, and had urged her to take a footman. However, knowing none of the servants would be excited about spending the afternoon surrounded by books, she'd opted for the maid, figuring the girl would be more easily reconciled than a footman by the promise of a nap in a chair while her mistress browsed and a stop for sweetmeats afterwards.

After purchasing their tickets, they were escorted by the porter into the library itself. Even the maid, Eliza thought, should be impressed by the soaring, coffered ceilings, and the tall windows beneath that provided bright illumination for the tables that ran between the long walls of bookshelves. She was pleasantly surprised to discover the librarian who met them in the Reading Room to be the same one who had supervised the room during her previous visits.

The man claimed to remember her, bowing and asking after her father's health. It might be more than a chivalrous courtesy, she thought; there probably weren't many *ton* maidens who visited the library, with or without their fathers.

An even happier thought occurred. 'Mr Quarles,' she whispered, 'as I am known to you as a serious student, would you allow me to dismiss my maid? Since you will remain in the room, a scholar eminently suited to stand in for my father as a chaperon, I could send her off to a tea room. I'm sure she would be happier waiting for me there.'

After a moment's hesitation, the librarian nodded. 'Better not to have a young person about who might, out of boredom, begin riffling through the volumes. Some are exceedingly delicate! You must notify me when you are ready to leave, though, so I may send a porter to summon your maid.' He shook a finger at her. 'Your father would not approve my allowing you to walk about the streets unattended.'

'You are indeed very kind. I will tell my father how diligently you saw to my care.'

Another visitor across the room, struggling to remove a heavy volume from a shelf, caught the librarian's attention. 'Excuse me! I must aid Lord Summerlin.'

As he bustled off, Eliza informed the maid of her good fortune, gave her a coin for her refreshments and told her the porter would collect her later. Her agitated spirits calmed at the prospect of immersing herself in a story, unhindered by knowing how impatiently her maid would be waiting for her to finish it.

For one blissful afternoon, she could set aside all the worries that bedevilled her days and troubled her sleep—the conundrum of what to do about Stratham, whether or not to encourage Fullridge, what choice she should make for her future.

She intended to make the afternoon a long one.

Chapter Eleven

But as Eliza proceeded to the shelves with French literature that Mr Quarles indicated, she found thoughts of Stratham continued to bedevil her. Why had confirming his suspicions been so upsetting, when in her heart of hearts, she'd known from the first that he had only taken up with her to prevent her 'pursuing' his father? Had she really expected a duet, a dance and a handful of conversations to change that view? More important, why was she still so blasted attracted to him, regretting even now the end of the relationship, when she couldn't trust what he said or did?

On the other hand, that believe-the-best-about-everyone side whispered, he had frankly admitted his fault and asked for another chance with every appearance of humility. There'd been no note of condescension, no overtones that he was tendering the apology for form's sake, and no hint he felt forgiveness from one of her humbler position was his due, as she might have expected from one of his wealth and stature.

Given that he'd misrepresented his intentions before, could she trust him enough to believe what he said, if she should allow them to begin again?

He'd conceded in his note that he now believed she

wasn't trying to entangle his father. But why would he wish for *her* friendship? As she was well aware, given their respective stations, he wouldn't be interested in a more serious connection. She might be socially beneath him, but she was gentry-born, so he couldn't have illicit intentions.

And with time so short and her attraction to him so strong, could she afford a friendship with someone who would distract her from concentrating on the urgent problem of settling her future?

Irritated with herself for wasting another half-hour in the same circular arguments instead of embracing the calm of scholarship she'd come here to find, she selected a volume of French poetry and carried it to a reading table.

She had succeeded so well in submerging herself that when, several hours later, she heard a voice behind her, she didn't immediately realise it was her name being called.

The bewitching, beguiling tenor of the voice so reminded her of Stratham that a shiver rippled over her skin and her heart leapt. Irritated, she reined in the response. Goodness, could the echo of his voice not stop bedevilling her even here?

Frowning in annoyance, she whirled around to face the caller—and froze.

Standing behind her, looking down with a slight smile, was Lord Stratham.

'What are you doing here?' she whispered furiously.

'Looking for you,' he whispered back.

'I mean why—how did you even know to look here for me?'

'I called at your sister's to see if I could persuade you

to see me, since the bouquet I sent was obviously not compelling enough. Lady Dunbarton said you'd gone out, and when I asked her where, said only that you'd gone to a place that comforted you when you were troubled.'

Eliza felt her face heat. Apparently, her sister was more perceptive than she'd imagined.

Stratham smiled ruefully. 'She looked like she wanted to blister my ears but refrained, instead sending me away coolly. When you'd come home distressed after riding with me, and a large bouquet arrived soon after, I suppose it wasn't too difficult to piece together the connection. Father told me you'd mentioned that you enjoyed visiting the King's Library. So I thought what better place to seek solace after being upset by a boorish and insulting gentleman than in a library?'

Having him stand so close—a necessity when they must whisper, but none the less a proximity that awakened every nerve and set her pulses pounding again—made it difficult to concentrate on anything beyond his physical presence. She struggled for a moment to create some order out the muddle that awareness made of her brain, finally replying as the realisation emerged, 'I thought Lord Markham was in the country!'

'He—well…' Stratham flushed. 'He planned to go, but hasn't left yet. To make a full confession, his reason for leaving was to allow me to…get to know you better, without the awkward complication of his competing interest.'

She shook her head, trying to make sense of that pronouncement. 'Not to impugn *your* honour, but how can I believe you?'

Stratham's flush deepened. 'You have every reason to be sceptical. But I assure you, on the honour I consider sacred, what I'm telling you now is the truth. Noticing that I had an…inclination towards you, my father, who admires you greatly, wanted to give me time to see where that inclination might lead. Now, will you forgive his maladroit and impertinent son?'

At that moment, Mr Quarles startled her by appearing behind them. 'Is this gentleman disturbing you, Miss Hasterling?' he whispered.

'No, Sir. He's a…a family friend, come to check on me,' she replied, not wanting to delve into the complicated dynamics between them. 'Lord Stratham, this is Mr Quarles, one of the senior librarians. Mr Quarles, Lord Stratham.'

Nodding, he whispered, 'You may continue your conversation, then—but keep your voices low. Scholars are at work.'

Eliza waited until the librarian was out of earshot before saying, 'Do you wish to regain my good opinion only to prove you can win it back?'

Stratham winced. 'I suppose I deserve that low assessment of my character. But I defend at least my initial behaviour by asking you to think about your own father. Were he widowed and grieving, would you not feel compelled to protect him, even though he is a man, supposedly well able to care for himself?'

He had her at that. There was little she wouldn't do to safeguard those dearest to her.

At her reluctant nod, he continued, 'I only sought to do the same for my father. Much as you look for the good in others, surely you are realistic enough to admit there are ladies prepared to use any stratagem to become the wife of a rich viscount.'

She didn't have to think hard to bring to mind several females on the Marriage Mart—or their ambitious mamas—who'd be willing to scheme and plot to obtain a rich, titled husband. 'Perhaps. But I'm not such a lady.'

'I know that now. I suppose I've known it from the first. I owe you a profound apology for maligning your character. Won't you allow me to make it up to you?'

It was oh-so-tempting to agree. But after spending hours in exhaustive self-argument, she knew it would be safer to put an end to their association. She was far too vulnerable to his insidious attraction. Which, despite his intriguing mention of an 'inclination' for her, she knew could not end by assuring her future.

'I accept your apology. There's nothing else you need do to "make it up to me".'

Stratham smiled. 'But I'll not believe you have truly forgiven me unless you allow me to call on you again.'

Why was he making this so difficult? 'I can't imagine why you would wish to,' she said with some exasperation.

'Because I genuinely like you. It's as simple as that.' After looking around quickly to make sure no one observed them, he took her hand.

'I feel a…connection between us. Don't you feel it, too? I want to explore it further. If you truly want to terminate our association, I'll respect your wishes and not trouble you again. But I hope very much you will permit me to see you.'

Eliza looked down at the hand he still held. She could feel the warmth vibrating from his fingers to hers, then a tremor that flashed all the way to the core of her when he lifted those fingers to his lips and kissed them, his gaze never leaving her face.

Her mind went blank, her chest so tight she could scarcely breathe. Desire intensifying, she wished he were touching those lips to her own, rather than to her hand.

Time seemed suspended until he raised his head again, his gaze moving to her mouth. She felt her lips tingle and burn...and wondered if he would kiss her.

As he leaned closer, the excitement pulsing in her veins made her dizzy. Until suddenly he stepped away—and bowed to two elderly gentlemen approaching them.

Too absorbed in their own conversation to do more than nod as they passed, the men walked on to the other side of the room.

Stratham waited until the gentlemen were well beyond them. Voice still at a whisper, but vibrating with intensity, he said, '*Will* you see me again?'

Despite all the excellent reasons for her to refuse, somehow she heard herself saying, 'Y-yes, you may call on me.'

He gave her a smile so warm it would have thawed the frostiest maiden. 'Thank you. Now, you may prove your good intentions by allowing me to escort you home once you've finished your reading.'

She blinked. 'You would...wait for me?'

'For as long as necessary.'

'But you've said you're not much of a reader. Surely you would be bored.'

'Perhaps I'll become a better reader. If you and Father find the classics so inspiring, I should brush up on my rusty Latin.'

She was still having trouble concentrating, her brain bouncing between the giddy knowledge that Stratham wanted to know her better, the vague disappointment of having perhaps missed his kiss, and the panicky warning that allowing herself to see more of him was a mistake.

But another voice, the one that kept her gaze on his lips, impatiently dismissed that cautious voice. She'd already given permission, so what was the point of worrying over it? She should savour the attentions of this handsome, compelling man who made her lips burn and her senses sing for the probably short time those attentions lasted.

After all, she would likely have a lifetime to settle either for the bland security of a marriage of convenience or a passionless life whose only warmth was the love of family.

'I'll let you get back to reading,' he said, giving her a wink before heading off to the shelves.

She couldn't help but watch him under lowered lashes as he paused in the Latin section and selected a volume. And then had to look quickly back down at her own book as he began walking back in her direction, lest he catch her spying on him.

To her mingled delight and consternation, he settled into the chair beside her.

Though she kept her gaze on the page, she was all too aware of his presence. Eddies of sensation seemed to dart and dance between them as they sat side by side, close enough to touch but not touching.

She stared at the words, willing them to make sense, then realised she'd translated the same sentence four times. Stifling a sigh, she knew maintaining her concentration was hopeless. Not with Stratham beside her.

Had he taken that seat deliberately, knowing how much his nearness affected her?

Or…delicious, novel thought…because her nearness affected *him*?

Though she kept her face over the book, her eyes stared unseeing at the pages while she wondered what might have happened if, instead of being in a library of scholars, they had been walking down a path in her sister's garden, alone but for twittering birds. Would he have leaned down and kissed her? What would his lips have felt like, caressing hers?

Heat flushed her and a curious melting feeling began in her belly, along with the now-familiar tingling all over her body.

She blew out a breath, reining in her marauding thoughts with difficulty. She'd come here to recover tranquillity, but with the person who was disturbing it sitting beside her, she might as well give up the attempt.

Not daring to let him see whatever he might read in her eyes if she looked at him now, she kept her face lowered, forcing herself to count silently to a thousand. Then, somewhat calmer, she closed the volume.

'I've reached the end of the passage,' she whispered. 'We can go now.'

He nodded, then rose and followed her as she walked over to Mr Quarles. 'We left the volumes for you to reshelve. Thank you for your kind chaperonage, Sir. Lord Stratham can escort me to collect my maid.'

'I'll take good care of her,' Stratham assured him.

'I shall look forward to your next visit. Perhaps with your excellent father.'

'Thank you and good day, Sir.'

After they exited the building, Eliza said, 'My maid is waiting at the tea room next door, so you needn't see me all the way home.'

'Mr Quarles would be displeased if I abandoned you at the tea room,' Stratham protested. 'While you fetch your maid, I'll summon a hackney.'

'Very well,' she replied, once again giving in. As they walked to the tea room, Eliza wondered what her sister would think when she arrived home under Stratham's escort. What excited chatter would erupt in the servants' hall when the maid told the other staff about her mistress's escapade.

And into what folly her rashness in disregarding the voice of prudence was going to lead.

Eliza's nonchalance at tempting fate had lasted through the giddy delight of sitting beside Stratham in the hackney bearing them back from the British Museum, the initially surprised but approving Lady Dunbarton, who invited the Baron to stay for tea, and through the family dinner during which her brother-in-law, in town for one of his occasional visits, teased her about her conquest, despite her laughing denials.

But once laid down upon her bed, sleep eluded her as the doubts and worries crowded back in. The very fact that she spent the afternoon and evening wrapped in the glow of spending time with him instead of planning how to engage Mr Fullridge in conversation at the Countess's upcoming dinner should warn her how easily his attention distracted her from the urgent task of settling her future.

Once again, she went round and round the facts that argued for her to terminate their pleasant but pointless friendship, without succeeding in convincing herself to give it up. She finally fell asleep, exhausted, after compromising that she would indulge herself by continuing to see Stratham, but only on expeditions that displayed her true interests.

He said he wanted to get to know her better; she would let him. Once he discovered how little she resembled the proper *ton* maidens from among whom he expected to choose a wife, he'd turn his attentions elsewhere. Finally freeing her to concentrate on more pressing matters.

Chapter Twelve

Two days later, Giles arrived at Lady Dunbarton's to escort Miss Hasterling on the sketching expedition she'd proposed. When she'd first mentioned the park, he'd thought she meant to suggest another ride, something he'd been eagerly anticipating so he might replace the memory of the acrimonious ending of the previous outing with a happier experience.

It appeared Miss Hasterling not only excelled as a scholar, played the pianoforte beautifully, rode well and uplifted all those around her with her optimistic outlook—she was also an artist. Was there any limit to her abilities? Since he now trusted that she would not try to impress him by pretending to be something she was not, she must be at least modestly talented, else she would not have requested the outing.

He wasn't exactly sure what he would do while she worked, as he had no pretensions to artistic skill. But he'd figure out something.

She'd also requested that he escort her to the park in his phaeton, after confirming that her sketchbook and paints would all fit within the limited space in the vehicle. Another request he was happy to fulfil, hoping that displaying his driving skill wouldn't make him seem too vain.

Once again, he arrived at the designated hour to find Miss Hasterling ready to depart. Having had almost always to wait on Lucinda to complete her toilette before they left for some event, he appreciated her promptness.

As he helped her into the vehicle, he let his hands linger on her waist as long as he dared. Though she never wore gowns that emphasised her figure or were cut low enough to reveal a daring decolletage, his fingers confirmed the pleasing curve of her waist, shadowed by the swell of her breasts. He clenched his jaw to stop his rampaging imagination from visualising what delights her slender body would reveal, could he see it without the layers of clothing.

But earning that right would mean marriage, and he wasn't ready to consider that—yet. Still, it was the first time he'd thought of wedlock in terms of any woman but Lucinda.

Regardless of how their relationship progressed, perhaps Miss Hasterling was the one who could help him 'look elsewhere and begin healing', as his father hoped.

He climbed up beside her, savouring as he took his seat an immediate, charged sense of sensual connection that played over his skin like the soft brush of silk. Fortunately, driving through the busy streets required him to focus his attention on his horses, helping to keep his simmering ardour under control.

He had to admit, as he guided the team around a heavily loaded dray, he still longed for the kiss he'd almost given her in the King's Library—unwise as that would have been. Had she regretted as much as he did having yielded to prudence?

How soon would he have another opportunity? And would she be as eager for it as he was?

It wouldn't be today, in a park where riders, carriages and strollers could pass by at any moment, not to mention his tiger's presence on his perch behind them.

Nor should he kiss her, he reminded himself. There could be no trifling with an unmarried maiden; taking such liberties would imply a level of commitment he wasn't yet prepared to offer, no matter how much she intrigued him.

'Is there any particular place in the park you would like to go?' he asked, turning his attention back to the matter at hand.

'Along the bend of the Serpentine. The reflections on the water create intriguing combinations of colour and movement. Watercolour is one of the best mediums to capture that, the colours easily blended and drying to their final hue quickly. There's a softness one cannot achieve with pastels or oils, perfect for the moody blend of sky and cloud.'

'You play, paint, ride—do you have a monopoly on all the feminine accomplishments?'

She laughed. 'Goodness, no! My sisters considered me hopeless, and even my mother often despaired of me. Rather than walk decorously, I was always chasing frogs and hopping over streams, returning with my sleeves covered in grass stains, my hems muddy, and my hair full of tangles. I love working with hue and shade in watercolour, but loathe creating pictures in needlework—it is so tedious and takes too long!'

He looked away from his horses for a moment to give her a quick glance. 'I can't comment on the quality of your needlework, but your sleeves and hem look pristine, and your coiffure is very neatly bestowed beneath your hat.'

She grinned. 'Only after years of practice—not to mention, the maid my sister assigned to me here, who was charged not to let me out of my chamber until she was sure my appearance wouldn't embarrass Maria in front of her friends. I do enjoy fashion, one feminine attribute, I suppose. It's another play of light and colour, shape and symmetry. Though much of current fashion is too exaggerated. Ladies' sleeves so wide it is impossible to do anything with one's hands! Gentlemen with nipped-in waistcoats whose hems flare out like abbreviated ballgowns! I'm glad you prefer more traditional attire.'

'Does that mean you think I look handsome in it?' he teased.

She tapped his sleeve. 'Don't be vain. You know very well you are handsome.'

He chuckled, pleased with the compliment even if he did have to solicit it. 'No flaring waistcoats for me to blow about in the breeze. It would frighten Midnight.'

'I might know you would consider the well-being of your horse. You drive well, too,' she observed. 'You took that last corner faster than I would have guessed possible, but without causing the least bit of sway in the carriage. Skilfully done!'

He found himself inordinately pleased by her compliment—the first he could recall her giving him. Not for Miss Hasterling the extravagant flattery offered by so many young ladies trying to ingratiate themselves with eligible gentlemen. Her praise was the more valuable for being rare. And as he knew by now, more valuable still as it represented her absolutely honest opinion.

A few minutes later, he guided the phaeton through

the park gates. 'Where to now? Is there a particular location you prefer?'

'If you could pull up just there…' she gestured '… where the Serpentine is closest to the carriage way.'

Giles obligingly halted the vehicle where she indicated, the tiger coming to the horses' heads while Giles handed her down, once again letting his hands linger as long as he dared.

Drat, but he wanted that kiss!

He fetched her bag from the tiger and told him to walk the team while he strolled with her to the river's edge and helped her set up her easel and painting supplies.

'Thank you,' she said, smiling—one of those sweet, glowing smiles that poured over him like warm honey and heated him from the inside out. 'I prefer not to have someone hovering over me while I work. You can stroll if you like, or sit on a nearby bench.'

Well, that was him neatly dismissed, he thought, amused. 'I'll stroll, but keep watch to make sure no one disturbs you.'

Leaving her to her paints, he set off at an idle pace on the footpath that bordered the water. The sky boasted a mix of sun and clouds, and a soft breeze blew across the lake's surface, whipping up small rivulets that, as she'd pointed out, served as multi-faceted mirrors of the sky above them.

The melancholy he'd been fighting for weeks now whenever he wasn't focused on some particular task seemed to ease under the spell of the golden sun and lapping waves. As he listened to the birdsong, the clop of hooves and jingle of harness from the carriage way, the laughter and shouts of two small boys playing hoops, a sense of peace and calm he'd not felt in a long time settled over him.

He looked back to where Miss Hasterling stood at her easel, her gaze flitting from her sketchbook to the river, the sky, and back. There was something so…intense, and yet serene about her. She made a charming picture, her absorbed profile and upraised brush silhouetted against the water.

Who would have thought he could find such contentment in the simplicity of a sunlit stroll? Admiring a lady who was ignoring him in favour of her art, who gave him freely only her smiles? But one who also asked nothing of him, trying neither to entice him into wedlock nor to wheedle favours from him. Who, in fact, told him pointedly she had no desire for gifts. Who must know by now she held sensual power over him—but made no attempt to use it.

For a while he stood at a distance and simply watched her, appreciating her total absorption in her task.

Then he strolled back, halting a few steps away so as not to seem as though he was trying to peek at her work uninvited. 'Is the painting going well?'

She startled, then looked up.

'Sorry, I didn't mean to disturb you.'

She waved the hand not wielding a paintbrush. 'No harm done. I do become…rather preoccupied when I'm working. I shall need a bit longer to finish, I'm afraid.'

'Take as much time as you need. Do you mind if I take the horses for a circuit around the park? I don't like to let them stand too long. I'll leave Finch to keep watch.'

'Drive if you wish. Though I would be happy to exercise the team for you later,' she added with an impish look.

He chuckled. 'Kind of you, but I must refuse.'

'I thought you'd been cured of doubting me,' she said with a frown. 'I'm quite a skilled driver.'

'Can you truly claim to have experience driving a high-perch phaeton?'

'Perhaps not one as high as yours, but I can certainly drive a phaeton. As I told you, I often drove my family. Since I never knew what sort of transport might be available, depending on whether Father had driven out and which vehicles were being used for the farm, I learned to handle all sorts, from a pony cart to a farm wagon to a phaeton to our neighbour's barouche.'

'A barouche!' he exclaimed. 'That usually requires a strong-armed coachman! Your neighbour allowed *you* to drive it?'

'Well, she allowed the family to borrow it,' she amended. 'I confess, I coaxed her coachman to teach me. An elderly man who had been with Lady Marsden for many years, he preferred to sit in the sun in front of the public house on a warm day, or by the fire with a mug of ale in winter rather than bounce about on the driver's box when our family wanted to go visiting.'

Giles shook his head. 'What a risk he took! I imagine his employer would have sacked him if she knew.'

'It was excellent practice in handling a team. I can drive up to four horses with confidence.'

'In the country, perhaps. London, with all its noise and congestion, would be a different matter. Horses, nervous creatures that they are, are far too prone to shy or bolt.'

'The country also has its distractions,' she countered. 'Rabbits darting across the road, leaves blowing into their eyes, gamekeeper's gunshots in the woods. Horses take objection to those too.'

'Is that experience speaking?'

She sighed ruefully. 'Hard-won experience.'

'Perhaps you have developed some skill,' he allowed.

'Gracious of you to concede it,' she said drily, giving

him an aggravated look that suggested she would have liked to pitch her paint brush at him. 'Go, then, exercise your horses. I will try to have my scene finished by the time you return.'

Smiling, he walked back to reclaim his team and dispatched his tiger to stand guard over Miss Hasterling. As he drove off, the lad was loitering by the water's edge, skipping stones, the lady once again absorbed in her painting.

He had to chuckle when he considered how their outing had progressed. He couldn't imagine squiring any other young lady and then having her voluntarily send him off, especially not in Hyde Park at the beginning of the promenade hour, when he would almost certainly encounter parties with young ladies who would try to detain him.

Miss Hasterling was proving yet again to be unlike any other society lady he'd known.

After several circuits around the Park's carriage trails—nodding to acquaintances, but *not* stopping to talk or flirt with any of the ladies—his horses were sufficiently exercised. Slowing their pace to let them cool down, he headed towards the place by the Serpentine where Miss Hasterling was painting.

Perhaps he could provoke the kitten to once again unsheathe her claws. It was bad of him, but he found it delightful to disturb a surface calm he was beginning to discover required a good deal of effort on her part to maintain. The spirited response he'd occasionally roused gave him a glimpse of a passion that intrigued and excited him.

Would he ever be privileged to unleash it?

He found her as absorbed in her work as she'd been when he left her. Motioning the tiger to come take the team, he approached quietly so as not to disturb her—getting in the process a good look at her painting.

She'd created a view of water and sky that mirrored and repeated each other, the small, sharp curves of the waves seeming to vibrate with motion against the white caps and the reflection of the scudding clouds. It was, not surprisingly, very good.

Charmed by her skill, he stood silently watching until at last, she put down her brush and noticed him.

'You do paint as well as you play pianoforte.'

She flushed slightly. 'You…you've looked at the picture. You like it?'

'It's lovely. I wouldn't have thought you could capture the movement of waves and their reflections so well in watercolour. In oils, yes—the glisten of oil catching the light.'

She nodded. 'Whereas in watercolour, it is the absence of paint, the white paper showing through, which creates the light.'

'Exactly. Beautifully done!'

Her blush deepened. 'Thank you. I think it came out well. It's a challenge to try to capture the beauty we find everywhere.'

'Do you find beauty everywhere?'

'Do you not?' At his raised eyebrows, she pointed to the canopy of leaves behind them. 'Only look at the colour of the trees!'

He did, and shrugged. 'Green?'

She waved an impatient hand. 'No, truly *look*! Yes, the leaves are "green", but it's not a single hue. There's the deep green and black of the trees in deep shade, which lightens to emerald and grass-green as the sunlight they receive increases. Then there—' she pointed '—the leaves turn apple-green and brighter still, to lime and almost shimmers of gold where the breeze ripples them in full sun. Every object teems with colour in that way—and it changes with the medium, too. Come, look.'

She seized his hand, the intensity of her motions magnifying the burn of her fingers clutching his. Powerful sensation shot to the core of him, igniting a flare of desire.

While he struggled to control his unexpectedly strong reaction, she tugged him to the edge of the Serpentine. 'See the seaweed along the bank? Bright green at the water's edge, with the spray from the breaking waves outlining it in a sparkle of crystal drops. Then below the surface, the colour is muted, darkened, the shape of the leaves distorted by being submerged.' She looked back up at him. 'How can you not find that fascinating?'

Giles stared at the water's edge, truly seeing for the first time the kaleidoscope of colour in a simple seagrass above and below the water's surface. Then back to her avid face, her eager expression urging him to see the wonder as she did.

And what a wonder he did see. A lady who could be transfixed by a simple weed and utterly intent on sharing its beauty. Passion pulsed through the fingers twined with his; a passion in that chaste and innocent creature that moved him more deeply than the studied techniques of his experienced lover.

'It is fascinating. I suppose I never looked closely enough,' he murmured—though his gaze encompassed much more than just the flowing seagrass.

He silently thanked the guardian angel watching over him for the good fortune of meeting her and her good nature in forgiving him and letting him continue to see her. Each further glimpse she gave him of the woman beneath the initially reticent exterior made him eager to know more.

As he continued to stare at her, she seemed to suddenly realise she still clutched his hand. Her cheeks colouring, she dropped it abruptly, as if scorched by the intensity of the desire she'd evoked.

'Well, I hope you did find it interesting,' she said, turning to walk back to her easel. 'Not as much as I do, I'm sure. I tend to get...carried away by my enthusiasms.'

'Would that more people shared your appreciation for the world's simple beauties.'

As if afraid she'd stripped away too much of the veneer of maidenly restraint an unmarried girl was supposed to display, she turned away and began packing up her supplies. 'Thank you for your kindness in bringing me today. I only hope you weren't too bored.'

'I wasn't bored at all.' When she turned to give him a sharp look, he said, 'Truly. And you must accept *my* word when I say I speak the truth.'

'Very well.' Her face softening, she smiled shyly. 'I'm glad...you enjoyed it.'

He recaptured her hand and kissed it. 'More than you can imagine.'

She curled her fingers around his and pressed them. For a moment they stood, gazes locked, bound together by the beating pulse of their joined fingers. Then she seemed to remember a maiden was not supposed to clutch the hand of a gentleman to whom she was not promised, and released him.

'We should get back. I'm sure you have other commitments.'

He did—a meeting at his club, cards, dinner. But at this moment, none of that appealed. He didn't want to quit her unique and unusual presence. 'Nothing until later. But I'll drive you back, if you are ready.'

She gave a little sigh. 'I shall have to be.'

Meaning what? he wondered as he carried her bag of supplies to the phaeton, then helped her up. That tasks awaited her at Lady Dunbarton's she needed to address? That she should terminate this meeting before she revealed herself even more fully? Or better still, that she was as reluctant to end their time together as he was?

She was silent on the drive back. With the increase in traffic, the *ton* headed to the park for the Promenade Hour along with the usual drays, horses, carriages and pedestrians, he had to focus too much attention on driving to be able to question her.

After pulling up the carriage in front of her sister's town house, he jumped down to assist her. No way was he going to cede to his tiger the opportunity to touch her again.

He hoped she might invite him in, but as he escorted her up the stairs, she said, 'Forgive me for parting in haste, but I must hurry. I've promised my niece and nephews a round of stories before supper.'

'Mustn't disappoint the young ones.' Though he was disappointed. 'I'll see you again, then. Soon.'

She gave him a slight smile. 'If you like.'

'I do.'

'Then I suppose I will. Good day, Lord Stratham. Thank you again for the drive.'

'My pleasure, Miss Hasterling.'

And it had been. He watched her enter the house and walk down the passage, not taking his leave until the door closed behind her.

She'd seemed…withdrawn those last few minutes in

the Park, after she'd pulled him to the pond and trapped his fingers in hers.

Was she embarrassed to have revealed that glimpse of her passionate, impulsive nature? To have seized and held his fingers while he gazed into her eyes, seeing in them the same desire that was flooding him?

He supposed the mother and sisters who'd criticised her for skipping on rocks and muddying her hems would have deplored such uninhibited enthusiasm.

He loved it. Her passionate conviction and complete devotion to the task she was engaged in. Her determination to find beauty and worth wherever she looked.

Oh, yes, he wanted to see more of her.

Chapter Thirteen

Eliza stood at the upstairs window, watching as Lord Stratham mounted his phaeton and drove off, still surprised by the ardent expression which had lit his face when he affirmed he wanted to see her again—soon—and his avowal that he'd enjoyed an outing during which she'd not paid him much attention.

Could such a sought-after, high-born society gentleman truly have enjoyed a simple sketching expedition?

She'd been surprised when he returned so quickly from driving his horses around the park. She'd rather expected such an eligible man would have been waylaid by one or several parties of society ladies and gentlemen making their afternoon promenades, and lingered to chat and flirt.

She cringed as she recalled her lack of restraint as she tugged him about, urging him to see as she did the wonder of the variation in colour and shape of objects brought about by the change in the sun's intensity, the water's density.

So much for remaining calm and serene, as a well-mannered young maiden was supposed to be.

Her mother would have sighed, her perfectly behaved sisters been embarrassed.

But Stratham…had seemed appreciative.

Could he truly have been as enchanted by those wonders as she was?

It was unlikely. She tried to tamp down her delight that he'd seemed to appreciate what moved her so deeply.

Maybe this elegant, well-born gentleman did have more in common with her than just that always simmering, inexplicable physical attraction.

But he *was* a high-born gentleman, a fact she must never lose sight of. Whatever they might share, friendship would be the extent of it. She couldn't afford to throw herself into a relationship which was almost certainly temporary to the neglect of planning for a future that would be permanent.

It would be wiser to end their association before she invested too much more time in it. Or forgot herself completely and let the desire he generated prompt her to embrace him, as she very nearly did at the King's Library.

He was like a whirlwind gusting through her life, disturbing all her settled thoughts and expectations, whipping up eddies of passion and desire she didn't need and shouldn't act upon. Awakening longings she probably would never be able to fulfil, yearnings that could only lead to sadness and disappointment.

But oh, how thrilling that prosaic expedition had turned out to be! She had the memory of the pure beauty of sharing something that inspired her with another soul who seemed to recognise and appreciate it, something she had previously experienced only with her father. She could treasure that, even if Stratham did reconsider the wisdom of befriending a clergyman's over-exuberant daughter and decided not to call again.

But she would honour this afternoon's enjoyment by

doing exactly what she'd told the Baron she intended, weaving fantasies for the enjoyment of her niece and nephews. And put out of mind for tonight any dutiful, practical considerations about her future.

Eliza wasn't sure whether to be thrilled or alarmed when the following afternoon, the butler interrupted her study to report that Lord Stratham had called. As they hadn't arranged another meeting and it wasn't one of her sister's at-home days, she hadn't expected him.

Why had he called, and what should she do with him?

With her sister out visiting, she brought her maid down to play chaperon. He rose from the sofa as she entered and she paused, the acute awareness his presence always aroused in her rippling through her nerves and warming her skin.

'Lord Stratham, how kind of you to call. I'm afraid my sister is out, however.'

'I don't mean to inconvenience you,' he said with a smile. 'But I accompanied a friend to Hatchard's this morning. When I saw this, I knew you should have it.'

He handed her an embellished, tooled leather copy of Petrarch's *Canzoniere*. 'Aficionado that you are, I thought you should have a volume of your own to keep when you give back my father's.'

She looked down at the book with reverence. 'It's beautiful! But far too costly! I'm not sure I can accept so extravagant a gift.'

'Nonsense,' he said, dismissing her protest with a wave of his hand. 'A book is an entirely appropriate gift for a gentleman to present to a lady. Even more so when that lady is a notable scholar.'

She ought to refuse. But now, in addition to the memories she was collecting to savour when he walked away, as he surely would sooner or later, she would have this beautiful volume to remember him—and the heady days when she'd had the delicious excitement of his company. Realising that, she couldn't make herself refuse it.

'Very well, thank you. It is exquisite.'

'I know you can't entertain me in your sister's absence, but might we walk in the garden? She allowed you to stroll with my father, after all, and your maid can accompany us for propriety's sake.'

The presence of the maid should ensure she wasn't carried away by his nearness. She hoped. But to have another chance to spend time with him, virtually alone, to bask in his nearness without the necessity of making proper drawing room conversation with her sister and other interested parties looking on… She couldn't make herself deny herself this treat, either.

'I suppose I can pause my studies long enough for a walk. If you can wait until I fetch my pelisse.'

'As this is the only occasion when you were not ready to depart the instant I arrived, I'll allow it.'

'Good,' she said drily. 'You can read the Petrarch.'

She could have sent Jane for her pelisse, but it wouldn't be proper to remain alone with him in the morning room. Given her recent behaviour, she couldn't be sure how far from proper behaviour she might stray with opportunity and his encouragement.

Stop thinking about kissing and just enjoy being with him, she scolded herself.

A few minutes later, properly garbed, Eliza led Stratham into the garden. To distract herself from that constant, simmering sensual awareness, she would use this opportunity to learn more about him.

'I've told you most everything about my home and

family, but I know little about yours,' she said as they headed down a path bordered by late-spring daffodils and roses about to bloom. 'I know you've taken over managing your family estate, Stratham Hall, which is located in Hampshire, but nothing else. Did you grow up there?'

'Yes, with three sisters who were the bane of my existence.'

She chuckled. 'All married now, I believe your father said.'

'They are. Anne, the eldest, married Lord Hadley and resides with their three sons at his estate in Northumberland. Sarah, Lady Austin holds sway over her husband, son and daughter in York and the youngest, Constance, recently wed Lord Wisborough of Stoughton Manor, outside Portsmouth.'

'Were you the eldest?'

'No, next eldest after Anne.'

'Good. Had you been the youngest, *and* the longed-for son and heir, you would have been so coddled and spoiled as to become insufferable.'

'Whereas instead, I'm personable, honourable and obliging?'

'Sometimes,' she said with a chuckle.

'Your brother is the youngest, you said—and the longed-for son and heir. Is he coddled and spoiled?'

'Coddled, certainly. But both parents are too conscious of their duty to raise a compassionate, responsible man to spoil him. Though of course, Papa cannot help being thrilled to finally have a son to share all his favourite pursuits.'

'The ones he used to share with you?' Stratham said softly.

She looked at him sharply, surprised by his perceptiveness. 'It wouldn't have been reasonable to expect I could continue to play a son's role once Papa actually had a son. I did have five or six years to adjust to giving up that special place in his life. What was hardest was losing the companion with whom I'd enjoyed studying, driving, riding, and shooting. Losing the refuge to which I formerly had been able to retreat when I was weary of all the attempts to press me into the mould of a conventional maiden. Especially since I now had to try to fit into that role constantly.'

'Surely your father still welcomed you into his study.'

'Y-yes. But once my brother was old enough, Papa started tutoring him and several other boys. My presence was…a distraction, so I was no longer permitted to slip into the library whenever I wished. Particularly after the boys started boarding with us.' She sighed. 'I was relegated to the "ladies' parlour" with my mother and sisters.'

'No wonder you escaped to chase frogs and hop across streams.'

She smiled at his perceptiveness. 'Yes. For years longer than my mother thought I should indulge in such follies. But I wanted to know more about you. Did you spend all your growing up years at Stratham?'

'No, I went to Eton, then to Oxford. Then spent most of the next few years in London after coming down from university, with periodic stays at the estate, so Father could instruct me in the duties I would one day assume. It wasn't until last year, after…when my father was incapacitated with grief, that I returned to Stratham for an extended time.'

'And took over management completely?'

'Yes.'

'How did you find it, after spending so many years away?'

'Challenging, to be sure. My previous stays had mostly involved going over the estate books with Father and the steward, so I was aware of the various income streams and knew the tenants by name. But it was my first experience at riding out daily to inspect fields and cottages and talk with farmers about their needs and crops. Getting to know them as individuals rather than just names in a ledger. Making note of repairs and improvements I thought needful in addition to those the tenants and the steward brought to my attention.'

'A daunting workload. Did it make you want to ride straight back to the city?'

'At first, I felt…overwhelmed. But as I got to know the people better, I found myself enjoying the work more than I'd imagined possible.' He smiled. 'You find delight in analysing and reproducing the exact colour of water and sky. I found satisfaction in knowing that tenants had the tools and equipment they needed, the repairs and supplies necessary to make their jobs easier. In watching crops grow, helping to harvest them. In assisting the herders and farmers with the sheep and hogs. Even helping pack the baskets of watercress into wagons for shipment into London. Although after our trip to the Serpentine, I will never again look at watercress without noting the shades of green, above and below the water of the brooks beside and in which it grows.'

'Brook water tumbling over rocks, sunlight playing over leaf and stream? There must be a rainbow of hues!' she said. 'How fortunate you enjoy the work that is both your heritage and your responsibility.'

'I am blessed to eventually inherit a property that has been well managed for generations. Although when

I first left university, I thought I would spend only as much time as I had to at Stratham, now a life of aimless pleasure in London seems…hollow. Oh, I enjoy seeing friends and acquaintances at various entertainments, playing cards and dining at my club, but those activities are essentially frivolous. They don't accomplish anything useful.'

His gaze went to the far distance. 'I clearly remember the day I first realised that. We'd helped a tenant rethatch his roof. As the sun went down, gilding the thatch, and smoke emerged from the chimney as the man's wife cooked the family's dinner, I felt a warmth inside at knowing Thacker, and every man who toils on the estate, had a dry, comfortable cottage to shelter himself and family. I've found I love playing my small part in the ancient cycle of the seasons, sowing in spring, tending crops through the summer, harvesting in the autumn, even the fallow fields of winter. But what of you? Do you hope to remain in London?'

'I enjoy the city, but I too love the rhythm of life lived close to the land. And I prefer the smaller society of a town or village. Though I love the theatre and bookshops, visiting modistes and haberdashers and the King's Library, I find London society and the Season… intimidating.'

'Intimidating?' he echoed. 'The lady who conquers the music salons with her mastery?'

'Well, perhaps not "intimidating".' She laughed. 'But I'm still the girl who reads Petrarch, chases frogs and hops over streams. My hems may be clean and my hair tidy, but I'm hopeless at the sort of clever chat that dominates society. I know few of the people about whom others are talking or exchanging witticisms. And if those witticisms are mean-spirited, as they often seem to be, I don't want to master the knack of uttering them. Which leaves me feeling out of place and silent.'

Stratham raised his eyebrows. 'Silent? You seemed to converse easily enough with my father.'

'Perhaps because I've spent so much time with *my* father, I find older gentlemen more approachable. Most are already married, there's no pressure to impress, and they have a wider range of interests. My happiest times are spent, though, with my family and close friends. Telling stories and playing with my niece and nephews. Performing on pianoforte. Riding and sketching in the countryside. And yes, driving.'

'So you hope to wed a country gentleman, manage his household and dote on your children?'

She smiled softly. 'A goal beginning to appear unattainable for a girl who reads Petrarch, chases frogs, jumps streams…but has no clever conversation to attract young gentlemen.'

'And older gentlemen?'

Was he probing again about her intentions towards her father—or Fullridge? 'I wouldn't be averse to marrying an older gentleman, if I liked and respected him.' She sighed. 'Not everyone is lucky enough to find a peerless love.'

'You would settle for less?'

'I—I don't know,' she admitted. 'Lady Margaret and I recently attended the wedding of our friend, Lady Laura. Her radiant joy inspires one to hold out for similar bliss. Failing to find such a compatible union, remaining on my own does have appeal. I enjoy the independence of having no husband to answer to…but I'm realistic enough to realise the freedom I've relished up till now has been made possible by my father's indulgence. With no income of my own, if I don't marry, I will become a burden he, or some other family member, must support for the rest of my life.'

'They would be compensated by your unpaid service,' Stratham said drily.

'I would never resent helping my family. But to be dependent for ever, with no establishment, no children of my own...' She shook her head. 'Gentlemen are so much more fortunate. They can choose to marry or not, as young men or old, and still be independent, able to earn a living or inherit one.'

As they turned the bend of a path, heading back towards the house, the butler appeared at the end of the walkway, waving to her.

'It appears you are being summoned,' Stratham remarked.

'I expect my sister has returned and has need of me.'

'Let me escort you back, then.'

She took his arm, savouring the contact, slowing her steps to make the transit last as long as possible. Once in the house, discovering Lady Dunbarton did require her, she thanked Stratham again for his gift and bid him goodbye.

As she went up to change into an afternoon gown to accompany Maria on her errands, Eliza mulled over the walk in the garden. Under the maid's watchful eye, she'd been able to push the sensual awareness into the background and found she had enjoyed the conversation— honest, with no innuendo and no argument, more than any other she'd exchanged with the Baron.

It was illuminating to learn more about his background, discover what he loved, where he saw himself ending up, and something of the experiences that had made him into the man he now was. Though initially she'd been wary of his beguiling charm, through the course of this conversation, she'd begun to view him more as an individual than as Lord Stratham, heir to a viscount, highly eligible marital prospect.

And she very much liked what she'd learned.

Which was not a useful development. She didn't need to find him even *more* appealing. She didn't need to realise that in enjoying riding, driving and a country life, they had yet more in common. Not when that growing sense of ease and camaraderie was layered atop the already potent physical pull he exerted on her.

As the maid assisted her into her gown, she admitted that she still hadn't the will to send him away—yet. But if she wanted to protect herself and concentrate her attention where it should be, on her future, she should set a limit on how much longer she allowed herself to see him. How many more times would she allow?

Unable to set a number, she pushed away answering that question. But while she indulged herself by spending time with him, she'd need to keep a close watch over her vulnerable heart. She didn't need to compound what was already the mistake of liking him into the disaster of falling in love with him.

Chapter Fourteen

Two mornings later, his tiger behind him, Giles drove his phaeton towards Hyde Park. To his note inviting Miss Hasterling to borrow Ginger for another morning ride, she'd replied that she would be accompanying her sister's children to the park, but he would be welcome to meet them.

He chuckled, thinking what the gentlemen at his club would say if they knew one of their smartest members was driving off, not to the afternoon social hour where he might impress the ladies and inspire envy in other drivers, but to play nursemaid to a pack of children.

Nor could he imagine any other female suggesting an outing with a gentleman that involved playing ball and rolling hoops with squealing youngsters.

But Miss Hasterling had told him how much she valued family and proved it by her attention to her sister's children. Once again, not showing an image carefully cultivated to appeal to gentlemen, but a true picture of who she was. With the *ton* so often a world of artifice, members appearing as pasteboard cut-outs embodying the traits society valued, Giles appreciated that simple honesty.

Like most single gentlemen, he had little experience

with children. His sisters' offspring were brought down to visit their parents at teatime and otherwise kept out of sight, confined to the nursery or the park under servants' care.

But he could throw a ball and roll a hoop. He guessed Miss Hasterling would not look kindly on him if he merely stood by, observing, rather than taking an active part.

A moment later, he swept through the gates and drove along Rotten Row, looking for the spot near the Serpentine where Miss Hasterling had written she would bring the children.

He soon spotted her party in the distance—three small youngsters and Miss Hasterling, who was tossing a ball between them, their nursemaid seated on a nearby bench. As he pulled up the team, excited voices, too far away to understand the words, carried over to him. There was a shout of laughter as she jumped up to catch a ball thrown over her head.

Giles smiled. It seemed their aunt played the game with as much enthusiasm as her charges.

Giles tried to imagine Lucinda, with her elegant ballooning sleeves and perfect coiffeur, leaping into the air to catch a child's ball. And failed utterly.

Hopping down, he handed Finch the reins with instructions to walk the horses and bring them back to the same location, and set off towards the group.

What unique vision of Miss Hasterling would be displayed for him today?

As he called a greeting, the game halted. Miss Hasterling beckoned the children to gather around her, the nursemaid rose, and both women curtsied to his bow.

'I'm surprised you were able to join us,' Miss Hasterling said.

'But pleased, I hope.'

'Of course,' she replied, a flush on her cheeks. 'I wasn't sure such an outing would be of any interest to you.'

'Everything you do interests me, Miss Hasterling.'

'Indeed?' she said, her flush deepening. Giles repressed another smile. Did she realise he must have seen her jumping after the ball? Realised once again her behaviour had not displayed the decorous, maidenly restraint the females of her family urged on her?

'Let me present the children, Lord Stratham. Master Andrew Dunbarton, the eldest. His brother Stephen, and this little hoyden is my niece, Miss Louisa Dunbarton,' she finished, tweaking the little girl's long curls. 'And this is Nurse Green.'

'Your Lordship,' the woman said, curtsying again.

'An honour to meet you, my lord,' the oldest said for others, the boys making him credible bows and even the little girl, who looked hardly old enough to be out of leading strings, managing a wobbly curtsy.

'Pleased to meet you, sirs and miss,' he answered.

The little girl's eyes growing wide, she leaned towards Miss Hasterling to whisper, 'Does he mean me, Aunt Liza?'

'Yes, and you must show him what a proper little lady you are,' she whispered back.

Reminding herself, too?

'I didn't mean to interrupt your game.'

'We were about to stop. Stephen adores playing ball, so Andrew, like the supportive big brother he is, agreed to begin with that, but he's eager to try out his boat. Shall we, children? There's another bench there—' she pointed to one adjacent to the one on which the nurse had returned to her knitting '—where you can watch for the return of your phaeton. I imagine you'd prefer to spend your time here driving.'

'Later, perhaps. First, there's some sailing to be done.'

'Do you have a boat, Your Lordship?' Andrew asked, taking his wooden craft from a basket beside the nurse-maid, then handing another to his brother and the smallest to his sister.

'Our streams back home are too swift and full of rocks for poling boats.'

'You may borrow mine, if you like.'

Touched, he replied, 'A generous offer, Master Dunbarton. But I'd not deprive you of the pleasure your aunt says you've been eagerly anticipating.'

Miss Hasterling handed out the long sticks used to move the boats across the water. 'Remember, boys, no swordfights, or boating is over,' she warned, then took her niece's boat, stick, and hand and set off towards the Serpentine.

'It's never me starts it,' Andrew protested.

'But you're quite happy to continue it,' she retorted, earning a guilty grin from her nephew. Looking surprised that Giles followed them to the water's edge, she said, 'There's another bench just there, my lord.'

'May I cut in with the lady?'

Her expression went blank for a moment, then her eyes widened. 'You wish to participate?'

'Of course. Why else would I have joined you today?' he replied, tickled at having upset her evident conviction that he would consider himself above interacting with children. 'Besides, how could I resist assisting the prettiest girl in the park?'

Beaming, Louisa said, 'He can help me, Aunt Liza. He's not a stranger.'

She raised her eyebrows, but said, 'Very well—if

you're sure. Assisting mainly consists of guiding her hand to move the boat while keeping her from falling in.' As she passed him the stick, the boat, and her niece's hand she murmured, 'Apparently no female is immune to your charm. I see I've been replaced.'

'Only temporarily,' he said. 'So you may leave off weeping.'

'I'll try,' she said drily, moving on to her nephew. 'Don't push too hard, Andrew! I don't fancy wading into the Serpentine to retrieve the boat if it goes beyond range of your stick.'

Giles had never before poled a child's boat. He'd really only offered to assist because Miss Hasterling so clearly did not expect him to participate. But he found the children's pure enjoyment of this simple activity surprisingly endearing. When his small charge succeeded in moving the boat on her own—without falling into the water—he shared her triumph when she shouted, 'See, Aunt Liza! I did it all by myself!'

'Excellent, sweetheart. You'll be outstripping the boys soon.'

Andrew made a disgusted face. 'Never. She's just a girl.'

'Girls can do almost anything boys can do, young man.'

'Your aunt will be the first to prove it,' Giles said, amused.

For another half-hour, the children guided their boats up and down the water's edge while Miss Hasterling made up stories about their imaginary passengers and cargo.

He recognised some of her fabrications, such as the tame version of Odysseus sailing past the sirens she produced as the boats rounded a rock. From the vast repository of lore she'd accumulated from her reading, she reassembled bits and pieces, augmented by her own imagination, into something relevant and appealing to them.

No wonder the children begged for her tales. They certainly adored her, their admiration evident in every glance.

Missing out on having a home and family of her own would be a tragedy. She'd make some lucky man a fascinating wife and be a superb mother to his children.

Might that man be him? The notion no longer seemed so far-fetched.

'Enough boating, children. We must return soon, and I promised Stephen another round of ball.'

The child eagerly gathered up his boat and stick and ran to replace them in the baskets. Andrew followed more slowly, while Louisa offered her boat to Giles. 'You may carry mine for me,' she said solemnly.

Like a princess gifting her favour to a jousting knight, Giles thought, amused once more.

'Usurped again,' Miss Hasterling murmured as they walked back. 'Carrying her boat is usually *my* privilege.'

'She would never prefer my stories to yours,' Giles said. 'How cleverly you weave together what they are doing with snippets of heroic tales!'

She shrugged. 'With all those story bits floating around in my head, it's easy to gather together the pieces when something they do reminds me.'

'Not easy at all, I wouldn't think. Bravo again, Miss Hasterling.'

She smiled, looking both surprised and gratified by his praise. 'Now to start the game of catch. They do need to be home soon.'

She plucked up the ball and directed the children to scatter. They scrambled to spots at a distance to her relative, he guessed, to their abilities to catch and throw, the speed of their assembly indicating they must often play this game with their aunt.

'Where should I stand?' he asked.

She swept a glance over his immaculate driving attire. 'You might get mud on your jacket.'

'Only if I miss a catch. But I won't,' he said.

She lifted her eyebrows. 'You think I throw like a girl—not hard enough to make you miss?'

He chuckled. 'I think answering that question would get me into trouble.'

She sniffed, giving him an irritated look. 'We shall see. Andrew can field quite well, Stephen less so. You'll need to roll the ball to Louisa. You can stand there—at the north corner of the triangle the children have made.'

He trotted off, chuckling, anticipating at some point she'd give him her hardest throw. Though he doubted she 'threw like a girl', he was confident he could catch anything she tossed his way.

What fun it was to tease the kitten into baring her claws!

The game proceeded apace until Andrew noticed Finch leading the phaeton back and abandoned his place, walking over to watch as the vehicle drew closer.

'That is your carriage, my lord?' he asked, his tone awed. 'What a bang-up rig!'

Giles chuckled at the slang, wondering where the child had heard it. From the reddening of his aunt's cheeks, he suspected from her.

'Thank you, Master Andrew. It's quite well sprung and handles beautifully.'

'May we ride in it?' Stephen asked, dropping the ball.

'I drove the boat. I want to drive the carriage,' Louisa announced.

'This time, I agree with your brother, young lady,' Giles said. 'Females can drive certain types of equipages, but never a high-perch phaeton. At least, not in town,' he added to Miss Hasterling's probable indignation. 'It's far too dangerous. See how high above the ground the driver sits? The carriage is so light, it bounces over any rough surface and sways alarmingly if the horses suddenly swerve. Which often they will, as they are easily startled by loud city noises or sudden activity in the street. But...' he reached down to pull one of Louisa's long curls '...perhaps you can have that ride another day.'

'I hope I have a carriage that splendid to drive when I grow up,' Andrew said.

'Perhaps Louisa will, too. In country and in town,' Miss Hasterling said in a militant tone as she picked up the ball and shooed the players back into position.

'Come now, Miss Hasterling,' Giles said as he loped back to his place. 'I know you claimed to drive a phaeton, but you admitted it was not a high-perch version.'

'I didn't *claim* it, I did drive one. And a little extra height shouldn't make that much difference.'

He watched the storm clouds of annoyance building on her face. She looked so adorably affronted, he couldn't resist teasing the scowling kitten a little more. 'A female wouldn't have the strength to hold my horses if they should have a mind to bolt—or bring them under control if they did.'

'Is that a challenge?'

'Certainly not! Drive that and you'd likely ruin the carriage and break your neck,' he pronounced, putting into his tone every bit of male condescension he could muster.

'Oh, I would, would I? Just like I throw like a girl?' At that, she pelted the ball at him.

He was laughing so hard, he missed it, the ball ricocheting off his shoulder and bouncing into the distance. He ran off after it, needing several minutes to locate it under a leafy branch fallen from one of the trees overhead.

He was still laughing when he turned and saw Miss Hasterling standing beside the phaeton, talking with Finch. His mirth faded when the tiger helped her up. And deserted him entirely when she snatched the reins from the boy's hand and set the team off at a trot.

Condescending, arrogant and presumptuous! Eliza fumed as Stratham chased after the ball she'd hurled at him.

'You shouldn't drive the phaeton, you know, Aunt Eliza,' Andrew said solemnly. 'You might get hurt.'

'Not you, too. I told you girls can do anything boys can, didn't I?'

'Not everything,' he said with such precocious masculine superiority she felt tempted to whack him with one of the boat sticks.

She wasn't sure when the idea seized her, but in a rush of furious determination, she found herself walking up to the vehicle. Smiling sweetly, she said to Finch, 'Lord Stratham is going to drive me home. Would you help me up to wait for him?'

'Certainly, Miss.' The tiger assisted her up into the tall vehicle and stepped back, his gaze going to Stratham as he disappeared into the trees. 'That was some throw, Miss!'

As soon as the tiger moved out of the way, Eliza jerked the reins out of the boy's hand and set the horses in motion. She heard his cry of alarm, and in a quick glance over her shoulder, saw him chasing after her— and emerging on to the pathway, a shocked Stratham.

She turned back to concentrate on directing the horses. In truth, she had to pay careful attention, for the path back to the carriage way was uneven, and once there, she had to manoeuvre around several other vehicles.

She quickly concluded that it was already too crowded to spring the team, as she'd hoped. But even keeping them at a trot, the speed was exhilarating, especially perched so high above the ground. She revelled in the excitement and the pleasure of directing such a well-matched, responsive pair. This bit of thievery was going to earn her a blistering scold, but it would be worth it!

But as she took a side road, turned the pair and began returning to the spot on the carriage way where the frantic tiger, Stratham and retribution waited, exhilaration was replaced by remorse.

What had she been thinking? This stunt showed she'd definitely not overcome the much-regretted impulsiveness of her youth. This drive might have proved her point about her driving competence, but Stratham was going to be furious and she really couldn't blame him.

In for penny, in for pound, she thought wryly. So, catching the thong of the whip, she brought the vehicle to a halt almost at Stratham's feet. As soon as its motion stopped, the tiger flew to its side and grabbed the reins.

Knowing her prank was well and truly over, she descended with as much dignity as she could muster.

The Baron was stone-faced with fury, his tiger looked miserable, and even the children, who'd followed Stratham, trailed by Nurse Green, were wide-eyed and wary. Punishment for her sins was about to be meted out.

'Just what did you think you were doing?' Stratham asked icily.

'It would appear I was driving your phaeton.'

Her flippant reply seemed to incense him further. Turning to Nurse Green, he barked, 'Escort the children to the Dunbarton carriage. I'll drive Miss Hasterling home.'

Andrew stepped to her side. 'Do you wish to go with him, Aunt Liza?'

He might have vexed her by exhibiting an irritating masculine superiority, but she couldn't help being touched by his protectiveness. 'Yes, it will be great fun, won't it? Perhaps you may have the treat of riding in it one day. Children, help Nurse Green load your things into the carriage. I'll see you at the house later.'

After growling at the tiger to walk the horses, Stratham took her arm and practically dragged her off. As soon as they were out of earshot of the others, he said furiously, 'Have you taken leave of your senses?'

'Not a bit. You all but dared me to drive. I merely took you up on it to prove my point.'

'I should sack Finch for letting you take the phaeton. Damn the boy!'

'Since I stole it out from under him, it's not his fault.'

'I thought you tried to set a good example for the children. Is this what you would have them emulate? Dashing off with someone else's property without permission, risking life, limb, and damage to said property?'

'I admit, this incident did not provide the…best example. I failed to meet my own standards, which happens sometimes when I get angry, but don't take my lapse out on poor Finch. Besides, would you have him telling the staff at his next post that he got the boot because his master was embarrassed by having a female drive his phaeton? It's certain to come out, and once the staff knows, it would be all over town in a flash. Or…

you could forgive him for something that was really not his fault, and have no one the wiser.'

'Except for everyone who saw you driving just now?'

'Who would think, naturally, that I was doing so with your permission.'

'That's blackmail,' he said after a moment.

'Negotiation,' she amended. 'But let me forestall the lecture I certainly deserve by tendering my sincere apology. I had no right to abscond with your vehicle, knowing you had expressly forbidden me to drive it. But having you unjustly denigrate a female's ability, I just…didn't think.'

'You could have been killed,' he said hotly. 'Injured or killed others! Not to mention harming the horses and, least important but still dear to me, damaging the carriage itself!'

'Pish tosh,' she said with a dismissive wave of hand. 'You saw me drive. I was in complete control the entire time. Yes, it was wrong of me to have stolen the team, but you have to admit, I drove it well. Didn't I?'

Stratham said nothing for long moments, then gave a deep sigh. 'Very well, I will reluctantly agree, on this occasion at least, you drove it well.'

Eliza grinned, relieved to have blunted the edge of his anger. 'Let me drive with you up beside me to intervene if necessary, and I'll show how well I drive on any occasion.'

'You are incorrigible!' He looked down, shaking his head at her. 'I suppose I should be glad I didn't say anything that made you feel it necessary to prove your proficiency with a pistol.'

'Alas, the park is normally too full of people to practise shooting.'

He gave her a stern look. 'If you wish me to forgive

you, you'll refrain from any more statements like that. How did you learn to drive a phaeton, by the way? Given its tricky balance, manoeuvring it is more difficult than a wagon, cart, or even a barouche.'

She didn't like admitting her youthful folly, but she had wronged him, so she supposed he deserved the whole story. 'When I was sixteen, we had a boarder studying with Papa; I'll call him "George". An earl's heir, he was provided ample pocket money, a riding hack—and a phaeton. I teased him to teach me to drive it.'

Despite the ever-present ache, she smiled wistfully, remembering those halcyon early days. 'We drove around the countryside when we both could get free, discussing the literature Father was teaching him. He told me all about his family and his plans for university. We fancied ourselves very much in love...or at least, I did. I went about in a glow of happiness for about a month...until suddenly, he began avoiding me.'

Pushing down the pain, she forced herself to continue, 'When I asked Papa if something had happened, he told me as gently as he could that George was to leave soon and go home to prepare for university. Shocked, I finally cornered George and asked what that meant for our plans. He...he laughed at me. A vicar's daughter was not a suitable match for an earl's son; it was presumptuous of me to have ever imagined our "casual flirting" meant anything serious.'

'You must have been...devastated,' he said softly.

'Oh, I refused at first to believe it! How could my judgement have been so wrong? But George left a week later without another word...and I never heard from him again. Though I didn't confess my folly to anyone at the time, not even Papa, I believe he suspected. I finally concluded George must have been...testing out his charm on me. I was crushed, but it was a good thing; I learned early to put away girlish dreams and look at my future with sensible expectations.' She smiled wryly. 'So you can be doubly sure I never had any thought of enticing your father.'

'How did you weather such a betrayal?'

'After hiding myself away with my books for a time, I decided there was no point moping about, nursing my grief. The only thing to do was to move forward and make the best of what could be.'

She looked away from the sympathy in his gaze. She might have learned her lesson, but even now, her lover's betrayal still stung.

'Did your heart finally heal?'

She forced a smile, submerging the residual pain with an effort. 'And my injured pride,' she said, her tone determinedly light. 'Now that I've humbly admitted my fault and begged forgiveness, are you no longer angry? I'll not be audacious enough to ask again for your approval, even though my skill merits it.'

Stratham laughed, as she hoped he would. 'Hoyden! I ought to ring your impetuous neck for scaring me half to death.'

'But you have forgiven me? I'd hate to forfeit your good opinion.'

'Very well. You are forgiven. As long as you don't do anything else outrageous.'

She felt a surge of relief that her impulsive stunt hadn't destroyed his regard. 'I'm glad we are friends again. But come now, can you claim to have never done anything foolish? I can recall all too many episodes in my youth.'

He'd been smiling, but at that, his expression sobered. 'Foolish?' His short laugh held an edge of bitterness. 'Sadly, yes. It's beyond foolish to continue running after something you want so desperately, you make yourself ignore all the signs that shout it cannot be in order to hang on to the dream far beyond when even your own common sense begs you to let it go.'

The ache in his voice was so compelling, it brought tears to her eyes. 'It's not foolish to believe in dreams,' she said softly. 'It's only foolish to never dream at all. What is the point of life, if not to aspire to achieve one's dreams? One should always strive after the beautiful, true, and worthwhile. Always believe it achievable. If one fails, at least one knows one has tried.'

He was staring at her as if he'd never seen her before. A strange, uncomfortable warmth rose in her. She had to look away and break the intensity of the moment before she ignored the other strollers, Finch waiting with the phaeton, and threw herself into his arms.

'I suppose I'm foolish to hope I shall ever become the perfect, ladylike maiden,' she said in a lighter tone, ending the fraught moment. 'It's true, I draw, play, and paint. But though I avoid—usually—muddy hems, torn sleeves and untidy hair, I never manage to be as impeccably behaved as my sisters.' She sighed. 'My next eldest sister, now Mrs Needham, the elegant wife of a baron's youngest son, always said I was the most boyish girl she knew.'

Stratham's eyes widened. 'Boyish? Ridiculous! Has she no eyes?' To her surprise, he took her hand and kissed it. 'I don't find you boyish in the least.'

Shock at the compliment as electrifying as his touch, for a moment, she simply stared at him. 'I believe that is quite the nicest thing anyone has ever said to me.'

He stared back at her, the heat between them intensifying. Her gaze fell to his mouth, and once again she thought with a thrill that he might kiss her.

But this was Hyde Park, with a sizable portion of the *ton* strolling or riding by. Besides, as a gentleman, he would consider it taking disreputable advantage to kiss a girl towards whom he didn't have serious intentions.

She turned away before she could forget herself and kiss *him*. 'I'd better get home. The children will have arrived, and heaven knows what they will tell my sister about what happened. She may worry I'm trapped in the wreckage of your carriage—or that you've strangled me and thrown my body into the Serpentine.'

Stratham took a shuddering breath, as if he'd felt the same compelling but impossible desire. 'I wouldn't want Lady Dunbarton to worry. Or forbid me the house.'

'There's little chance of that. After displaying your expertise with balls and boats, you are more likely to be kidnapped by the children and dragged to the nursery if they discover you've called. In one short outing, you've become a great favourite. Thank you for your kindness to them.'

'I enjoyed their company.' He grinned. 'I especially enjoyed their aunt's exuberance in playing ball...at least until she saw fit to steal my carriage.'

'I thought you'd forgiven me.'

'Just reminding you the episode must not be repeated. Promise?'

She gave an exaggerated sigh. 'Promise.'

'No fingers crossed behind your back?' He peered around at her hands despite her indignant look. 'Just checking.'

'No dissembling. Just honest remorse.'

'Good. I should never forgive myself if something happened to you while riding my horses or driving my carriage. And...' He sighed again. 'You are right that it was partially my fault. I did…tease you into it. Even if I definitely did not intend it as a dare.'

'Handsome of you to admit it,' she said, surprised and touched that he'd allow her to diminish her own blame by claiming some himself.

'It is, isn't it?' he said, grinning.

So much for being grateful. Giving him aggravated glance, she said, 'Better take me home before we find another topic to brangle over.'

He chuckled. 'I don't want to brangle. I'd much rather do…something else.'

She felt his heated glance rove over her face, her mouth, until her skin tingled. Do something—like kiss her?

She wished she had enough experience with gentlemen to be sure of his intentions. Although if she had, she would doubtless realise that comment was just idle flirtation.

Don't run after something you can never have.

Wise advice then and now, she thought as Stratham escorted her back to the phaeton and handed her up.

Chapter Fifteen

The following morning, Eliza sat at the desk in her chamber, staring down at the note the butler had just delivered, her name inscribed on it in Stratham's bold script. She couldn't help savouring that it had come from his hand even as she chided herself for being affected by the fact.

That delight was yet another indication that she should force herself to set a limit on how much longer she would see him, lest she grow still more attached. Especially since, to her continuing surprise, the glimpses he'd been given into her true nature hadn't yet seemed to discourage him from seeking her out.

For her own part, quite frankly she had expected as she adjusted to the shock of being in the company of such a handsome, compelling man, his allure—and the thrill of sensual attraction—would dim. But then he had appreciated her enthusiasm for the wonders of colour and hue and even seemed to share it. He'd not only deigned to talk with Andrew, Stephen and Louisa, he'd joined in their games with every appearance of enjoyment.

He was seeming less and less the wealthy viscount's heir, the sort of autocratic, self-absorbed aristocrat Maggie and her own experience had warned her about. Instead, she saw a responsible landowner who cared about the welfare of his land and tenants, a man who seemed to appreciate children's directness and charm.

Which augured well for him becoming the sort of engaged, encouraging father she'd had. The sort she'd want for her own children—if she were ever fortunate enough to have any.

Sighing, she told herself to remember the advice she'd heard from his own lips about not running after something she could never have.

Quickly she scanned the note, then put it down, frowning.

Before parting yesterday, they had compared social calendars and noted that prior obligations would prevent them from meeting in the evening for at least a week. His note proposed taking another morning ride, but with one task or another, she was occupied in the mornings as well.

So it would be a week before she saw him again. *Too long*, her heart whispered. *Not long enough*, the voice of prudence answered. If they spent enough time apart, he would likely become sidetracked by other events or charmed by another lady, freeing her from the need to force herself to part from him.

Unless…

The evening before Lady Knightley-King's ball, she was to participate in another musical evening at Mrs Chiverton's, for which she needed to practise. Why not suggest that he join her and assist? They could even work on a duet together, if he liked. Warmed by the possibility of once again sharing the music she loved, she penned a note asking if he could join her for a morning music practice session in three days' time.

Her spirits raised at the prospect of that potential

treat, she dutifully turned her thoughts to a more pressing matter: considering what topics she might discuss with Mr Fullridge at the dinner Maggie and the Countess had arranged in two nights' time.

On the designated evening, Eliza accompanied her sister to the Portman Square residence of the Earl of Comeryn. She smiled as she approached the front entry, remembering how cleverly Lady Margaret had manoeuvred her father into allowing his wife and daughter to reside at the family manse—after virtually imprisoning his daughter at their country estate the previous year for refusing to marry her father's choice. The very handsome return her railway investor brother had earned for Maggie on a small bequest from her aunt had subsequently made her financially independent of her father.

She then informed the Earl that she was moving with her mother to London permanently and would engage a house for them. Realising the gossip and speculation it would cause in society if his family resided somewhere else, the Earl had grudgingly permitted them to move into Comeryn House, their London town house.

Though Maggie had never revealed any details about her exile at Montwell Glen, Eliza feared the conditions had been abusive enough to solidify Maggie's determination to eschew marriage and never again put herself under the control of any man.

She hoped some day Maggie would meet a kind, generous, understanding gentleman who would convince her that sharing her life offered more benefits than risks. A kind, generous, understanding gentleman like the one she wished to find for herself.

Might Fullridge be such a man?

The image of Giles Stratham slipped into her mind

and with a sigh, she banished it. She simply must stop even considering such a possibility. Had her humiliation at George's hands not taught her not to reach above her station?

Fullridge might not be the man, either. But she would try tonight to determine whether he might be a possibility. Maggie had arranged this dinner so the two might converse at more length than was possible at a rout or ball. She, who claimed to Stratham that one must always be sensible and make the best of one's circumstances, needed to act upon her own advice.

Eliza entered the drawing room to discover the dinner party included several of the Countess's friends, two amusing gentleman friends of Maggie's and Lord Atherton, a widower who'd befriended Maggie during her first Season—and one whom Eliza privately suspected would like to be more than a friend to her. Conversation was general in the drawing room before dinner, Atherton describing a hunting trip at his estate and the two gentleman giving a commentary on several of the plays currently being presented in London theatres.

Eliza's nerves tightened as their hostess led them into dinner, but once again Maggie had anticipated her concern and seated Eliza beside her with Fullridge opposite, so she was not obligated to carry the whole conversation with him. Fullridge, too, seemed content to let Maggie direct their exchange.

Not until after dinner, when the gentlemen finished their brandy and cigars and re-joined the ladies for tea, did Fullridge approach her. 'Miss Hasterling, I've been wanting all evening to tell you how charming you look in that gown.'

Eliza felt herself blush. 'Very kind of you, Mr Full-ridge.'

'Not to imply you do not always look lovely,' he added hastily. 'Just that the hue of this gown is particularly complimentary.'

'No offence taken,' she assured him. Apparently he was as nervous about this occasion as she was.

'It is awkward to feel everyone's eyes upon one, try-ing to evaluate the progress of one's relationship,' he murmured, nodding his head towards Maggie, who though chatting with a friend, kept glancing in their direction.

'Rather like being a specimen under microscope,' she agreed. 'You feel it, too?'

'Very much. Shall we ignore them all, and only con-verse if and as we wish? I assure you, you have no need to "impress" me.'

'Nor you, me,' she answered, grateful for his under-standing, and warming towards his kindness. 'Yes, let's ignore them all.'

'Get our tea, repair to chairs by hearth? Sip, talk if we wish, or remain silent?'

'Excellent suggestion.' As Fullridge escorted her to the tea tray, carried her cup for her to the chairs indi-cated, she concluded that so far, she was favourably impressed. He'd showed no need to monopolise conver-sation at dinner, nor had he tried to impress by talking of his accomplishments, wealth, or property. He'd re-plied to Maggie's questions without seeking to embroi-der his answers or prolong being the centre of attention.

He seemed the sort of easy-going, quiet gentleman who might make her a congenial companion.

Even if his proximity didn't make her nerves tingle or set swallows soaring and dipping in her stomach.

He'd been so accommodating, rather than sit in companionable silence, she felt he deserved to have her make an effort at conversation.

'When required to chat with a gentleman, and unsure what to say, ask about his interests,' her friend Lady Laura always advised.

'Lady Margaret tells me your home is in Westmorland, near Kendal.'

'Yes. My family was involved in the wool trade, the manufacture of Kendal green.'

'Ah—the colour of archers and foresters. Did one of your ancestors march with the victorious bowmen at Agincourt?'

He laughed. 'My family comes from good yeoman stock; we don't own any fancy pedigree. My great-grandfather established the business. Grandfather expanded it, making it profitable enough that he was able to buy land and a manor house, Greenlands, where the family now resides. Father passed on to me the management of the land, mainly given over to sheep, and also invested in Mr Harrison's snuff business.'

'A profitable enterprise during the Georgian era! Even now, one does see gentleman taking snuff, though the practice is not as popular as it was.'

'Yes, tobacco is preferred now. Which Harrison's firm also produces to good profit. I fear my family has not been reluctant to be associated with trade, even after we became landed gentry.'

'I have only admiration for men who build successful businesses through their own skill and hard work. It requires just as much expertise as the more "genteel" business of managing land. A man should be judged on his character, not on whether or not he chooses to indulge in an occupation.'

Fullridge gave her a slight smile. 'Quite broad-minded of you, Miss Hasterling.'

'Your children still reside at Greenlands?'

'My eldest son and his new wife do; Jeffrey is currently learning to manage the estate he will one day take over. My younger son is at the Inns of Court, preparing for a career as a barrister. My two daughters have married gentry in neighbouring counties.'

'Do you enjoy your sojourn in London?'

'My son's managing the estate allows me to spend the entire Season here, something I've not done before. Frankly, I prefer the hills and lakes and clean fresh air of the north country! But it's been some years now since I lost my lady wife, and I find… I'm ready to look for companionship again. I'm fortunate that Constance was one of the Countess's friends. She and Lady Margaret were kind enough to welcome me to town and give me entrée to various entertainments.'

'Lady Margaret has a kind heart.' Eliza smiled. 'If a bit…managing.'

Fullridge chuckled. 'She is that.'

'But only because she wants the best for those she befriends.'

'I cannot complain. She introduced me to you.'

Eliza felt her face flush, not sure what to answer. She didn't want to be too effusive and give him the idea that she was eagerly seeking his pursuit. She wasn't sure yet that she wanted him as a serious suitor, even though he was the most practical, even the most attractive candidate.

He saved her from replying by saying, 'Will you play for us tonight?'

'Only if I'm bid. I don't wish to put myself forward.'

'I'll suggest it to the Countess, then.' He gave her another slight, almost self-deprecating smile. 'It will save you having to converse any further with me.'

'I've enjoyed conversing with you,' she protested, not wanting him to think she found his company distasteful just because she hadn't returned a more enthusiastic response to his overtures. 'It's always good to have another friend in London, and I think we could be…friends.'

Which was the most she could agree to at this point, and she wanted to be honest with him about it.

He nodded, seemingly not offended that she hadn't offered more. 'Friends is always a good place to start, Miss Hasterling. May I return your cup for you?'

'Please.'

He collected her teacup and carried both back to the table, then went over to speak with the Countess. Eliza watched him, glad she'd been able to talk with him— but glad the conversation was over.

Her impression of Fullridge as a kind, companionable, perceptive man was confirmed. His oblique indication of interest in her was understated, not putting her on the spot. And he'd exhibited a certain finesse in making his exit before she became uncomfortable. Everything she had thus far learned about him confirmed there was no reason to rule out a potential relationship.

If he'd not inspired her to yearn for his company or his touch, he'd certainly not made her inclined to dismiss him.

The Countess approached a few moments later and asked her to play. Fullridge returned to offer to turn pages for her; she granted the request and made her way to the pianoforte. For the balance of the evening, she played easy airs and familiar ballads. Although Fullridge had disclaimed any musical ability, she discovered he possessed a fine baritone voice, with which he accompanied her soprano on some of the songs.

Occasionally the gaze she felt lingering on her bare neck set the skin there tingling. That, and the brief touch of his hand on hers, or on her shoulder as he adjusted the music for her, was enough to let her know he found her physically attractive without making her draw away or requiring any response from her.

She wasn't sure she could give one.

She allowed herself to escape into the music, grateful to Fullridge for making an awkward situation easier and permitting her to drift, free of thoughts about the future and worries over what to do next. Putting off answering the questions of whether, or how much, to encourage him.

'What did you think of the gentleman?' her sister asked in the carriage on their way home. 'Can you see him as a serious suitor?'

'I find nothing disagreeable in him. I learned more about his home and family, but not enough yet about his interests to determine if we would be compatible.'

'But you're not prepared to dismiss him?'

Fighting an instinct to say 'yes', she replied, 'No. I'm not ready to dismiss him. But neither am I ready to lead him on, so don't be inviting him to dine!'

Her sister laughed. 'It's early days for that. But I'm encouraged. Last Season, you never progressed even to the point of agreeing you'd met an eligible gentleman you *wouldn't* discourage.'

'As we both know, if I'm to marry at all, I must seriously consider the few prospects I have now. All I know for sure is we can rule out Henry Alborne. I'd have neither hems nor toes left if I had to dance with him for a lifetime.'

Her sister chuckled. 'I agree to ruling out Alborne. Having even one approved suitor is progress.' She paused. 'And what of Stratham?'

Eliza felt a ripple of longing, followed by irritation that she had not yet squelched such ridiculous hopes. 'We both know he couldn't be a serious suitor. He's been seeking my company for the present, but I don't expect his attentions to continue much longer. Miss Eliza Hasterling is not a suitable candidate to become the wife of a future viscount.'

'Not suitable, true,' her sister agreed with a sigh. 'Not *wholly* unsuitable either, for you are gently born, if not of his rank. It would be terribly romantic if he fell in love and simply *had* to marry you!'

'When the cow jumps over the moon,' Eliza said drily. 'I won't deny I enjoy his company. I intend to continue enjoying it for…a time. But it will be a temporary pleasure, surely. Mr Fullridge…might be a permanent solution.'

Even though she could view that solution with only mild enthusiasm. But she did like the quiet, unassuming man. Their initial friendship might grow into something warmer. When she was no longer distracted by Stratham.

She was just glad, she thought as she leaned her weary head back against the squabs, that she'd not been forced into an immediate decision.

And that she had that music session with Stratham to look forward to.

Chapter Sixteen

Three mornings later, Giles sat at his desk, rereading Miss Hasterling's note inviting him to join her music practice session today, to which he'd returned an immediate acceptance. He'd kept it on his desk in the intervening days, next to a charcoal sketch of his gelding, Midnight, that she'd sent with the note as a thank you for the copy of Petrarch he'd given her.

She'd caught the elegance in the curve of the horse's neck, the sense of controlled energy in the body. The Petrarch was a handsome volume, but he valued the sketch even more, for it was something she had created herself.

He chuckled. And not the typical piece of feminine needlework, or a painting of flowers on a china plate.

Nor was her invitation to practise the pianoforte the sort of activity one would expect a young lady to propose to a gentleman. An invitation to view her performance where she might display her skill, perhaps, but not to observe her possibly stumbling over chords or playing dissonances. But by now he should expect the unexpected from Miss Hasterling.

A sudden vision of her dashing off in his curricle recurred, and he shuddered. She had scared him to death with that little stunt, even though he'd soon realised she seemed able to control the team with ease. His initial terror had been a fitting rebuke for him succumbing to the impulse to goad her; one he should recall any time the imp on his shoulder was tempted to suggest she indulge in risky behaviour.

Though he regretted they wouldn't be able to ride this morning, sitting beside her on the piano bench would bring him much closer to her tempting body. After the practice, he could hope to persuade her to walk in the garden and perhaps learn even more about her unconventional upbringing.

He recalled the unexpected disclosures at their last meeting. Anger and a deep sympathy filled him at learning of her betrayal and abandonment by a young man she'd fallen in love with. He'd had a few stanzas from that Petrarch sonnet himself. Yet…rather than weep and bemoan fate, she'd pulled herself together and set that sweet, heart-shaped chin towards envisaging another future.

He should follow her good example when it came to emerging from heartache.

He frowned, recalling her sister's hurtful comment calling her 'boyish'—and cringed he had not come up with a finer compliment, one that stressed how lovely and desirable he found her. Perhaps because he found it hard to concentrate when he drew close to her, getting lost in the depths of those big brown eyes and having to submerge his keen desire to kiss her.

He'd wanted to kiss her then, to show her just how un-boyish he found her.

It was eloquent testament to how overlooked she had been that she seemed absurdly pleased by such backhanded praise. Society might not have appreciated her as it should, but he vowed to let her know just how lovely, talented and unique he found her.

She was a bundle of contradictions—often gentle, yet with a fiery temper that prompted her to rashness. Unnoticed and silent in society, but talkative and ready to hold her own in a small group when she felt at ease among friends. Willing to dream, yet eminently practical about assessing her future. A girl who drove phaetons, fired pistols, and translated Petrarch; an adored aunt who poled boats with children in the park while weaving fantastical stories about the boats' crews and destinations.

He shook his head wryly. And to think, upon first meeting, he'd thought she was only a clever, possibly scheming, but altogether ordinary young lady.

The clock on the mantel sounded the hour, jolting him out of his reverie. He must leave at once, or he'd be late for their appointment.

He couldn't wait to see what he'd discover about her today.

A short time later, Giles hastened up the steps of the Brook Street town house, where the butler ushered him to the music room. He found Miss Hasterling engaged in playing a scale, her maid at the window seat mending. Breaking off, Miss Hasterling looked over and smiled.

'Prompt as usual, my lord. Shall we get started?'

'I'm ready to practise that duet, or do you need to work on your solo performance first?'

'I don't imagine you want to twiddle your thumbs while I practise.'

'I wouldn't mind at all. I enjoy listening to you play.'

'Then if you are sure you won't mind, I should like to practise first.'

'What piece have you chosen?'

'I just received a new volume that includes several transcriptions of string music for pianoforte. After warming up with scales and intervals, I'd like to play through a few and see if there are any that would be good performance pieces for Mrs Chiverton's.'

'I'd be interested in hearing them. By the way, have you chosen a duet for us?'

'I thought perhaps the Schubert *Fantasia*. Do you know it?'

'I don't believe so. After you work on your solo, would you play it for me?'

Giving him a nod, she said, 'I'll be as quick as I can.'

'Take your time.'

Giles settled on the sofa, content to watch Miss Hasterling, who soon appeared to have forgotten he was even in the room, so intense was her concentration. One might consider listening to scales rather dull, but her complete focus on the music, her evident enjoyment in playing even those basic exercises, and the varying tempos and volume at which she played them made even these commonplace exercises interesting.

After a time, she opened the volume and played a few pieces at random, stopping after each to ask what he thought of them. Giles found several interesting, and recommended she play one or both. Nodding agreement, she turned back to the pianoforte and began a methodical study of each piece, first sounding the chords slowly, then gradually increasing speed until she could play the work at the correct tempo with no mistakes.

She continued for over an hour. Though Giles had suspected, despite his assurances to the contrary, he would start to chafe at waiting, he discovered somewhat to his surprise that he did not. Her concentration on the music offered him a rare opportunity to study her with an intensity that, in any other situation, would have been deemed rude.

So he indulged himself, mentally tracing the outline of her cheekbones, the pert nose, the pointed chin. Observing the occasional frown of concentration that creased her forehead, the times when she flicked out her tongue or bit down on her lip in concentration. And couldn't help wishing he could trace those features with his fingertips, and meet that questing tongue with his own, that observation setting up a low thrum of awareness in his body.

At last, she lifted her fingers from the keys. Flexing her shoulders, she looked up at the mantel clock and gasped. 'I'm so sorry! I had no idea I'd taken so long. You must think me terribly uncivil.'

'Not a bit. As I said, I enjoy watching and listening.' And he had, in more ways than she could imagine.

She jumped up and headed to the bell pull. 'At least I can reward you with tea for your patience. Will you have enough time to practise the duet before you must leave? I don't want to make you late for your other engagements.'

'My morning is at your disposal,' he confirmed, not at all eager to quit her presence. 'Tea would be welcome. And I'm looking forward to learning the Schubert piece.'

They moved to the sofa, Miss Hasterling pouring after the butler brought in the tea tray. 'Father often attended Philharmonic Society concerts in the Argyll Rooms when he visited London,' she said, handing him his cup. 'Such a shame Nash's lovely building burned down.'

'Yes, regrettable. One hopes another concert hall will

be constructed soon. In the interim, my father thinks the Hanover Square venue quite sufficient.'

'Did you often accompany your parents to performances?'

That question evoked a wry smile. Giles had generally avoided his parents when they came to London, as he was dancing attendance on Lucinda, a circumstance that irked his father and distressed his mother. 'Not often. I did come with them when Mr Mendelssohn conducted the performance of his new *Italian Symphony*, as my mother had particularly urged me. I'm glad she insisted, for it was splendid!'

'I wish I could have witnessed it.'

'Have you attended any of the Philharmonic Society concerts?'

'Several, when my father had to be in London for some reason. Such extended performances are not to my sister's taste, so I've not been these last two Seasons. I particularly enjoy Beethoven. Papa later obtained sheet music of some of his pieces for me.'

'Difficult to play, I'm sure, but superior musicians should attempt music worthy of their talent.'

'With melodies and harmonies they love,' she agreed.

'One should always indulge in beauties one loves,' he said, looking at her. *Like time spent in your company.*

His eyes must have lingered on her a bit too long, for her face coloured. 'If you've finished, shall we begin?'

'I'm ready.' Especially ready to join her on the bench, where he might inhale the lavender scent she always wore, feel the warmth of her body close beside his. He'd have to rein in the physical response her nearness triggered, though, or he risked making a hash of his performance.

It was worth the risk to be close to her.

Giles settled on the bench, closing his eyes for a moment so he might let his other senses savour her nearness. Then, after she arranged the music, he nodded to indicate he was ready to begin.

Giles might not have lost himself in the music as completely as Miss Hasterling, but he profoundly enjoyed playing it with her. When she announced they had probably done enough, as the hour was growing late, he only regretfully concurred.

'That was splendid,' he told her as he rose from the piano bench.

'I think we can perform it creditably at Mrs Chiverton's next event,' she agreed. 'Thank you so much for helping me practise.'

'You hardly needed my help to excel, but I'm please to assist.' Loath to leave, he said, 'Can I tempt you to a walk in the garden before I go? After the glory of the music, returning to the mundane business of getting my horse shod is too great a let-down.'

She chuckled. 'Is that the task that awaits you?'

'It is. What will you do next?'

'My sister wants me to go with her to look at dress lengths.'

'An endeavour you will enjoy?'

'Immensely. To run one's hands over the material, feeling texture and weight, evaluating bright hues…'

'Like painting with cloth?'

'Exactly,' she said, looking surprised that he understood her fascination.

'Then there's the choosing of designs. Equally compelling.'

She nodded with enthusiasm. 'The evaluating of shapes and styles and matching them with the colour and texture of the cloth… It seems you have more than nodding acquaintance with the process.'

He was about to say his expertise stemmed from sitting in on many a dressmaker's session—before realising he hardly wanted to admit the time spent with Lucinda. Thinking rapidly, he said instead, 'A gentleman's choices of fabric and style are not nearly as vast, but one still has some discretion.'

'Colours and fabric for waistcoats, especially, I imagine.'

'Indeed,' he agreed, suddenly thankful for the variety available for that garment.

'Before being trapped within the confines of the dressmakers' shops, I had planned to walk in the garden,' she admitted. 'I can only tolerate so much time sitting still in one spot. Let me fetch my pelisse and bonnet.'

'I'll await you here.'

She hurried out, followed by the maid, leaving a trail of soft lavender scent.

Giles walked to the window and gazed out over the garden. He recalled how at first, he had thought her so still and serene. He saw now how much effort she expended to give that impression, while under the surface her active, questing mind teemed with restless energy.

One of the many impressions that had altered since their first meeting.

Her promptness, however, had not. Within a very few minutes, she hurried back in, suitably garbed for a walk. 'Shall we go?'

As she took his arm, he stifled a sigh. A good thing they would be trailed by the maid. That surveillance would help him control his ever-increasing desire to kiss her.

'Do you feel restless, when forced to remain indoors?' he asked, picking up on her last remark as they walked out the doors and took the first pathway.

She sighed. 'Fidgeting is a fault I've worked hard to control. I've always aspired to be like my mother, but I'm afraid I've not succeeded very well. She *is* calm, serene and in control, the perfect lady. My older sisters seemed able to master the behaviour easily, but it's always been difficult for me. Especially sitting over needlework! I'd tolerate it as long as I could, then escape to the nursery. I'd much rather entertain my younger sisters than prick my fingers. Mama usually excused me, knowing the little ones enjoyed my visits, and it gave Nurse a chance to catch up on her other duties while the girls played with me.'

'Spillikins and tops?'

'The girls preferred dolls. Rather than play household, we would have them be characters from the fairy tales—Cinderella oppressed by the wicked stepsisters and rescued by the prince, Sleeping Beauty put to sleep by the evil witch and awakened by the prince's kiss.' She grinned. 'You see a favourite theme in the rescue of princes? Then, when my little brother was old enough, we'd dress some of the dolls in boy's garb and act out pirates capturing princesses, or Leonidas and the Spartans blocking the pass at Thermopylae.' She chuckled. 'We even constructed a horse out of straw in which to put Timothy's toy soldiers, so we could enact the storming of Troy.'

'I see that your siblings profited from all your study. Though I must point out that while reading, you were sitting still.'

'That's different. One's body may be motionless, but one's mind is transported. To ancient Greece, the siege of Troy or the Greco-Persian wars. It is rather unfair, though, that in most of the tales, it is the gentlemen who get to do the travelling, while wives like Penelope are stuck at home fending off unwanted suitors, or becoming stakes in a wager, like poor Helen, or mournful prophets of doom, like Cassandra. I prefer stories about the Amazons.'

'As one who drives phaetons and shoots pistols, I can well imagine.'

'You were not much of a reader, you said. But boys can act out adventures. Did you involve your sisters in them?'

'Not really. As far as I know, they confined themselves to dolls, needlework and china-painting. When not chained to study by my tutor, I exercised the horses, hunted with the dogs, tromped the fields, fished, or just went exploring. Of course, I also accompanied Father when I could, riding the acreage with him, learning the basics of sheep and hog-raising, farming techniques, and how to become a competent manager of the estate.'

'And in the evenings? Your father said your family enjoyed music.'

'Yes. My sisters played as well. Mother taught us— she had a wonderful touch. From your description of your own mother, it seems they were much alike. Serene and competent.' He felt a familiar pang of sadness. 'The household ran so smoothly under her supervision, I never noticed how much work went behind it. Until she was gone. Oh, our housekeeper is efficient, our meals are well prepared, and the rooms are as spotless as ever. But there's something...missing at the heart of it.

'It's the main reason, I believe, that Father came to town. They didn't spend as much time together in London as they did at Stratham Hall, so he feels her absence less keenly.' Looking at Miss Hasterling, Giles smiled. 'I think she would have liked you.'

'With all my faults?' She shook her head. 'I imagine she would prefer an exemplary young lady. Accomplished. Elegant. A competent housekeeper, a gracious hostess.'

'You are accomplished.'

She shrugged. 'In some things. Music, I'll grant.'

'Painting and sketching.'

'Very well, that too. But the others…one look at my needlework, and she would send me back to my governess with a stern reprimand.'

'She'd forgive you once she listened to you play.' He sighed. 'I do miss listening to *her* play. And so many other things…' he said, his voice trailing off as lingering grief tightened its noose around him again.

'Losing a mother is a grievous blow,' she said softly, putting a hand on his arm.

'It was. It is.' He looked down into those dark eyes, captured by the compassion filling them. Until the tingling contact of her hand fanned the smouldering passion back to flame. He saw in her eyes the moment when she, too, went from sympathy to awareness to desire.

The shared confidences and the sense of closeness evoked by her sympathy slipped the leash that had been restraining him. Seizing her arm, he tugged her around the bend of the garden path, out of sight of the maid who trailed some distance behind them.

'Thank you for understanding,' he murmured. And kissed her.

He meant it to be swift and gentle, just a soft brush of her lips—she was an innocent, he reminded himself, and he didn't want to alarm her with passion's fervour. But the intention to keep the kiss light and brief disappeared the moment his lips met hers.

She gasped, and thinking she meant to pull away,

he steeled himself to let her go. Instead, she angled her head up and wrapped her arms around his neck, pulling him closer in an invitation he couldn't make himself refuse.

Instantly, he deepened the kiss, binding her tightly against him as he intensified the pressure, finally tracing her mouth with his tongue. Which elicited another shocked gasp, and finally prompted him to release her.

'Oh, my!' she whispered, her hand going to her reddened lips as she stared up at him, her dark eyes enormous.

'A good "oh, my" or a bad one?' he asked, knowing he should offer an immediate apology.

In answer, she pulled him back to her and kissed him again.

This time, at the probing of his questing tongue, she opened readily. He explored her mouth, then sought her tongue, showed her the teasing dance of thrust and parry while his pulse drummed in his head and a liquid fire of need coursed through him. Not until passion urged him to slide his hands to her breasts was he able to make himself step away.

For a long moment, they both stood motionless, the only sound their frantic breathing. 'Now you can harangue me for taking advantage,' he said at last.

'Or should you harangue me? I kissed you the second time, after all. But oh, my, you kiss so much better than George!'

He laughed, breaking the sensual tension. So she was not quite the innocent he had believed her. But then, that made sense. Unconventional Miss Hasterling, whose deep reserves of passion he was just beginning to plumb, wouldn't have held back if she believed herself in love with her George. He felt an uncomfortable stab of something that might be…jealousy?

Ridiculous to resent the hold another man had over her long ago. He was here and now. 'Glad I passed muster.'

She frowned. 'I probably should have slapped your face for effrontery—shouldn't I? I have very little experience with kissing, you see, and don't always remember the exact rules of proper behaviour, but kissing a gentleman to whom one is not related or engaged is doubtless not permissible.'

'Kissing a proper young lady is doubtless not permissible for me, either. You may slap my face if you wish, but I don't regret it.'

'It wouldn't be very sporting to slap your face when I mostly wish you'd do it again.'

How he wished to as well! 'Probably not a wise idea.'

'No, probably not.' She chuckled. 'Now you really could ruin my reputation.'

'Only if someone found out. But I won't tell, if you won't.'

Her eyes gleamed with amusement. 'It will be our secret. But you must also promise to help me.'

'Of course. Help you how?'

'Help me resist kissing you again. Because I want to, very much.'

There was no restraining himself then—he had to kiss her, deeper still this time, exploring her lips, her mouth. He managed to retain some control, but with desire running through his veins thick and fast, he wanted ever more, even as the brain warning this was madness finally made him break away.

She stared up at him, her eyes smoky, her lips moist and reddened from his touch.

'Wonderful!' she breathed. 'I understand now why women become courtesans. Imagine, indulging in this all the time! Though I suspect a courtesan is not always able to kiss only charming, handsome young men. They probably have to accept rich old men sometimes, to find someone who can afford them.'

Initially astounded, he then had to laugh. 'You are the most outrageous creature!'

'Why? I'm only being honest. But I suppose that is not an acceptable remark for a proper young lady either?'

'Certainly not!'

'It comes from reading ancient literature, I suppose. Mama always thought the influence suspect. All those frolicking gods and goddesses, females being carried off to be ravished, sirens luring married men on to the rocks. Not very moral.'

In the face of her gravity, Giles fought to suppress his amusement. 'Certainly not for the daughter of a clergyman. Nor tales to repeat to innocent nieces and nephews.'

'Goodness, no! My sister would have my head. Speaking of whom, it must be nearing noon. Maria will be back from visiting her ill friend, ready to collect me for that trip to the dressmaker's. I must go back in and school myself to be proper again.' She grinned. 'Alas, no more kissing,' she said, waving an admonishing finger.

Giles caught and kissed it. 'Are you sure about that?'

She sighed. 'Not in the least. But I will *try* to be good.'

The discreetly trailing maid caught up to them as they exited the pathway and crossed to the French doors into the sitting room, then proceeded into the hallway.

'I'll say goodbye here. I must go up and change,' she

said, the regret in her tone matching his, that their private interlude had ended.

'When will I see you again?'

'Lady Knightley-King's ball?'

'I will be there.'

'Thank you again for practising with me.'

'I'll look forward to our next performance.'

Look forward to anything I can share with you, he thought, watching her mount the stairs.

After collecting his hat and cane, Giles walked down the town house stairs, smiling, his senses still simmering from her kisses. Yes, there were depths of passion there waiting to be fully awakened.

No excessive maidenly modesty for Miss Hasterling, just a straightforward admission of desire. No coquetry, nor did she try to use the passion she could arouse against him.

Though she described herself as ordinary, claiming she just wanted to be a normal wife and mother, there was nothing at all 'ordinary' about her. She'd be an excellent mother, certainly. An exceptional wife as well. Adored by her children who would thrive on her stories, she would run her house efficiently, amuse and entertain family and guests with her intellectual, musical and artistic talents. A girl who loved country, she would make an ideal countryman's wife.

He would need a countryman's wife himself some day. Might she be the perfect choice?

He wasn't quite ready to make such a leap. But he was more than ready to spend all the time necessary to explore the possibility.

He would look forward to Lady Knightley-King's ball…and helping her resist kissing him again.

But who was to help him resist kissing her?

Chapter Seventeen

On the evening of the ball, not wanting to miss Miss Hasterling's party when they arrived, Giles alighted from his carriage at the Knightley-King town house before the main crush of guests.

He relished the opportunity to talk with her again, and with his control over the desire she aroused uncertain, was grateful the meeting would take place in a crowded ballroom, which would limit their opportunities to be alone. Especially knowing she was as eager for his kisses as he was to give her them, he kept reminding himself it would be dishonourable to indulge in too much kissing—or be tempted to take even greater liberties—until he committed to asking for her hand.

He planned to secure at least one waltz, to console himself for the ban on kisses by whirling her around the ballroom in as close to an embrace as was possible while in company. Attractive as that prospect was, it wouldn't be wise to stand up with her for more than two waltzes; the attention he'd already shown her, playing the duet at Mrs Chiverton's musicale, doubtless had already created a buzz of gossip and speculation. He didn't wish to subject her to more malicious remarks like the one he'd overheard Mrs Anderson deliver after the musical performance.

But tonight, he'd not worry about anyone else. Tonight, he would just enjoy dancing and talking with her.

He felt his spirits soar with effervescent delight as he saw her enter the ballroom with Lady Margaret and the Countess of Comeryn. As his feet of their own volition headed towards them, he noted the Earl of Atherton also approaching the party.

Then she turned and saw him, her face lighting with that sweet, glowing smile, and he exulted. Finally, he'd won from her the brilliant, heart-stirring warmth he'd seen her gift Fullridge the first night he met her. Selfishly, he now wanted her to keep that expression only for him.

He and Atherton met them, the company exchanging bows, curtsies and greetings.

Giles was grateful to Atherton, who soon engaged Lady Margaret while the Countess was claimed by another friend, allowing him to speak almost privately with Miss Hasterling. Though he had been waiting two days to do just that, with the secret knowledge of the kisses they'd shared shimmering between them, he found himself suddenly feeling awkward.

'You are well tonight? You look lovely,' was all the clever repartee he could muster.

'Quite well, though my sister, suffering from a trifling cold, remained at home. You are also well, my lord?'

'In excellent health.'

For a moment, both tongue-tied, they stared at each other, the air between them charged with unspoken yearning. Then Miss Hasterling uttered a trill of laughter, breaking the tension.

'I wouldn't have kissed you if I'd known it meant we would become so stilted with each other,' she murmured.

He grinned. 'Shall we forget it, then, and be ourselves?'

'Let's be ourselves, yes, but I don't want to forget it.'

'Neither do I.' *I want to repeat it, soon and often.* 'Do you want to practise again before the next musicale? We have only a few more days, but I could squeeze in another morning session.'

'I think we did well enough. In any event, I must look after my sister. I wouldn't have come tonight, except she insisted…and I knew I'd be seeing you. I didn't want to fail to appear and have you think something about our last meeting had made me alarmed or regretful.'

Their kisses, she meant. That intimacy had certainly complicated their relationship, but he couldn't make himself regret it either. Not when it confirmed the depth of passion he'd sensed in her, the depth of passion he wanted in his wife.

'Miss Hasterling, how lovely you look! Good evening, Lord Stratham.'

'Mr Fullridge,' Giles said, irritated to have their tête-à-tête interrupted.

Fullridge stepped closer and bowed. 'Will you do me the honour of dancing with me later?'

'Of course.'

'I must pay my respects to Lady Margaret and the Countess. I'll come by later to claim you,' he said and after another bow, walked away.

'You must dance with me, too, you know,' Giles said.

'Only if you promise me a waltz,' she replied, a mischievous gleam in her eyes.

'Gladly.'

That turned out to be the end of their private chat, as

Lady Margaret turned to include them in her conversation with Atherton. To his delight, he only had to wait for three numbers before the waltz was announced.

'I believe this is our dance,' he said to Miss Hasterling, who nodded and put her hand on his arm. Eager to feel his hands on her waist, her shoulder, he led her on to the floor.

The dance was just as exhilarating as he'd expected. The warmth of her side and her hand burned beneath his fingers and the sweeping turns brought her so close, their torsos brushed, that glancing touch jolting him as if striking sparks. He clasped her tighter, while the whirling motions turned the rest of the room into a kaleidoscope of colours, a blur of shapes, the only thing in focus her rapt face, looking up at him.

So absorbed was he, he hardly noticed when the music stopped.

Finally, she tugged his hand, breaking the spell. 'You should let me go now.'

With a start, he was conscious of voices, movement, glances directed towards them where they still stood at the centre of the dance floor. 'Must I?'

'I'm afraid so.'

'If I must.'

As he led her off the floor, Fullridge met them. 'I hoped to have that waltz, but by the time I found you, Lord Stratham had already claimed it,' he explained, a trace of resentment in the glance he sent Giles. 'May I have the next dance instead? And hope for a waltz later.'

Miss Hasterling looked back at Giles, gifting him again with that special smile that warmed his heart. 'I must honour my promise to Mr Fullridge.'

'Then you must promise to dance again with me, too.'

She nodded, then gave her hand to Fullridge. Giles watched the older man lead her off, his attention remaining on them as they took their places. Until suddenly, his gaze struck that of a tall, dazzlingly beautiful blonde lady standing at the opposite side of the ballroom, staring at him.

Unpleasant shock zinged through him. What was Lucinda doing here?

She hardly ever deigned to attend a mere ball, unless it was hosted by someone from her favoured coterie of high-born politicians. But his speculation about the reason for her presence ceased when he realised she was walking towards him.

Something akin to panic chilled him.

He'd never said anything to Miss Hasterling about Lucinda. He'd seen no reason to explain about her—yet. If their relationship progressed the way he hoped it would, he would have to tell her about his former love.

But Lucinda had a keen eye. If she had been in the ballroom during that last waltz, she would have seen him dancing with Miss Hasterling—and would doubtless have noted how absorbed he'd been in his partner.

He must intercept her before the country dance ended and Fullridge left the floor with Miss Hasterling. Because after watching him dance with her, he couldn't trust Lucinda not to approach Miss Hasterling, introduce herself and make it clear just what her relationship to Giles had been.

With a few well-chosen words, she could destroy the future he was beginning to envisage with Eliza Hasterling before it could begin.

They met near the edge of the dance floor, she making him a very proper curtsy to his bow.

'Giles, darling, I've missed you,' she murmured. 'It's been almost two weeks.'

'Has it?'

She made a moue of displeasure. 'You mean you haven't been counting the days? I have.' She looked out to the dance floor, her speculative gaze resting on Miss Hasterling. 'You seem to be in a dancing mood tonight. Perhaps you'll lead me out for the next.'

He'd probably have to, if he didn't want her to cause a scene. It would also give him a chance to figure out how to persuade her to leave the ball. 'Unusual for you to be in a dancing mood. At least, at an entertainment given by a hostess as relatively obscure as Lady Knightley-King. Not quite the rarefied atmosphere in which you prefer to move.'

'When my favourite person has abandoned me, I need to seek him out. It took quite a bit of searching to discover where you'd be. I never thought I'd be reduced to…hunting for you.'

He could remind her that he'd told her at their last meeting that the relationship was over, had been steadfast in affirming that despite her pleading and her anger, and said his final goodbye one more time before leaving. Anger smouldered in him that she was blithely disregarding his decision. And seeking him out to complicate the new path he'd chosen without her.

Or had he only become essential to her when she realised she could no longer control him?

As the music ended, he was relieved to see Fullridge escort Miss Hasterling in the opposite direction, towards the refreshment room. Hopefully he would keep her there long enough for Giles to give Lucinda the dance she'd requested, reaffirm—again—that their relationship over, and escort her out—all without her causing an embarrassing scene that could ruin his chances of deepening the attachment to Miss Hasterling he was beginning to believe might be the key to his future happiness.

As the master of ceremonies called the couples to take their places, he reluctantly led her out. It was to be a pattern dance, so they would not be together during the whole of it, but enough to exchange some conversation. He'd have to make every word count.

'I'd wondered what you've been doing the last few weeks,' she said as they waited for the music to begin. 'Not dancing attendance on that pale little thing you were waltzing with, I hope.'

'If you'd been listening two weeks ago, you'd know that what I've been doing is no longer your concern.'

'Have you been courting her? I can understand you trying to punish me by paying attention to another lady, but...*her*? The nobody daughter of a nobody clergyman? Do you think to annoy me by singling out a female of such...meagre attractions?'

Lucinda's networks of information must be extensive if she'd already identified Miss Hasterling. But her arrogant dismissal just increased Giles's anger. 'Have you always disparaged other females, and I just didn't notice? Granted, you are the most beautiful woman in the room. But what do you do, beyond that? Play or sing?'

'I suppose she does that.'

'With superior skill. Do you ever put yourself out for anyone?'

'Put myself out? What do you mean?'

'Oh, call on a friend who is ill, tend a sick child?'

She frowned. 'You're joking, aren't you? An ill friend would prefer to recover in peace. Anyone with a sick child has staff to attend them. Is that what she does? Nurse her friends, cuddle children?' As she laughed, the movements of the dance separated them, giving Giles a few minutes to master his anger—and strong desire to throttle her.

'I never thought you'd develop a taste for the domestic,' she said when they drew back together.

'You certainly haven't.'

'I beg to differ. I have an excellently run household, as you well know!'

'It's run by your housekeeper.'

'Which is her job, with me to oversee her. What, you expect me to don an apron, dust the library or displace Cook at her stove to make eggs and kidneys for breakfast?'

'You wouldn't know how if you had to.'

'This whole conversation is ridiculous. I admit, I was…too cavalier, taking your affections for granted. I've missed you…more than you can imagine. I've learned the error of my ways, once and for all, I promise you! Surely we can begin again? After so long, would you give up on everything we've had?'

He sighed. 'Did you hear nothing of what I said when I called on you? Go back to your courtiers and diplomats. That's not the world for me; it never was. And a man whose destiny is to manage his acreage is not the man for you.'

'You think that little nothing chit is for you? She'd bore you in a month.'

Holding on to his temper with an effort, Giles said, 'Since you seem determined to ignore everything I tell you and continue to disparage a lady I hold in esteem, this conversation is over. Once the dance ends, I'll walk you out.'

'Giles! You cannot mean it.'

She glared at him, tears glittering in her eyes, but

when she realised Giles was truly not going to say anything more, she closed her lips in a grim line. They performed the rest of the dance in angry silence.

As soon as the music ended, Giles took her arm in an iron grip and walked her towards the door of the ballroom.

'If what we shared means anything to you, leave quietly and don't embarrass me—or yourself. Lady Evans would not make a spectacle of herself over a man, would she? A Beauty who can have anyone she wants with a snap of her fingers? You don't want to spoil that illusion.'

He felt the heat of her fury, but fortunately pride triumphed and she let him lead her out. No, Lady Evans wouldn't allow it to be said that she would run after any man.

He didn't halt until they reached the entry hall, where he instructed the butler to bring her evening cape. He held up a hand to forestall her speaking.

'I'm not trying deliberately to hurt you. But nothing has changed since I called on you two weeks ago. You are beautiful, charming, desirable and sought after. While that remains true, make the most of it, and your life, with someone else. Goodbye, Lucinda.' Giving her a final bow, he turned his back on her and paced back upstairs towards the ballroom.

Too agitated to talk with anyone, he crossed the room swiftly and slipped out the door on to the balcony beyond, his hands shaking.

For a long time, he paced the empty terrace, his impassioned strides criss-crossing the golden pools of light cast by the chandeliers inside. But when at length he grew calmer, he realised his agitation stemmed from anger rather than hurt or yearning.

He'd been more worried about Lucinda interfering to

destroy his future than agonised by the reminder of her loss. He'd always known she was rather self-absorbed. Which, he'd told himself, wasn't unusual when the lady was as beautiful and sought-after as she was, everywhere praised and admired. He hadn't realised until tonight how truly uncharitable she could be to others.

He remembered how Miss Hasterling tried to see the best in everyone. Could there be any more telling contrast between the society Diamond and the lady most would describe as a quiet wallflower?

Lucinda was like a beautiful bauble brought from a street vendor: gaudy, bright and shiny, attracting the notice of everyone who passed by—but having little of substance beneath. Not valuable through and through, but only tin lightly gilded.

Whereas Miss Hasterling was gold unrefined, but solid. Not as beautiful on the outside as Lady Evans, but precious to the core.

What had his father said? In time, a man realises there are more important qualities than beauty. Virtues like compassion, kindness, and gentle wit that would sustain a relationship over the long haul. Nourish the soul. Such solid gold, he was now certain, Miss Hasterling possessed.

He glanced back through the French doors into the ballroom, to see the lady dancing again with Mr Fullridge. He wasn't the only one to recognise her sterling qualities. If he wanted to win her, he'd better make his move quickly, before someone like Fullridge recognised her for the gem she was and stole her away.

A short time earlier, Eliza had walked with Lady Maggie, Lord Atherton and Mr Fullridge from the refreshment room back towards the ballroom. As they stood watching the dance underway, Atherton said, 'I must leave you for a time, ladies. I promised a dance to Lady Chesterton.' As the Earl walked off, Fullridge said, 'I fear I'm promised for the next dance as well. May I hope for another later, Miss Hasterling?'

'I would be delighted,' Eliza said automatically…but already, her gaze was scanning the crowd of dancers, looking for Stratham. He hadn't been in the refreshment room. Had he already left the ball?

Then she spotted him—dancing with the most beautiful blonde woman she'd ever seen. With a sinking feeling in the pit of her stomach, she tapped Maggie on the arm. 'Who is Stratham's partner?'

Maggie turned to inspect the dancers, then her eyebrows raised. 'Lady Evans! I wonder what she's doing here among us unimportant folk. The young widow of a very wealthy baronet, she's enjoyed being the reigning beauty of society since her husband's death allowed her to return to London. A darling of the political set, one of Melbourne's flirts. She favours Privy Councillors and High Court officials, which means she seldom attends ordinary *ton* gatherings like this. Gossip says she may be named one of the ladies-in-waiting when young Victoria comes to the throne.'

'She seems…quite cosy with Stratham.'

Maggie laughed. 'She's led him a merry chase for years!' She turned back to Eliza with a look of concern. 'I know you've danced with Stratham several times lately, but…you're not developing a *tendre* for him, I hope! For one, he's just the sort of rich, entitled, arrogant aristocrat I've been warning you about.

'Then, he and Lady Evans have been *chère amies* for ever. They fight and break off, fight and break off, but he always goes back to her eventually—just like in the figures of that dance! I suppose their dance will continue, even if he marries someone else. After all, a man of his rank is unlikely to be faithful, whatever his marriage vows promise—only look at my esteemed father.'

A wave of heat washing over her, Eliza was fiercely glad she'd never told her friend about her meetings with Stratham or revealed how often he had called. Frozen, she watched the two dancers re-joining as the figures brought them back together. Lady Evans looked up at Stratham through long lashes, smiling, holding his arm a bit too tightly, pulling him a bit too close.

Unable to bear any more, she looked away, sickness rising in her throat.

Then scouring anger burned away the nausea. How ridiculous she'd been, even dreaming something serious might develop between modestly attractive clergyman's daughter Eliza Hasterling and viscount's heir Lord Stratham!

She made herself look back at them, noting how elegantly the graceful Lady Evans danced. She was the focus not just of Stratham's attention, Eliza noted after a quick glance around, but that of every gentleman not currently engaged with a partner—and quite a few who were. She probably manipulated every man she'd ever met like puppets on a string.

Stratham was certainly dancing to her tune.

Which was none of her affair. Watching him with the beautiful Lady Evans was a fortuitous reminder that there could never be anything beyond casual friendship between her and Stratham. He might enjoy playing pianoforte duets or riding in the park with her, but their relationship was just a friendly...camaraderie, like something he shared with his sisters.

Suddenly she recalled Mrs Chiverton's upcoming

musicale. She had a strong, cowardly desire to send Stratham a note and cry off from performing with him. But no, that would be another signal opportunity to underscore the true nature of their relationship. Light-hearted, warmed by shared interests, even some flirting and those stolen kisses, but nothing lasting. She vowed to stifle her silly daydreams and think of him hence-forth only as an amusing friend.

If she kept telling herself that long enough, numb-ness would replace the sickness inside and she would be comfortable again.

The dance was about to end; she didn't want the music to stop and have Stratham discover her watching him.

She seized Maggie's arm. 'I drank a bit too much punch. I'd better visit the ladies' withdrawing room before we return to the ballroom.'

'I could do with a stop, too,' Maggie said. 'Atherton and Fullridge are both engaged for the next dance any-way.' Linking her arm with Eliza, she led her off.

'I'm feeling rather weary,' Eliza told her friend as they walked. 'Would you be willing to leave the ball soon?'

Maggie stopped, giving her a look of concern. 'Are you feeling well? Not sickening with something, are you? Tussling with children, you're always exposed to something.'

Silently thanking Maggie for providing her with an excuse, she said, 'No, I'm feeling fine. But I did spend several hours romping with the children this afternoon. I suppose it fatigued me more than I realised.'

'Very well. You must stay for the dance you prom-ised Fullridge, but we can leave after that.'

'You're sure you don't mind?'

Maggie gave her hand a squeeze. 'Of course not, silly. There will be other balls. Besides, you know Mama plans another dinner with Fullridge. You have a better chance to charm him in that more intimate setting.' After a moment's pause, she added, 'Have you decided yet if you want to charm him?'

'I'm not sure…yet. But he is a most attractive candidate.'

'Good. I do like him, and I hope very much you will find him suitable.'

'Don't be planning my nuptials yet,' Eliza warned.

'I'll allow you to plan your own. And not push—too hard. You know I only want the best for you.'

They arrived at the ladies' withdrawing room, putting an end to the discussion. She could do with some cold water splashed on her face—a cold slap of reality, Eliza told herself as they entered. She needed to recover her equilibrium quickly, lest her perceptive friend realise how shaken she'd been by seeing Stratham with Lady Evans.

Though she shouldn't have been. She should have realised such a handsome, compelling, well-born man was bound to have admirers, to have admired other ladies. Yes, that dash of cold reality was just what she needed.

She'd remain for the dance she promised Fullridge and leave as soon as possible afterwards. She'd probably encounter Stratham again before she could depart; he'd said he would come back to talk with her and claim another dance.

She might not be able to refuse that request without him suspecting something was wrong, as he was perceptive and she was not very good at dissembling. But she was even more loath to have him realise she'd been upset by watching him with Lady Evans than she was to have Maggie figure it out.

So she'd dance again, if she had to, but not a waltz.

She couldn't face being that close to him, knowing her attraction had betrayed her into an intimacy she shouldn't have permitted. Not when she was now certain that for him, those kisses only represented another move in the teasing dance of flirtation.

Dalliance was not a game she knew how to play, nor did she wish to learn.

Better instead to make a serious study of moving ahead into the future. In which Stratham would soon be just a pleasant memory.

Chapter Eighteen

A week later, Eliza stood in her chamber, her sister's maid helping her into a carriage dress. She'd managed to make pleasant conversation before escaping Lady Knightley-King's ball without dancing again with Stratham. Then survived sitting next to Stratham on the piano bench, determined to use the occasion of Mrs Chiverton's musicale to 'practise' being just a friend to him. She'd focused on trying to enjoy his skill, his witty conversation, and his presence while repeatedly reminding herself he meant nothing more by his attentions to her than casual flirtation.

She'd also tried to act upon the resolution to finally begin weaning herself from his company. When he asked about her plans for the coming week, she'd responded vaguely that she would be busy, maintaining that fiction when he proposed a morning ride or another early music practice session.

She'd done well until, as another performer began, he urged her into the nearly deserted refreshment room on the pretext of them both needing a beverage after their performance.

'What has happened?' he demanded in a low voice, glancing around to make sure they were not overheard.

'Happened?' she echoed, squelching a feeling of guilt. 'Nothing. What do you mean?'

'I don't mean to press, but you seem…decidedly distant tonight. Have I offended you in some way? Or is there some problem with your family—your sister's children?'

'No, the family and the children are fine.'

'Thank heavens for that! Then is it something I've done?'

'Of course not. What could you have done?' she asked, trying to navigate her way through this minefield of questioning while being as honest as she could.

'That's what I've been asking myself. Never before have you seemed quite so…disinclined to allow me the pleasure of your company.'

Because I'm in grave danger of becoming too fond of you, the immediate answer flashed into her head.

Scrambling to come up with some explanation other than the bald truth, she said, 'Time is growing short. I need to think carefully about my future. I've been spending time with Lady Margaret and the Countess, discussing it.'

After a quiet moment that sparked the wild hope that he might offer a solution by pledging himself, he said, 'You really shouldn't worry. I'm positive all will work out well for you—as you deserve. In the meantime, let me divert you from all those weighty thoughts.'

It wasn't the declaration she needed. Was it even the hint of one? She felt a flash of anger, deeply vexed that she liked him so much and yearned so for his company that she would parse even words as innocuous as those to try to imbue them with meaning on which to pin her hopes.

Give up foolish, girlish dreams, Eliza, told herself sternly.

Since she was so susceptible to him, her resolve to avoid his company was wise.

Yet she didn't want to insult the friendship they'd shared by seeming to spurn him. What outing could she offer that she was reasonably sure he would refuse?

An answer springing to mind, she said, 'One thing could tempt me to be diverted.'

He smiled. 'And that would be?'

'If you'll escort me to the park and allow me to drive your phaeton.'

His smile vanished. 'After once frightening me within an inch of my life, you have the audacity to propose to do so again?'

'It's not my fault you were frightened. I wasn't at all,' she tossed back, thinking it wouldn't hurt to add a little coal to the flame.

From the thundercloud of a frown on his face, she thought for a moment he was going to give her another blistering scold. Then, to her surprise, he laughed.

'You are the most incorrigible female I've ever met. Very well, if it will "divert" you, we shall go to the park. And I'll let you drive the phaeton.'

His unexpected capitulation left her speechless. She'd been so certain he would refuse, enabling her to wriggle out of another meeting, that she was left groping for words. While she floundered, he said, 'What morning can you make free for this folly?'

Caught now in own trap, she didn't see how she could refuse without admitting her suggestion had been a ploy.

And quite frankly, she didn't want to refuse. She'd enjoyed immensely the heady excitement of driving his phaeton that time she'd stolen it and counted the experience fully worth the scold she received. The opportunity to drive such a splendid vehicle and team might well not come her way again. She found she simply could not deny herself the pleasure.

Besides, with his tiger behind them and the necessity to give all her attention to the horses while driving, she'd be distracted enough not to be so dratted conscious of the powerful allure he held over her.

There would be no opportunity for kissing, either.

That temptation she simply had to resist. Kissing might mean little to him, but despite her making light of it to him, it meant far too much to her.

So she'd named a date—this morning—and now prepared herself to receive him, vowing this time, there'd be no kissing. And after this final outing, no more excursions.

She'd accepted the invitation from the Countess to the dinner Maggie had mentioned, which would take place in a week's time. Mr Fullridge would be present, and by the end of that evening, she needed to have made a final decision about whether or not to actively encourage his suit.

She felt the burden of answering that question like a lead weight pressing down on her chest, sometimes making it hard to breathe. With her whole life's happiness hanging in the balance, it was desperately important to make the correct choice.

A footman rapped at the door. 'Lord Stratham is here, Miss.'

The nervousness swirling in stomach warred with excitement.

Make the best of what life offers, she reminded herself.

She would enjoy this drive. She would maintain her

resolve, evade giving answers to Stratham's questions about her schedule and return home without any promise of seeing him again.

She pictured Lady Evans smiling up at him as they danced, a dull ache throbbing in her chest. It shouldn't take many evenings of smiles like that—and the intimate entertainments that surely followed—for him to move on from his friendship with odd, boyish Eliza Hasterling with few memories and no regrets.

She must try to do the same.

Time to begin.

With a deep breath, she settled the bonnet on her head, pulled on her gloves and descended the stairs to meet Stratham.

Despite that resolve, when he smiled at her as she walked into the parlour, she couldn't help smiling back.

'Delighted to see you again!' he said, bowing over her hand. 'It seems like an age.'

'Only a week. But I'm happy to see you, too.' No harm admitting it or allowing herself a buoyant leap in her spirits at being near him again, anticipating both the pleasure of his company and the treat of driving the phaeton.

'I've brought the team here, as requested. It might have been wise to see my solicitor and make sure all my affairs were in order before undertaking this drive,' he teased.

'I'm insulted you have such a poor opinion of my skill,' she protested as he escorted her out to where his tiger held the horses. 'I thought you'd agreed upon watching me last time that I knew exactly what I was doing.'

'Perhaps I did. I was too paralysed by terror while you were driving and too overcome with relief when you and team returned unharmed to remember.'

'I shall have to refresh your memory today, then,' she said tartly.

'I've agreed to give you the opportunity. But only once we reach the park, so don't even try to wheedle me into letting you drive on the city streets there or back,' he warned.

'I wouldn't dream of it,' she said loftily—even though she hoped to persuade him to allow her to drive back.

She savoured the rush of pleasure at the touch of his hands as he assisted her up into the carriage. She noted wryly Finch's wooden response to her greeting and refusal to meet her gaze. Stratham might have forgiven her for the theft of the carriage, but his tiger obviously had not.

As they set out for the park, she asked, 'At what age did you begin driving, my lord?'

'Almost as soon as I learned to ride. We had a small pony cart Father allowed me to drive my sisters in, from the stables down the long drive to the gatehouse and back. Like you—' he gave her glance '—I persuaded the coachman to teach me to drive the family's barouche. After learning to handle a full set of reins, it was an easy matter to transition to curricle and phaeton.'

'Not so much difference in driving. Only the height of the high perch makes it seem more difficult,' Eliza said.

They broke off the conversation as they entered a busier area, Stratham concentrating on guiding the high-bred horses through the congestion until they were through park gates, where he pulled up the team.

'I'm pleased to see little traffic on the carriage way this morning,' he observed.

'Will that lessen your terror while I drive?' Eliza asked.

'Somewhat. But I don't want to take years off my

poor tiger's life.' Looking over his shoulder, he said, 'Hop down, Finch. We'll meet you back here after several circuits around the park. I'm sure you will spend a much more tranquil half-hour skipping stones on the Serpentine.'

Still avoiding looking at Eliza, the lad nodded and walked off towards the river.

'I don't think your tiger likes me,' Eliza said.

Stratham laughed. 'He did all but prostrate himself on the stable floor after the previous episode, saying he would understand if I felt I must dismiss him. I told him you'd insisted that it was your fault and he should get to keep his job. But he has very high standards, Finch. He believes he should have been able to prevent you from stealing the carriage.'

'Oh, dear. I suppose I shall have to think of some way to make it up to him.'

'I suspect he will be suspicious of you for some time.'

Eliza was about to laughingly agree before she remembered she would not be around Stratham long enough even for a 'next' time, much less 'some' time. Before that sad fact could depress her spirits, she shook the thought away, determined to focus only on the delight of this excursion.

'Very well. We're here at the park, and the carriage way is mostly deserted. Do I get the reins now?'

Stratham sighed and gazed skywards. 'Lord have mercy,' he muttered and handed over whip and leathers.

'Oh, ye of little faith,' Eliza retorted. Then, grasping the whip in her right hand, she settled the reins in her left and gave the horses the office to start. 'I'll hold them to a walk, then a trot, until your nerves settle,' she told Stratham.

'My nerves thank you,' he retorted.

Dismissing all other concerns, she gave herself over to the pleasure of driving such a responsive team and such a beautifully balanced vehicle. After one circuit, as the park remained relatively deserted, she said, 'Can I spring 'em now?'

At Stratham's nod, she flicked the whip and the team charged off. Stratham remained silent, allowing her to revel in the excitement of driving at a spanking pace, the ground flashing beneath the wheels while suspended nearly at tree-branch height above the ground. At last, seeing the horses were beginning to tire, she eased them back to a trot, then a walk, before pulling the carriage to a halt where the tiger awaited them.

'Right fine driving, miss,' he admitted as he came to hold horses' heads.

'Thank you, Finch,' she said, surprised and gratified by his approval.

'We'll stroll a bit while you walk the team,' Stratham said, hopping down, then offering Eliza his hand.

Once again, she savoured his touch, knowing this would be one of the last times she would experience that pleasure. And again pushed away the sadness of that fact. Today was for enjoyment only. She would have plenty of time later to mourn the loss of his friendship.

'Finch is correct, you're a very good driver,' Stratham said as they strolled the footpath bordering the Serpentine.

'Does that mean you'll allow me to drive the team back to Brook Street?'

'There's too much chance for calamity to happen on the street. But...' he held up a hand to forestall her protest '...I refuse only to fulfil my duty to protect you. You possess remarkable skill with the reins, a light touch with the whip and were able to catch the thong with the best of them. Your tutor may have been a blackguard, but he taught you well.'

She sighed. A timely reminder of another man she'd foolishly let herself care too deeply for. 'You are the superior driver.' Stratham was better at kissing, too, but it wouldn't be wise to remind him of that.

'I hope I am superior to him at many things,' Stratham said, a more serious note to his voice. 'Have I managed to divert you from your sober reflections?'

A bittersweet sadness tightened her chest. 'Wonderfully. But I shall have to return to them soon enough.'

'You are concerned about your future?'

'How can I not be?' she said frankly. 'I cannot have another Season, and this one is nearing its end. I must be settled by then, one way or another. Much as I love my family and my sister's children, I've always hoped for a family of my own.'

'Don't you think you will have that?'

'I don't know. I have to be realistic about how I might be able to achieve that. Or decide it preferable to remain unwed.'

'I have no doubt whatsoever that you will achieve it. You have every quality a man could look for in a wife.'

Shock jolted through her. Did those words mean what…what she hoped they might?

While she stood frozen, he continued, 'I've not always been wise in the past. I had an…unhappy experience of my own and have had difficulty in moving past it. You've been of tremendous help in easing that transition and opening my eyes to new possibilities. Possibilities of happiness I hadn't thought would ever be mine.'

She swallowed hard. Was this an oblique reference to Lady Evans? She wished she dared ask him. 'I'm glad if I have been of help. As Petrarch wrote so well, loving can be torment as much as delight.'

'With you, there has only been delight. I want you to know how deeply you have affected me, how you've completely woven your way into my thoughts. My heart. How very dear you've become to me. I hope…hope you have come to have warm feelings for me as well.'

Eliza shook her head, trying to retain some degree of calm despite her racing pulse. Was this just appreciation for helping him recover from disappointment in love? Or…was he actually about to make her a declaration? The prospect seemed too impossibly wonderful to be true.

'You…have become very dear to me, too,' she whispered, her heart beating so fast she was almost dizzy with hope, anticipation and the dread that she was vastly overreacting to his words.

He'd just clasped her fingers, opening his lips to say more, when a strolling group approached them. Abruptly he dropped her hand as one of the ladies cried, 'Lord Stratham! We've been missing you at our soirées.'

Stratham turned and bowed. 'Lady Lansdowne, Lady Carlisle, so good to see you. And you noble gentlemen.'

As the men bowed and the ladies curtsied, he continued, 'I've only recently returned to London. Ladies, gentlemen, may I present my companion, Miss Hasterling? She's spending the Season here with her sister, Lady Dunbarton. Miss Hasterling, this is Lord and Lady Lansdowne, Lord and Lady Carlisle, Lord Althorp and Lord Barth-Thomas.'

A reminder of the circles in which he moved, Eliza thought, a bit intimidated as Stratham introduced her to the high-ranking members of the cabinet and their wives.

Elevated company for a simple clergyman's daughter indeed!

After an exchange of polite greetings, Lord Lansdowne said, 'Tending the estate for your father, I understand. How is Lord Markham? I know losing your dear mother was a severe blow. Has he recovered yet?'

'Not completely, but he is struggling towards that.'

'Now that you are back in London, how long do you plan to stay?'

'Most of the rest of the Season, though I will be back and forth to tend matters at Stratham.'

'We must include Markham in our next dinner, my dear,' Lansdowne said to his wife.

'He would appreciate that,' Stratham replied.

'Walk with us for a bit, won't you?' Lord Lansdowne said.

'Our pleasure,' Stratham said—the only polite response to a cabinet minister, after all.

While the gentleman gathered around Stratham, Lady Lansdowne and Lady Carlisle walked next to Eliza.

'Is this your first visit to London, Miss Hasterling?' Lady Lansdowne asked.

Eliza thought the wife of the Lord President of the Council was hardly interested in the thoughts of a simple country nobody, but it spoke well of her breeding that she was polite enough to ask. 'It's my second Season, Lady Lansdowne.'

'And your home is where?'

'Saltash, near Plymouth, my lady,' she replied. 'My father is the vicar of a parish there.'

'Ah, Plymouth, delightful area,' said Lady Carlisle.

While the men conversed among themselves, the ladies chatted about the area near the seaside, its attractions as compared to Brighton or Cornwall. Eliza had little to do but walk along, nodding politely…and regret the end of her tête-à-tête with Stratham.

Had he said all he intended? Was he just expressing appreciation for her friendship? Or had he meant to declare himself?

She knew he was a gentleman. He wouldn't trifle with her feelings. Surely he wouldn't have spoken so warmly and frankly unless he intended to suggest something deeper? If not an actual proposal, a request for permission to court her in earnest?

The party reached the end of the Serpentine path, then moved on to the carriage way where Finch was walking Stratham's team. Spotting them, the tiger brought the horses over.

'They're ready when you want them, Your Lordship,' Finch said, bowing to Stratham and the assorted guests.

'Best not to keep the team waiting,' Lord Lansdowne said. 'I'm pleased we happened to encounter you! Now that we know you and father are back in London, we will definitely have you to dinner soon.'

'It will be our honour, my lord,' Stratham said.

'Very nice to have met you, Miss Hasterling,' Lady Lansdowne said.

Her Ladyship was polite, but not stretching courtesy or credibility by suggesting an invitation might be forthcoming to her, too, Eliza thought wryly. With farewells from all parties, the group walked on.

Stratham looked at her apologetically. 'We probably should get the team moving.'

With his tiger looking on, there would be little opportunity to continue their interrupted talk. And given the nature of it…should she hold fast to her intention not to see him again?

It wasn't even a question; she knew she wouldn't be

able to end their association until she knew for sure exactly how he felt about her.

'Yes. We need to be getting back. My sister will be expecting me.'

He nodded, then offered to help her up. Did he let his hands linger at her hand and side a little longer than necessary, or was she only imagining that?

He climbed up beside her, the tiger handed over the reins and Stratham set the team in motion. 'You won't make me wait so long to see you again next time, will you? There's more to be said—but not here and now.'

'M-more?' she stuttered, hardly daring to let herself believe what he seemed to imply.

'Much more,' he affirmed. 'To say…and do.'

His gaze lingered on her lips for an instant before he returned his attention to the horses. More to do…like kissing? she wondered with a little thrill.

With the streets even more congested on their return, conversation ceased while Stratham concentrated on his driving. After reaching Brook Street, he helped her down and walked her to the door.

Before she could ask him in for tea and prolong the encounter long enough to perhaps prompt him to finish saying whatever he'd intended to tell her, he said, 'I'm afraid I must get back. Our solicitor is calling shortly. I'd like a good deal more than this,' he added, kissing her hand lingeringly. 'But that's not possible while standing on your front step in view of everyone on the street. I'll send you a note; we'll meet again soon. Promise me?'

'Yes. Soon,' she promised.

With another smile that warmed her all the way to her toes, he made her a bow and headed back to the phaeton.

Eliza proceeded to her room in a daze and shut the

door. She didn't want to speak with anyone yet, so she might first mull over the events of the drive.

Had what she thought happened actually occurred? Was Stratham really intending to court her in earnest?

She hardly dared believe it. But after going over his words several times, she couldn't construe any other meaning.

She wrapped her arms around herself, as if to contain the excitement and joy threatening to burst from her. She must be cautious, she told herself. Once before she had felt this expansive euphoria, sure she'd found the love that would sustain her for life, only to be cruelly disillusioned.

Having Lord Stratham court her was even more unlikely than securing George's affection all those years ago. Difficult as it was, she would keep her own counsel and rein in her hopes and anticipation until she saw Stratham again and he clarified where he stood.

At which time, she would discover whether she was racing towards heaven on a wild phaeton ride, or about to slam into the ground after falling from her high horse.

Chapter Nineteen

The following afternoon, after a mostly sleepless night filled one moment with excited expectation, the next chastising herself for harbouring ridiculous fantasies, Eliza begged off making calls with her sister. Too restless and agitated to sit still, she said she wished to spend time with the children, whom she'd neglected over the past week.

A good choice, for as soon as she entered the nursery, the youngsters' noise and demands claimed her attention, blocking out her speculation about when she might hear from Stratham, what he might say when she saw him—and what she should respond if he confirmed the incredible possibility that he wished to court her.

But the tiny bit of thought she managed despite the children's boisterous frolics confirmed she would welcome his attentions. They might not be equal in birth, certainly not in wealth, but she had discovered to her surprise that in many other ways, ways more important to her, they were similar.

She'd been struggling to hold her emotions on a tight leash to avoid the heartache of growing too attached to him, but if the need for that restraint were removed…

She could embrace loving him with her whole heart.

'Aunt Liza! Your turn to put a block on the tower!' Louisa said, frowning at Eliza's lapse in attention.

With an apology, Eliza tore her mind free of conjecture and focused back on the game.

After building and demolishing numerous towers, they were enjoying tea in the nursery when a footman appeared at the door.

Eliza's pulses leapt. Was he bringing the note she'd been waiting for—or had Stratham himself called?

'A Lady Evans to see you, miss,' the footman reported, handing her a card.

From exultation, her spirits veered to alarm. Lady Evans calling...on her? A vision of the blonde beauty smiling up at Stratham recurred, and her stomach lurched.

'Inform her that I'll be right down.'

She didn't really want to receive the woman, but had no valid excuse to refuse her. It would be rude to snub her simply because Eliza resented her—former?—relationship with Stratham. In any case, morbid curiosity about why the lady had called propelled her to face the visitor.

Good news or bad, she'd prefer to know sooner rather than later.

She was wearing one of her older gowns, but she supposed that didn't matter. Even attired in a dazzling new ball gown, she would fade into the background next to society's reigning Diamond. So, after a quick check in the mirror to tidy the crumbs from her sleeves, she descended to the parlour.

Lady Evans rose as Eliza entered. They exchanged curtsies, her visitor giving her appearance a frank appraisal, her slight sniff at the end of that confirming that she wasn't impressed with what she saw. While Eliza reached the disheartening conclusion that Lady Evans, viewed up close, was perhaps even more beautiful than Lady Evans viewed from afar.

No wonder rooms full of gentleman ceased their activities when she entered to simply stare at her.

After an exchange of greetings, Lady Evans said, 'You are probably wondering why I've called, as we have not been formally introduced. Though we do share a common acquaintance and, dare I say, a similar attachment?'

An icy dread settled in the pit of Eliza's stomach, but she refused to appear intimidated by her elegant visitor, that visitor's evident disdain for her—or what that opening speech might indicate about her purpose in calling.

'Indeed?'

'Come now, don't be coy, Miss Hasterling. You know very well to whom I'm referring. I must say, I cannot but sympathise with your attraction to him—is there any other man in London so handsome and appealing? Who can be so wonderfully attentive? I, who am also under his spell, can readily understand how easy it is for him to captivate others. So I felt it only my duty to warn you, that I might save you from heartache by informing you of the long-standing attachment between us.'

Eliza was already overcome by that sense of dread that strikes one after one's horse refuses a jump and sends one sailing over its head, knowing one will soon strike the ground. But she would not dissolve into dismay and make it any easier for her visitor. 'And this affects me—how?'

Lady Evans shook her head, apparently interpreting from Eliza's lack of distressed response that she didn't understand what her visitor was trying to tell her. 'Perhaps knowledge of our prior attachment comes as a shock. My dear Giles has been rather attentive to you lately. Drives in the Park, waltzes at balls. I know better than anyone how mesmerising those attentions can be! But I'm afraid they are soon to cease.'

She paused, but when Eliza remained silent, giving neither an exclamation of distress nor the denial she was evidently expecting, an exasperated frown marred the perfection of her face. Quickly smoothing it back to an expression of concerned sympathy, she continued, 'We've lately been parted by…a silly quarrel. My fault, I fully admit. I was a little too careless of his devotion, but I've learned my lesson and I assure you, I don't intend to let it happen again. He paid attention to you to punish me, you see.'

Could Stratham have singled her out simply to make his mistress jealous? The image of all her interactions with the Baron racing through her brain, she searched for motive and halted at what she knew to be true. Though it was possible he could have continued his attentions recently for other, less charitable reasons, she knew without question he'd begun them to protect his father.

'I doubt you are fully aware of the nature of our association,' she said at last.

'Oh, come now, my dear, how can you not understand it?' She gave a short laugh. 'You can't seriously expect that Giles would prefer you to me. A girl of, I'm sorry to be so blunt, only modest personal attractions. One whose talents run to shepherding children to the park and driving phaetons? You might amuse him for a while, but he'd be bored in a month.'

How had Lady Evans known about their meetings… unless Stratham had *discussed* her with the woman? Hurt, disbelief, and a gathering outrage kept her silent.

Though she held her tongue, her expression must have given her away, for Lady Evans continued, 'Oh, yes, he told me about your exploits. A little hoyden-ish, perhaps, but entertaining, I'll grant. Like those of a child. Holding a certain appeal, I suppose, in the short term. But I promise you, over the long run, he prefers the delights only an experienced woman can offer. Many other ladies of wit, beauty and charm have tried to lure him away from me over the years without success, so how could you possibly think *you* might accomplish it?' She sniffed disdainfully, making obvious her opinion of such a ridiculous presumption.

'Even suppose we accept for a moment the ludicrous possibility that he might actually marry you, can you imagine how ill you would fit into his world? He's used to moving in the first circles of society, at the highest levels of Parliament and the Court. He will be a viscount, sit in the Lords, and undoubtedly be called on to help direct the new regime when young Victoria takes the throne.

'He might even win a place in the cabinet…with a hostess who possesses the right contacts to assist him. Could you claim that? I hardly think so. Attaching himself to you would hold him back, not advance him. He is intelligent enough to know that.'

Lady Evans had her there. She had no political contacts at all, and her friendship with members of the higher echelon of society was limited to Lady Margaret and mother, the Countess. Even her friend Lady Laura, though her father was now an earl, had grown up as only minor gentry, her father inheriting the title unexpectedly when the title passed to a cadet branch of the family.

'There could be only one reason for him to marry someone like you. Coming from a family of no wealth or influence, you would make him a biddable, submissive wife to breed his sons, one he could leave in the country with impunity while he enjoyed the amusements of London.'

Before Eliza could respond to that, she swept on, 'Which brings me to the final way in which he is not at all a favourable match for you. Excellent as he is, Giles is but a man, with the appetites common to that sex. Indulging them is a failing widely accepted in his world. Not perfect myself, I can forgive his little…peccadilloes. But you, a clergyman's daughter, are probably painfully moralistic, poor dear. Could *you* forgive him, live with them?'

'He and Lady Evans have been chère amies *for ever…'* She heard Maggie's words in her ear. *'I suppose their dance will continue, even if he marries someone else. After all, a man of his rank is unlikely to be faithful…'*

She shook her head, trying to deny it. Stratham's parents had been devoted to each other. Surely he would be devoted to his wife…wouldn't he?

'I turned down his offer of marriage, you know,' Lady Evans was continuing. 'I might change my mind later—who can predict the future? But regardless of whether or not the link between us is formalised, he will always come back to me. Whatever he might pledge to anyone else.'

A married Stratham…who would not or could not be faithful? She'd never considered the prospect.

'I can see you don't want to believe me. I can't say I blame you—he's so devilishly attractive, who would want to give him up? But before you make yourself foolish in front of society by boasting of your conquest—or set yourself up for misery by encouraging his suit— why not see for yourself where things stand? You cannot disbelieve the evidence of your own eyes. Watch by my house on Hill Street tonight around seven. Now that we've made up our quarrel, Stratham will be joining me for an…intimate evening. We've much lost time to make up.'

Looking satisfied, she settled back against the sofa. 'Well, you look stricken. I'm sorry for it, but I couldn't have it on my conscience that I could have helped prevent, or at least lessened, your heartache by failing to warn you.' Lady Evans smiled kindly, as if consoling a child who'd dropped her sweet on the ground.

The woman wanted her to feel cowed, miserable, *diminished*. She might not be the lady's equal in birth or beauty, but, quietly furious, Eliza refused to bow to the woman's assumption of superiority. Even though she had no idea what to reply to it.

If Stratham had been honest with her, the failed relationship he'd hinted at with Lady Evans, and that lady realised she was losing him, she might want to strike back. Was that what was truly behind this visit? Telling Eliza the naked truth about Stratham's attentive and amorous behaviour he had concealed from her? Or simply lashing out to try to eliminate someone she saw as a threat?

One thing was sure: she was done listening. Rising, Eliza said, 'It was gracious of you to trouble yourself, but I think I've heard enough.'

'I thought it a kindness,' Lady Evans said, rising as well and bestowing on her a beneficent smile, like a queen deigning to recognise a lowly subject.

'I can well believe you felt compelled to come,' Eliza retorted. 'But out of *kindness*? I don't think so. Now you must excuse me. I have some children to tend. The butler will show you out.'

With that, she stalked out of the room, her head held high.

She went not back to nursery, however, but out into the garden, not bothering to stop for pelisse or bonnet.

Of course, the woman had struck at her vulnerability—she would never match Lady Lucinda in looks or appeal. But could she believe what she'd been told? Certainly not the *grande-dame*-dispensing-mercy act. Much as she tried to find the best in everyone, Eliza simply couldn't credit that this spoiled society beauty would possess any empathy whatsoever about what it was like to be an underrated wallflower. She felt a bit ashamed of being so uncharitable, but every instinct told her that if the woman's hold over Stratham were secure, she would never have bothered with a female as socially insignificant as Eliza Hasterling.

True, Eliza was not bred for the world of political power. She had no connections at Court nor was she the confidante of diplomats. But neither did she feel she would be a liability. As the daughter of a scholar, she could hold her own in any discussion, and as her mother's daughter, she could create a hospitable reception for visitors of any rank.

Besides, she wasn't sure Stratham actually possessed political ambitions. She'd never heard him mention a desire to do anything but manage his estate. Was a position in the cabinet his goal, or Lady Evans's for him?

She cringed at the idea that he had discussed her with the woman. But how else could she have known about Eliza driving his phaeton, about her caring for her niece and nephews? Would he have discussed her with the woman if he were serious about her? Surely he hadn't been…mocking her, though Lady Evans's tone had been derisive.

No, he wouldn't have given the appearance of courting her if he hadn't meant it; he wasn't that deceptive. But then, he had started out deceptive. Pretending at first to seek her company when he'd really just wanted to obstruct her relationship with his father. Maybe he had not meant to be deceptive at the beginning, had truly thought his affair with Lady Evans over, but then, as she claimed, had lately reconciled with her?

But her instincts cried out that they shared a genuine connection and a palpable physical bond. She might be inexperienced and know little about flirtation, might have questioned the depth of their connection even a few days ago. But after their last drive reinforced all her feelings, she'd been sure there was a well of deep affection to support his words.

She should trust them. Trust *him*. Dismiss Lady Evans's challenge to put her convictions to the test by lying in wait for him outside the woman's house, like a footpad lurking in the shadows, preparing an ambush. Wait instead for Stratham to fully explain what he had been about to broach to her in the park.

But the claims made about Stratham were not easy to dismiss. That his only reason to choose Eliza would be to obtain a biddable wife with no influential family to object if he neglected her. That he'd only taken up with her to punish his mistress.

The most troubling claim concerned the flexible morality that prevailed at the heights of society. Lady Evans had all but spelled out that they had been lovers and were content to remain so, with marriage possible in the future—if she chose it. But she claimed they would continue as lovers, even if he married someone else.

For one brought up with a belief in the sanctity of marriage and family, such a casual attitude was unacceptable.

She knew herself well; however much in love she might be with her husband, she could never overlook his infidelity. Tied by marriage to a partner like that, no matter how fulfilled she might be by running a house and raising her children, her inner being would be slowly destroyed. The wedge of her discontent would only drive the spouses further and further apart, until they ended up estranged and she miserable.

She wavered between telling herself to ignore Lady Evans's devastating visit and trying to see Stratham and ask him baldly about the woman's claims. But she could hardly expect him to admit discussing her with his lover. Or admit he'd marry with no intention of honouring his wedding vows. Could she believe his denials?

You cannot disbelieve the evidence of your own eyes.

It was disloyal to doubt him. But her future happiness was at stake here. She'd never puff off her 'conquest' as the lady accused, but more important to her, she mustn't risk her heart and future if she were wrong about his feelings—or mistaken in predicting his fidelity if they married.

She took several more agitated turns around the garden, only to end up knowing she couldn't live with this paralysing uncertainty. She would hate herself afterwards if she were wrong, but she would have to go to Hill Street tonight.

Now she needed to figure out how to manage it without taking a maid or having her sister find out.

Later that afternoon, Giles sat at his desk, going over the correspondence from his estate agent at Stratham.

He needed to make a trip back to Hampshire, but with his intention to begin courting Miss Hasterling postponed by that untimely interruption during their walk in the park, he had put off leaving London.

He smiled, picturing her wide eyes and rosy lips after he'd kissed her. Maybe he'd use more kisses to convince her that he was the answer to every question about her future. And what a future they might have together! His much-bruised heart filled with warmth as he considered the prospect of sharing a life together at Stratham.

Moving forward into that future, once he answered the letter from the Hampshire agent, he must pen a note to Miss Hasterling. Since evenings were already promised to various social engagements, he'd propose again that they take that long-delayed morning ride. He didn't want to wait until he had an evening free to see her again.

He'd just finished the note to the estate agent when the butler knocked at his door. 'Sorry to disturb you, my lord. A messenger brought this; said it was urgent and he would wait for a reply.'

A stab of alarm pierced him. Had something happened to Miss Hasterling or one of her sister's children? A swift vision of a galloping horse or a runaway carriage flashed through his head as he seized the note. But as soon as he looked at it, he recognised the paper and seal as Lucinda's.

Giles frowned; whatever she was writing to him about, he was pretty sure he was going to be annoyed by it. With a frustrated sigh, he broke the seal and unfolded the missive.

My darling Giles,
I know you are angry with me and feel I have not respected you or your views. I'm distressed that

you left me in such haste and irritation at Lady Knightley-King's ball. I hate to think our last exchange might end on such an unhappy note.

I ask that you would give me a few minutes of your time tonight, so I might say what you did not give me time to express at the ball. I think you will be inclined to refuse me, so I beg you, in honour of our long attachment and all we have meant to each other over the years, to grant this final request.

Though I would much prefer to make this farewell privately, if you fail to respond, I shall have to seek you out at some other ton *event.*

Please tell me by return note that I may see you tonight at seven instead.
Yours always,
Lucinda

He dropped the note, as irritated as he'd expected. His first reaction was to simply ignore the request and send the messenger back empty-handed. He'd already told her—twice!—that their affair was over; what more was there to say?

But on second reflection, he acknowledged the implicit threat in her otherwise pleading missive. If he did not answer her summons, she intended to track him down at some public venue and make an embarrassing scene. He'd hoped to avoid making a full disclosure of his past to Miss Hasterling until he wooed her enough to be fairly certain she would not reject him when he told her about the affair. For most *ton* females, the allure of his wealth and title would outweigh any transgression, but he was certain that would not be the case with Eliza. The odds of her accepting and forgiving him would dwindle to nothing if the disclosure occurred in public, at Lucinda's whim.

That prospect didn't really leave him any choice but to comply with her request.

He grimaced as he envisaged such a meeting. Though her note might *sound* as if she were resigning herself to the end of their liaison, she was so used to being able to manoeuvre him into doing whatever she wanted, she probably still believed she could change his mind. Her reaction when she finally realised that she could not was unlikely to be pretty. He also flattered himself to believe she felt a genuine affection for him and would be hurt to lose him.

He'd have to steel himself against any sympathy and his reluctance to cause her pain by reminding himself again that pain in the short term was preferable to a lifetime of regret. As it had taken him so long to realise, what each of them wanted out of life would never make the other happy.

Could he convince her of that?

Perhaps. But as long as he convinced her that he would not in future respond to either commands or summons, the discomfort of meeting her would be worthwhile.

Get this final meeting over and done, and he could pursue his darling Miss Hasterling in earnest. As he pictured the angelic smile he so loved, his irritation faded.

How could he have known when he set out to save his father that it would be he himself who was saved? That this sweet but feisty, fiercely intelligent, compassionate and caring lady would so invade his heart and mind that he now could not envisage a future without her?

First, he would meet Lucinda and relegate her to the past once and for all. Then, he would work to persuade Miss Eliza Hasterling that being together was their future.

* * *

At precisely seven o'clock that evening, Giles arrived at Hill Street. So focused was he on girding himself for the probably unpleasant scene to come, he gave only a passing glance to two heavily cloaked figures huddled near the corner of the street. Quickly dismissing them as footmen awaiting instructions to summon a hackney for an employer calling on one of the street's residents, he hastened up the entry stairs.

Perhaps Lucinda had resigned herself to the facts, for the butler greeted him with much less familiarity than normal before conducting him to her sitting room. No maid attended her, and though she sported his diamond and sapphire bracelet, as well as diamond earrings and the matching necklace he'd given her earlier, she was dressed to go out, not in a dressing gown designed to entice him into making love to her.

For perhaps the first time, he was pleased at the prospect of her *not* trying to seduce him.

She rose as he entered and walked over to kiss his cheek. 'Thank you for coming, Giles. Won't you take a seat?'

'Very well,' he said, choosing the wing chair by the fire. 'Don't bother with wine; I came for one reason only. To tell you that I will not come again, no matter how urgent the note you send. Our association is over, Lucinda. A quick, clean break will be easier on us both.'

'On you, perhaps. How am I to reconcile myself to losing you?' Tears welled in her china-blue eyes. Tears he thought were genuine, softening his resentment a bit. For all her lack of fidelity, he acknowledged that, in her way, she had loved him.

Her way just hadn't been enough for him.

'Come now, you can't tell me you haven't already got

someone in mind to replace me. I never expected to be a permanent fixture in your life.'

'Didn't you?'

'Very well, at one time, I'd hoped to. But the place I aspired to occupy wasn't available. That's neither your fault nor mine. To truly honour all we've been to each other, let us agree to that, and part amicably.'

'And now you think to occupy that place for someone else? That little Hasterling girl?'

Giles felt irritation revive. 'I advise you again not to speak slightingly of her, or this visit will be over before it's hardly begun.'

'Do you think you're in love with her?'

Giles was about to answer 'yes', then decided he didn't want to discuss with someone else what was private between the two of them. 'She is my future. We want the same things in life,' he said instead.

'Oh, yes. Your idyllic life in the country, tending crops and pigs and whatnot, while your dutiful wife fills the nursery with heirs and knits baby caps,' she said mockingly.

Frowning, Giles lifted hand to silence her, but she waved away his protest. 'I'll say no more. Except to point out that though you may want the same things, I doubt you want the same *people*. Oh, I don't doubt the girl has been as sweet as sugar, so encouraging and admiring, while you've been attributing to her all the feminine virtues. But a chit like that knows you are above her touch.

'She may gaze at you with big adoring eyes, but inside that little head, what she's really doing is calculating possibilities. She knows she stands little chance of keeping your attention, even if she somehow beguiled you into wedding her. Possessing neither the beauty nor the background to hold her own in society, she'd be shipped off to languish at Stratham Hall once you lost interest.

'But…if she can appear to attach a man of your stature, it makes her suddenly more attractive to other gentlemen. After all, if a viscount's heir finds her worthy of attention, should others not take a closer look? Having a noble suitor will attract prospects more at her level.'

Lucinda laughed. 'She's clever enough to know how out of place she would be in the higher echelons of society. Clever enough to avoid a situation that would see her out of her depth, ignored, pitied and exiled. Just see how long her cow-eyed gaze remains focused on you once a more reasonable suitor makes her an offer.'

Miss Hasterling encouraging him only to bring other suitors up to snuff? Giles couldn't believe it. 'That sort of duplicity might come naturally to some, but not her. She's not capable of deception.'

Lucinda gave him a sly smile. 'All women are capable of deception when the stakes are high enough. Just like that sweetheart you had before you left for Oxford. How many months did it take her after your departure, advertising her pursuit by a viscount's heir, to find another rich man to wed?'

It was surprising how much that betrayal still stung, even after all these years. Trust Lucinda, in pursuit of her own self-interest, to instinctively know how to strike where it hurt most.

'Ancient history. So also, my dear, are we. Let me state one final time, clearly and without equivocation, that I am not interested in continuing or reviving our relationship. The time for reconciliation, for realigning around a common purpose, came and went long ago. Our paths are too firmly set now, and they lead in different directions. Accept that, and it will make this easier. I do wish you the best. I'm just certain, now, that it isn't me.'

As the best for me isn't you, he thought, but didn't say.

Giles rose. 'I see you are dressed to go out, so I'll not take up any more of your time. Goodbye, Lucinda.' He bowed, but made no attempt to kiss her hand.

'Can we not at least remain friends?' she pleaded. 'Don't shut the door on me, Giles.'

'Sorry, Lucinda. That door is already firmly closed.'

'You may think so. You may think again, when your precious Miss Hasterling decides you've served your purpose and gives her hand to someone else!'

Not deigning to answer, Giles turned and walked out.

As before, he felt a mingling of relief, sadness at the ending of something that had once been so sweet and promising, and a slow, subtle rise of anticipation for the future. He dismissed the little niggle of doubt Lucinda's words had cast about Miss Hasterling's motives in encouraging him, then chuckled.

Given how very *un*encouraging she'd been at the start of their association, that accusation was hardly credible. Now, instead of trying to shoehorn into his hopes and dreams a woman who didn't fit, he could focus on winning the hand of a lady who did.

Someone he could readily envisage as a landowner's wife tending her garden, overseeing the housekeeping, calling on neighbouring gentry and bringing soup to sick children of tenants. Envisage playing with, loving his children, delighting him with her musical and artistic talent, encouraging him with her optimistic and unique point of view, satisfying him with her passion. Picture offering a loyal, steadfast, constant love like that his parents, and hers, had shared. The sort of love he craved, that would keep them both happy for a lifetime.

Now he just had to persuade her that he could offer her the same. Before one of those 'lesser' suitors Lucinda claimed his pursuit attracted could steal her away.

Chapter Twenty

The following morning, Eliza sat numbly at the desk in her chamber, staring at the note from Lord Stratham the footman had just delivered. She'd dropped it as if the paper scorched her fingers and let it remain there like a looming threat, not sure she wanted to touch it.

She'd hardly slept and didn't know how she was going to make it through the day without her sister noticing something was wrong. How could she dissemble and pretend that it was a normal morning, when all her dreams had come crashing down last night?

Her dreams destroyed, and also her heart.

She'd hated herself for giving in to Lady Evans's poisonous suggestions, but was too weak to resist the compulsion to creep to Hill Street and keep watch. She'd bribed a footman to come with her, explaining that she was to meet a gentleman but didn't want her sister to find out until she determined whether the gentleman's interest was serious. Quieting her conscience with the rationalisation that her explanation was mostly correct; she *was* going to determine whether a gentleman's interest was serious.

Rather a flimsy excuse to give the footman, though, since a gentleman with serious legitimate interest in an unmarried maiden wouldn't ask her to sneak out and meet him. The footman, however, seemed happy enough to pocket his coin and keep his observations to himself.

But after witnessing Stratham hop out of a hackney and mount the stairs to Lady Evans's town house, where he was immediately welcomed by a butler clearly accustomed to his visits, she hadn't needed to dissemble the disbelief and anguish with which she told the footman they could leave, that her suitor had broken faith with her and failed to appear.

That, too, was true; her suitor *had* broken faith, for the man who had trotted up the steps of the Hill Street town house wasn't the suitor she'd expected, but a man she apparently couldn't trust. A man who had said all the right things about what he wanted and valued, but who obviously did not value the loyalty and fidelity she considered essential for a marriage.

Or perhaps, as Lady Evans insinuated, Stratham had chosen her because, with her position in society so much inferior to his, he felt he could marry her, get children on her, and then send her away while he continued his former pursuits, knowing she did not have a family powerful enough to object or complain about his treatment of her.

She still could not believe it of him. Yet…how could she dispute the evidence of her own eyes?

What a fool she'd been, thinking she could win the affection of someone like Giles Stratham! Or compete with the sophisticated sensual pleasures offered by a Beauty like Lady Evans.

Almost as bad as the shocking revelations of the night was the unpleasant realisation that they came too late to protect her from heartache. The devastation she felt now was far worse than anything she'd experienced after

George's defection. Somehow, despite trying to armour herself against Stratham, she'd managed to fall in love with him.

No, she told herself resolutely. Not in love with *him*. With the man she'd thought him to be. But recovering from her disillusionment and from the loss of the beautiful dream lover she thought she'd found would not be easy or quick. Still, love him or not, she could never marry a man who would not be faithful to his wedding vows.

Taking a deep breath, she forced herself to break the seal and read his note.

> *My dear Miss Hasterling,*
> *As I don't want to wait to speak with you again until a free evening offers itself, might I prevail upon you to join Ginger and me for a morning ride in the next day or so?*
> *Please say you will, and please make it soon. Both Ginger and I are impatient to see you again.*
> *Stratham*

She dropped the note, feeling sick again. She couldn't ride with him, couldn't ride the gentle little mare he'd brought because he thought she'd enjoy and appreciate her. She couldn't listen to whatever sweet words he wanted to say, knowing if she asked him to affirm that he would honour his wedding vows, he would be certain to assure her he would. The interview with Lady Evans was too recent, and too raw, for her to even contemplate asking him about the lady—besides, once again, how could she trust his replies?

Which made her realise that not only was a serious relationship with Lord Stratham now impossible—she would have to break with him completely. Knowing she loved him, she could no longer pretend to herself that she could continue to see him just as a friend.

And loving him, knowing how susceptible she was to his touch, his smile, his charm, she *dared* not meet him. For despite how deeply held were her principles, she wasn't sure she would be able to withstand him if he tried to charm away her resistance. Refuse a marriage she had briefly thought would bring her everything she'd ever desired, that a heart yearning for him even now whispered would still offer so many pleasures, though she answered back that it could only end in misery.

She looked down at the note on her desk. She would have to reply, coming up with some answer that would not just turn down this invitation, but make clear she no longer wished to see him at all.

At that bleak conclusion, she lay her head on the desk and let fall the tears she'd been fighting since her heart-breaking discovery outside Lady Evans's house last night.

Later that morning, buoyed by his certainty that the problem of Lucinda had been solved and would trouble him no more, Stratham sat at his desk, busying himself with estate papers. He should leave for Stratham immediately to deal with the situations the estate agent had written about, but he couldn't leave before he saw Miss Hasterling—Eliza—again.

He tried her name on his tongue again and found it sweet. Or should he call her "Liza", as her niece and nephews did? As was true of his parents' marriage, there'd be none of that cold formality he too often witnessed in other aristocratic unions, the wife calling her husband by title, he calling her 'Lady Title'. He couldn't imagine his vibrant, impulsive, affectionate Eliza tolerating that.

He smiled as he called up the image of her leaping into the air to catch a ball Andrew had thrown her. And hurling it at him with such force when he teased her, it bounced yards away into the trees. He chuckled, recalling the angry sparkle in her eye when he disparaged a female's abilities…her cheeks flushed with excitement and guilty pleasure as she brought his phaeton to a halt with a flourish beside him…the sweet passion with which she'd grabbed his neck and kissed him in the garden.

Ah, yes, he thought, feeling his body stir, he was especially looking forward to more kissing in the garden. And to initiating her into the whole realm of lovemaking, once he'd persuaded her to marry him and he had the right to make her his completely. His mouth dried and desire hardened as he imagined her glorious response while he worshipped her body with his hands and mouth…

But for the moment, he would have to bank his ardour and wait with as much patience as he could muster for her response to the note he'd sent her earlier this morning. Looking back to the document whose first line he'd already read three times, he hoped it would be soon.

As the minutes dragged by with no reply, Giles thought perhaps Eliza had taken the children to the park again, or had been away on errands with her sister when his note arrived. As the mantel clock ticked later and later, past the time when he would have expected her to return from such outings, he began to worry she was ill, or that something dire had happened.

The clock had chimed noon, setting him nearly on the

point of going to Brook Street himself, when her long-awaited response finally arrived. He felt a huge wave of relief when Baxter entered, carrying in the note on a silver salver.

'This just came for you, my lord,' the butler said.

Barely waiting until the man walked back out, he impatiently broke the seal and unfolded it. But as his eyes scanned the page his smile faded, puzzlement and dismay succeeding it.

Dear Lord Stratham,

Thank you for your kind offer to lend me a mount for a ride in the park. As I've been a trifle unwell, I think it would be prudent for me to remain at home over the next few days and recuperate.

Although I have enjoyed our very diverting outings, with the Season soon to end, I shall have to forgo them in order to concentrate on activities that will settle my future.

I much appreciate your and your father's affable condescension over the few weeks of our acquaintance. Please accept my highest regards and convey them also to the Viscount.

Sincerely,

Eliza Hasterling

Giles read it over several times, trying to make sense of it while a kaleidoscope of emotions skittered through his brain. Concern that she confessed to feeling ill. Confusion at the polite and distant tone, as if she were writing to a slight acquaintance, and the very deferential language, as one of lesser stature thanking a higher-ranking person for graciously acknowledging them. So different was it from the intimacy of their recent encounters and the warm camaraderie they shared, if not for knowing the handwriting to be hers, he might have thought it had been penned by someone else.

And what did she mean by intending to 'forgo' their 'diverting outings' so she might concentrate on 'settling her future?' Confusion was succeeded by the stark realisation that the tone wasn't just odd—this note signified that Miss Hasterling did not intend to see him again.

Lucinda's spiteful words whispered in his ear. *'All women are capable of deception when the stakes are high enough... Having a noble suitor swells the ranks of lesser men and gives her a choice of suitors more at her level...'*

Confusion and dismay were succeeded by anger and disbelief. Had Eliza led him on only to deceive him even more profoundly than his first love? Seeming to enjoy his company, parading about with him to encourage 'practical' suitors closer to her in rank to declare their intentions?

'A chit like that knows you are above her touch.'

He couldn't believe Eliza thought herself unworthy of him—until he remembered her abandonment by George. The humble, almost humiliated tone in which she conveyed how she'd learned the difference between being worthy and being eligible. Did she truly not consider herself deserving of his regard and his hand?

Given her experiences, he supposed it was *possible*.

Surely she knew he'd been at the point of declaring his intentions. But…he hadn't spelled them out. Had she, in desperation at the prospect of becoming a spinster, felt pressed to encourage the courtship of a more promising suitor—like Fullridge?

He'd already dispatched a reply to the estate agent, indicating he would leave London tomorrow—after, he'd hoped, that ride with Eliza. Travelling by post chaise, he could arrive at Stratham Hall by late evening. The staff would be expecting him.

He sat for a few moments irresolute. Despite the finality in the tone of her note, Giles did not want to leave London without seeing her and having her tell him clearly to his face exactly what she'd meant by it. And he was concerned about the illness she'd mentioned. Over their month or so of acquaintance, he'd never seen her as anything but robustly healthy, but everyone knew of ailments that could attack without warning, laying low, even killing by nightfall, someone who'd arisen in the morning feeling quite fine.

If he were going to try to see her, it would be better to wait until tomorrow, but he really needed to leave London by mid-morning. But since he absolutely could not leave without calling on her again, it would have to be this afternoon.

And so, a few hours later, Giles presented himself at Brook Street armed with a large bouquet of white roses. He requested to see Miss Hasterling, but after a short wait, the butler returned to say the lady was indisposed and not receiving company. Then he asked for Lady Dunbarton, who did grant him few minutes and accepted his bouquet on behalf of her sister.

'How ill is she?' he asked, his level of concern rising at the worried look on Lady Dunbarton's face.

'I'm not quite sure what is ailing her,' Lady Dunbarton admitted. 'She's laid upon her bed, the curtains drawn, claiming a severe headache, but there's no sign of fever. It's somewhat alarming, for she is never ill.'

Short of storming her bedchamber, an unforgivable breach of decorum, there was no way he could force his way to see her. Frustrated as well as worried, Giles settled for telling her sister, 'Please convey my deepest regards. I am obliged to go to Stratham tomorrow to take care of estate business but will return as soon as possible—within the week, I hope. I will count on seeing her as soon as I get back and will pray that she is restored to her customary good health before then.'

Lady Dunbarton rose and curtsied, giving him no alternative but to bow and take his leave, none of his questions answered and uncertainty eating at him.

Lady Dunbarton had looked decidedly uneasy at his appearance. Because of the disturbing, unusual occurrence of her sister falling ill? Or because she was dissembling; Eliza was not really ill, but determined to concentrate on other suitors and had sent her sister to fob him off?

Had she betrayed him? But she couldn't betray him if he had never declared himself. Had she led him on, then, only with the intention of encouraging other men to pay her court? He still couldn't believe it—not of her. He heard again Lucinda's poisonous whisper, *'All women are capable of deceit...'*

Had he really learned nothing about females these last twelve years? Was he still capable of being completely taken in?

And if that was not the case, why was Eliza refusing to see him?

Frustrated, angry, confused and disheartened, Giles slowly walked down the hallway, accepting his hat and cane from the butler. Too dispirited to dine at his club and unwilling to explain his sudden depression to his father, he'd return to King Street, pack his kit and set out for Stratham Hall at once.

* * *

From her hiding place behind the curtains at her chamber window, Eliza watched Stratham walk down the front steps on to Brook Street. For a moment, he halted and stared back up at the town house before turning away and pacing towards the phaeton, where his tiger had been walking the horses.

With the ghost of a smile, she remembered the thrill of driving his team. Finch's grudging compliment, Stratham's laughter at her boldness in demanding to drive them again.

Would she ever again hear that laughter? Or thrill at sitting close beside him on the narrow seat of a phaeton, or a piano bench as they prepared to play a duet together?

Agony expanded in her chest and she swallowed another sob, feeling as if torn in two, trying to resist the nearly overwhelming impulse to rush down the stairs, run after him and call him back, while the image of him clasped in Lady Evans's arms froze her in place.

She had struggled with the decision to remain in her chamber, wondering whether it was better to confront him immediately and tell him why she could no longer see him, or stay away. But the almost irresistible strength of her desire for his presence, his laughter, his kisses, told her she had been wise not to see him now. She wasn't strong enough, yet, to be near him and still trust herself to be able to send him away.

But she hadn't been able to deny herself this chance to look at him. It might well be the last time she ever saw him.

Her gaze lovingly traced the broad shoulders, the erect carriage, the sweep of dark hair under the tall beaver hat. She noted the strength and grace with which he swung himself up into the vehicle, the easy command as he took over the reins and set the horses in motion, guiding them expertly around a coal wagon that was partially blocking the street.

A magnificent, handsome, virile, compelling man... who had almost been hers.

She watched at the window until his phaeton disappeared from view. Then walked slowly back to her chair before the fire, wrapped herself back in her blanket, and let the tears fall freely.

Chapter Twenty-One

A week later, Eliza was once again sitting in her chair before the fire in her chamber. Giving the excuse that she was ill with a cold and did not wish to infect anyone else in the household, she'd become a virtual recluse, refusing to attend any gatherings and remaining in her room, not even seeing the children. At least some good had come from all that weeping, she thought wryly; with red eyes and a running nose, she looked the part of a cold sufferer.

Her sister had seemed suspicious at first, especially when she'd not been able to completely conceal her agitation when she refused to receive Stratham the afternoon he'd called. Knowing it to be impossible to act normally if they went to the ball they were to attend that first night, she'd fobbed off her sister with the excuse that with her headache persisting, she feared she was sickening with something. Like a broken heart, she thought sadly.

On her desk rested a letter from Stratham she hadn't been able to bring herself to read. Even if she confronted him with Lady Evans's claims, what could she expect but for him to deny them, especially if he did want to woo her into wedlock to assure himself of a wife of lowly status whom he could treat as he wished? Despite that, she was still not sure she was strong enough to deny him if he did try to cajole her into forgiving him.

She would be strong enough soon, she promised herself. Once she marshalled her depleted resources and put back together the shattered pieces of her heart. She would have to emerge from isolation; with the Season ever closer to its end, faced with the alternative of spinsterhood, she must go back into society if she were to preserve a different choice.

Her best, really her only, prospect was Fullridge. She needed to act on the resolve she'd formed before she cancelled out of the Countess's second dinner, and seriously consider whether she could accept a marriage of convenience.

After that missed dinner, Fullridge had sent flowers and a note hoping for her swift recovery.

She was about to ring for a maid to bring her solitary tea when, after a knock at the door, a footman appeared. 'A caller for you, Miss,' he said, walking over to offer her a card. 'I told him you hadn't been receiving, but he asked me to bring it up anyway.'

Her heart leaping, she took it. But the name engraved on its buff surface was not Stratham, but Fullridge.

She should be relieved it was not Stratham. Despite knowing it showed her to be a coward, she still couldn't imagine facing him.

But Fullridge? Should she see him, or send him away?

She'd indulged her grief and despair for a week. With her last, best chance to wed come calling, she should act on her resolve to put away mourning and move forward. Turn her back on heartbreak and make the best she could of the future.

Which might mean marrying Fullridge.

'Tell him I'll be down directly,' she told the footman.

After he bowed himself out, she went to her dressing table and patted her hair, still as perfectly arranged as when the maid had pinned it in place this morning. She was wearing one of her older gowns, but Fullridge was well aware of her financial situation, so there was no need to change to try to impress him. Fortunately, she had finished crying out all the tears her body possessed several days ago, so her eyes were clear and her nose no longer red. Her nerves were unlikely to settle any more than they already had, so she might as well go down immediately.

Take the first step towards deciding your best future, she told herself firmly.

Fullridge rose as she entered, giving her a bow. 'I'm so glad you are feeling well enough to receive me! You are certainly looking well. Have you completely recovered?'

'Not yet, but almost.' That was surely true, wasn't it? She'd not quite accepted the loss deep in her bones, but she was getting closer. And she felt gratified that she was able to receive Fullridge with a tepid sense of warmth. 'I hope soon to be fully mended.'

'I brought this to sweeten your recovery,' he said, handing her a bouquet of fragrant pink roses.

She drew in a breath of potent rose scent. 'Very kind of you. I also appreciated your previous note and gift.'

'I was sorry to miss your company last week while you were confined to the house. Now…we've danced around the topic, but with the Season soon to end, may I speak plainly?'

She felt a glimmer of alarm. Was Fullridge about to give her a farewell speech? She'd only been concerned about her own worries and misgivings; it would be helpful to learn his thoughts and know where she stood.

Waving him to a seat, she said, 'I appreciate plain speaking, Mr Fullridge. Please, tell me what you wish.'

He nodded. 'Another thing I like about you. And I do like you, Miss Hasterling, very much. You are lovely and talented—I could spend many a contented evening listening to you play! You also possess selflessness—your sister told me of your care for her children. Compassion and concern for others, an almost total lack of vanity. Qualities I appreciate and admire.

'So let me be frank. I acknowledge that I'm...older. Though my children are grown, I'd not be opposed to having a babe in the nursery again, if my wife wanted children. I'm looking for companionship, a quiet glow of affection and camaraderie. Not the sort of exciting, heart-racing love a young woman would probably prefer, and if you feel you would rather hold out for that, I will withdraw and think no less of you. But if you could envisage a union based on warmth, friendship, respect and a gentler sort of love, I'd like to continue seeing you.'

He leaned towards her, giving her cheek a soft stroke. 'You deserve only the best, happiest of homes, my dear.'

Touched on the raw by his compassion and understanding, Eliza leaned into his soothing touch, her eyes tightly closed to prevent the tears burning at the corners of her eyes from escaping.

Fullridge ended by drawing his fingertip down to trace her lips. She opened her eyes to see him watching her, his gaze telegraphing clear signs of desire. Respectful, and restrained...but unmistakably sensual.

It was too much to say he stirred an answering response, but she felt…acquiescence. The possibility that she could accept what he was offering?

He held up a hand. 'I don't intend to put you on the spot, forcing you to give me an answer now. I only wanted to let you know clearly where I stand. I hope we can go forward. If not, I'll accept that and consider the time we spent together a lovely memory. Now, I'll leave you to continue your recovery. No, you needn't rise. Rest, my dear, and get well. I can see myself out.'

With a smile, he rose, bowed, and walked away.

Eliza remained on the sofa after he'd gone out, touching her finger to her lip where he'd stroked it. That wordless gesture said he might want a gentler sort of love, but he did not want to settle for a *marriage blanche*. As her husband, he would have the right to take her body whether she desired him or not. But such a kind, honourable man deserved a wife who eagerly welcomed, rather than just tolerated, his caresses. Could she?

She put a hand to her head, which ached with a maelstrom of thoughts and conflicting emotions. If she couldn't give herself willingly with some expectation of pleasure in their physical union, it wasn't right to marry him just for the security he could offer and the chance to have a house and perhaps children of her own.

Ah, yes, children. She recalled the joy she felt when her newborn niece first looked up at her, her tiny inquisitive eyes inspecting the new world around her. Her awe and wonder at that perfect small being had ignited within her a deep longing to some day hold a newborn of her own. Could she give up that dream?

If she did turn away Fullridge, it was likely she would never have children. Would being a doting aunt be enough?

It spoke well of Fullridge's kindness and compassion

that he had not pressed her for an immediate answer. So she'd not press herself either. Right now, she couldn't give one.

Eliza did take another step towards normalcy, for first time in a week dining with Lady Dunbarton, though she told her sister she was still not feeling strong enough to attend the ball to which her sister was promised later that evening. After dinner, she returned to her room, back to the familiar, comfortable chair before the fire.

Was this the night she finally let go of her hopeless love for Stratham? Cleansed her heart of past emotion, as she had with George, and faced the future unencumbered?

She thought she was done with weeping, but as the image of Stratham's face recurred, laughing down at her as she pitched a ball at him, she felt the sadness welling up again. Staring into the fire, she struggling to let go of her emotions, feeling the silent tears slipping down her cheeks.

She startled when the door suddenly opened, her niece and nephews tumbling into the room.

'Why are you sitting in the dark, Aunt Liza?' Stephen asked.

'Don't be sad, Aunt Liza, we love you,' Andrew said.

Smiling for them, Eliza wiped away her tears. 'I love you too. Sorry I've been dreary for so long.'

'You haven't told us a bedtime story in for ever!' Louisa said.

'Nurse warned us all week not to bother you, because you were sad,' Andrew said. 'But since you felt well enough to have dinner with Mama, she said tonight we could ask for a story. Will you tell us one?'

Trust the servants to discover the difference between sneezing and mourning, she thought ruefully.

'It makes you happy to tell stories,' Andrew persisted.

'You're right,' she said, impressed by his perception. 'Telling stories does make me happy. Very well, let's have a story.'

Eliza walked the children back to the nursery, cheered and warmed by their innocent, uncomplicated devotion. Could the love of these children suffice, even if she never had little ones of her own?

With the children settled in their beds, she told them the happiest tale she could devise, of brave princes and bold princesses who rescued each other, saved the kingdom from a dragon, and lived happily ever after.

Then, as she tucked in a sleepy Louisa, the little girl held out her stuffed toy. 'You can sleep with Bear tonight.'

'But Bear always sleeps with you,' she said, touched that the child would offer her most precious possession.

Louisa nodded solemnly. 'Bear makes me feel brave. Tonight, he'll make you brave, so you won't cry any more. But you must bring him back tomorrow. I can only be brave by myself for one night.'

Eliza swallowed hard, holding back tears. 'Thank you, darling. I'll bring him back first thing.'

Clutching the stuffed animal, she brushed another kiss on the little girl's forehead and tiptoed out.

Andrew was right; it was time to stop being sad. To put aside discarded dreams and regrets that could make no difference. She'd given herself time to mourn, and now must move forward.

She recalled again how she'd felt, holding the infant Louisa for the first time, and knew she wanted to experience a mother's joy for herself. She would allow Fullridge to court her and see if the relationship developed sufficient affection and passion for her to be able in good conscience to pledge to him her life and fidelity.

But as she snuggled in bed with Bear, Eliza decided she must also absorb the bravery Louisa believed the stuffed toy would impart. She'd been cowardly and indecisive too long; she could not accept Fullridge's suit until she had the courage to formally end her friendship with Giles Stratham.

She would meet him face to face and confront him about his duplicity with Lady Evans. If he did offer for her, she would let him know she could not accept a marriage partner who could not offer fidelity as well as love. She must arm herself not to let the love she felt for him and sensual power he held over her weaken her resolve and persuade her into a marriage that would ultimately end in misery.

Only after she purged herself of her attachment to him—proved to herself she *could* end that attachment—would she be free to give her loyalty to someone else. And be ready to make the best of whatever life might offer.

Meanwhile, Giles toiled at Stratham, filling his days with activities to limit the amount of time he had to think. Still, in the dark, sleepless reaches of the night, he was left with far too much time to rage, worry, speculate, wonder and try to imagine what had gone wrong so quickly in his relationship with Eliza. He vacillated between believing what her note seemed to imply, that as Lucinda warned, she had used his prestige to lure another suitor, to dismissing the possibility that she could be so calculating.

Her warmth, the connection he felt between them,

couldn't have been all lie and pretence. He'd felt the draw between them too strongly, had seen an answering commitment in her eyes, had recognised the passion in her kiss.

But he had been wrong before. Had he only deceived himself into believing he had finally found a woman who could give him the same sort of complete love and devotion his parents had shared?

He'd sent a letter asking her to let him know how he'd so offended her that she could imply she no longer wanted to see him. He'd had no reply—which should be answer enough.

Maybe Lucinda was right. Maybe he should take the dismissal she'd given him with good grace, and let her get on with her life—without him.

A withering bleakness filled his heart and soul at the thought. He'd known before their sudden estrangement that he cared about Eliza and wanted to marry her. But not until he faced the prospect of losing her for ever did he realise just how deeply and completely he'd fallen in love with her.

Whatever the outcome, he wouldn't give Lucinda the satisfaction of knowing she'd been right. Whether or not he tried to repair the breach with Eliza, whether or not he succeeded if he tried, he had no desire whatsoever to see Lady Evans again.

A week after he arrived at Stratham, Giles rode out to the far pasture with the estate agent to discuss replenishing the stock of Hampshire hogs, after which the agent proceeded on to the village to pick up a supply order. Feeling disinclined to interact with either tenants, the staff back at the Hall, or even his father, who had joined him from London, Giles rode along aimlessly, willing his mind to a blank.

Stopping beside one of the brooks, he dismounted to let his horse drink, wandering to the stream's edge and kneeling to trail his fingers in the chilly water. As he watched the play of light and shadow in the water tumbling over rocks and his submerged fingers, he noted the watercress growing along the brook's edge. Smiling, he lifted a leaf, observing the change in green hue of the plant above and below the water.

Suddenly, he was catapulted back to that day beside the Serpentine, Eliza pointing out to him the wonders of changing colour in the plants growing there while she extoled with passion and urgency the endless variety and beauty found in nature.

His longing for her became a physical ache. Despite the poisonous doubts Lucinda had planted in his mind, as he thought of all his experiences with her, he simply could not believe she might have been feigning affection for him, stringing him along to encourage other suitors. He might have been deceived by other women, but he was not, could not, be that mistaken about her.

But if she cared for him, the sudden decision to send him away made no sense.

Unless…unless, by not persevering that day in the park to reveal his love clearly, she was left to believe that, like George, he enjoyed her company but didn't think her status high enough to become his wife. If she did believe that, it might make sense for her to write that she could no longer spare the time to entertain a friend when it was so important for her to find a husband. And if her sister or her family were also pressing her to settle her future, lacking a declaration from him, she might feel compelled to accept another offer.

Was that the real reason behind her abrupt termination of their friendship? For, scrupulously honourable as she was, she wouldn't accept another man's suit and continue to encourage Giles. She might distance him even before a formal engagement, deciding it wasn't fair to allow a gentleman to begin courting her while she was still spending time with another man.

He was done with agonising over whether or not to try to see her when he returned to London. He *would* see her and learn the reasons behind her abrupt withdrawal. And then, unless she professed a sudden dislike for him, he would boldly make her an offer.

Though the prospect agonised him, if she had truly decided she no longer wanted him, or had pledged herself to another and could not in honour withdraw, he would have to respect that decision and let her go.

Impatient, he caught up his horse and leapt back into the saddle. He could finish the rest of the tasks that kept him at Stratham by tomorrow. He'd return to the Hall now and pack, so he would be ready to leave the instant his last chore was completed.

Leaving his mount outside the front entry for a footman to return to the stables, he hastened into the Hall. He encountered his father coming down as he was running up the stairs to his chamber.

'Where to in such a hurry, Son?' the Viscount asked.

'I'm returning to London tomorrow. Sorry to give you so little notice, but—'

Before he could say more, his father clapped him on the shoulder. 'Thank Heaven, you've come to your senses. Whatever went wrong between you and Miss Hasterling, you must go sort it out. I won't have my fondest plans shattered now.'

'Your plans?' Giles echoed, confused.

'I thought the moment I met her she might be the very girl for you. Why do you think I encouraged the connection? Now, no more spineless dallying. Get back to London, make things right and win the lady.'

'I shall do everything possible,' he promised, then continued up the stairs.

His father had envisaged Eliza for him from the beginning? Taking that as a good omen, he charged into his chamber to begin packing his kit.

Tomorrow he would make for London with all speed—and do whatever it took to persuade Eliza Hasterling to accept him back into her life.

Three days later, an impatient Giles trotted up the front steps of Lady Dunbarton's town house. The butler who admitted him barely had time to respond that Miss Hasterling was walking in the garden before Giles brushed past him and hurried to the French doors, frantic to find Eliza and confirm he hadn't returned too late.

Half running, he went down one pathway, then a second. Finally he spied her walking away from him down the next. Heart leaping with gladness and trepidation, he rushed after her and seized her shoulder.

'Please, tell me you haven't accepted his suit!'

Chapter Twenty-Two

Gasping as a hand grabbed her shoulder, Eliza whirled around.

'Stratham?' she cried, thinking at first her aching heart must have conjured him from thin air. 'You already received my note? Your butler said you wouldn't return until later today.'

'Note?' He shook his head. 'No, I haven't received anything. I just this hour rode into town and came here at once, still in all my dirt. Please, Eliza, tell me you haven't accepted Fullridge.'

She had to blink to believe he was truly here, standing right before her…though the stir in her senses, the leap in her heart testified that it was really him. Then she remembered why she had summoned him and tried to restrain those unfortunate longings.

'No, I haven't accepted him…yet.'

'Please, you can't. I know you care for me. I've been foolish, delaying too long in revealing my feelings. Despite your telling me several times how urgent your need was to settle your future, like an idiot, I remained silent, giving you no definite indication of my intentions. Not until after I had to leave London without speaking with you did I realise how vulnerable I'd left you.

I shall delay no longer in vowing I love you, Eliza. I can't imagine a future without you. I'm nearly certain you love me, too. Won't you tell me you do, accept my hand and end this misery?'

'I don't know that I can.' Swallowing hard, steeling herself against the regrettable feelings that still surged so strongly within, she said, 'I sent the note asking you to call because I wanted to tell you face to face why I intend to accept Fullridge's suit.'

'But…you do love me, don't you? I can't be that mistaken about your feelings!'

She bit down on her lip before finally saying, 'Yes, I love you,' the admission wrung out of her.

'How can you wed him if you love me?'

'Love isn't always enough. This is…awkward, but I must tell you the truth. I cannot marry a man who would not be faithful. No matter how much I love him. Especially if I love him. The betrayals would be too devastating.'

Frowning, he stared at her, looking puzzled. 'Not be faithful? Why would any sane man lucky enough to have you as his wife look elsewhere?'

'Even if "elsewhere" is a beautiful blonde woman skilled in the seductive arts?'

Perhaps in some deep, secret place, she still hoped she'd been mistaken. But as she watched his face redden, her hopes dissolved.

'You mean Lady Evans. Someone told you of our… liaison?'

'The lady herself called on me.'

His eyes widened. 'She did what?'

'She called, saying she wished to save me heartache by letting me know that you were in a long-term liaison and that no matter what happened—whether or not you married someone else—you would always go back to her.'

Muttering what sounded like a curse, Stratham swiped a hand through his hair. 'Damn her! I can well believe she told you that. She might even still believe it herself. But I broke with her weeks ago, whether or not she wants to accept that fact.'

A tiny spark of hope flared. 'You broke with her?'

He sighed. 'Perhaps I should have told you about her long ago. Our liaison began soon after I came down from Oxford. I loved her for many years. But I finally came to realise she could never be the sort of wife I wanted. She couldn't give up being celebrated by the many to settle for one man, especially one who preferred Stratham Hall to the political London she adored. Like you, I've witnessed a marriage blessed by love and fidelity and knew I couldn't settle for less. I broke with her before I ever started calling on you.'

'When I saw you together at Lady Knightley-King's ball, you seemed very much enchanted.'

He grimaced. 'By the time of the ball, it had been several weeks since I'd ended the relationship. I'd left her before and always came back, so when I didn't this time, she sought me out—at the Knightley-King's ball. I told her again that the relationship was over and I had no interest in reviving it.'

'Then why, if the relationship was over, did you return to her house?'

'What are you talking about?'

'The day she came to see me, she claimed you had reconciled and that you would call on her that night. After the ball, after…after you'd said things that made me think you might have serious interest in me, I couldn't believe it. But deciding it was too important to know whether or not she was telling the truth, I came to Hill Street at the hour she named and stood at the corner, watching. I saw you go into her house, just as she'd said you would.'

'You…were watching on the street?' His eyes widened. 'The two muffled figures… You were *spying* on me?' he asked, his voice indignant.

She felt a flush of shame, but said hotly, 'Yes. It looks like I had good reason to, doesn't it? After having you practically made me a declaration, just a few days later, I watch you warmly welcomed into the home of your *chère amie*! That's not the sort of marital fidelity I could tolerate.'

He shook head, looking furious. 'I knew she was angry, but I never thought she would go that far! She called on you that very morning, you say?'

'Yes.' She gave a short laugh. 'To warn me of where your true affections lay, that I might not be deceived into making a disastrous union.'

'Will you let me explain?'

Crossing her arms, Eliza glared at him. 'How can you explain? I saw you enter her house with my own eyes, just as she predicted! You just admitted you did so!'

'Ah, but you don't know *why* I called—and it wasn't for some romantic tryst. You must have left immediately, for if you'd remained for half an hour, you would have seen me leave.'

'You…didn't spend the night?'

'No.'

'But you…discussed me with her. She knew about my driving your phaeton. About the excursion with the children. How could you so betray my trust?' she cried, trying to hold back the angry tears.

'I never discussed you with her!' he replied hotly. 'Unless…' He took an agitated turn around the small space of the garden aisle. 'As I told you, I broke with her weeks ago, but being so used to having me at her beck and call, she wouldn't accept it. To track me down at Lady Knightley-King's ball, she must have found out a good deal about our friendship. Which would have been easy enough; she has connections all over the *ton*.

'But I swear to you, the only mentions I made of you to her were during the ball, when I praised your talent, wit and charm. I went to Hill Street because she threatened if I didn't see her privately, she would make a public scene—and I didn't want to risk that, risk losing you before my courtship had even begun. I stayed only long enough to tell her again, for once and for all, our relationship was over. She no longer has any hold on me…because I've found the true love of my life. You.'

'You…believe that?'

'With all my heart. I intended to tell you about Lucinda straight away, but I never got the opportunity. Why did you not let me call and ask me the truth of the matter? Why send me away with no explanation?'

'If it were true, would a man admit it? You hadn't been completely honest with me before, you know. Pretending to pay me your attentions only so your father wouldn't; telling me your father was out of town when he wasn't.'

He started to protest, then fell silent. 'You are right,' he admitted. 'How much damage those small evasions caused! But can you believe me now? Or have you formed so ill an opinion of my character that you cannot accept what I tell you is the truth? That I have broken with Lady Evans, for good and all. That I love you, only you, and if you give me your hand, will be faithful and true to you, only you, for rest of my life?'

'I couldn't at first believe I could be so mistaken in

your character,' she said softly. 'Not until I saw you walk up those steps… I think part of me died that night. I'd steeled myself to move forward without you, but all my joy and anticipation of the future were gone. I should have come to you sooner. I'm sorry I didn't trust you more.'

'Then…you believe me now? You forgive me?'

As she nodded, too overcome with joy and relief, too humbled by the love he expressed to speak, he tipped her chin up. 'You'll marry me then, my heart?'

With a tremulous smile, she said, 'I will, my darling Giles.'

Stratham seized her in a hug, then kissed her so fiercely she went dizzy, her whole body sizzling with arousal. When he finally released her, he said, 'I thought I was terrified the day you stole the phaeton. That was nothing compared to the agony of thinking I might have lost you for ever.'

Clasping her arm, he said, 'Come, you must inform your sister you are leaving as soon as you can get packed.'

'Leaving?'

'Yes. I must go ask your father for your hand and have him post the banns. I want to marry you as soon as possible. I don't want to chance Lady Evans making another run on your belief in me or Fullridge carrying you off.'

Eliza halted, forcing him to stop. 'Mr Fullridge! I can't leave before I see him. Kind as he has been, it would be shabby to fob him off with only a note of farewell.'

Giles frowned. 'You're sure you can't send just a note?'

Eliza shook her head. 'It wouldn't be honourable.'

'Can I be present when you see him?'

She laughed. 'You don't trust me?'

'I don't trust *him*. He might try to steal you away.'

She shook her head. 'I'm sure he'll do no such thing.'

Giles sighed. 'If it were me, I suppose I'd feel insulted to learn the news second-hand. Very well, but bid him to call immediately, for we must leave no later than to-morrow. On second thought, while you see him, maybe I will call on Lady Evans again. When I consider how close she came to ruining both our lives, I would like to strangle her.'

'No, there's a better revenge. We live our lives together and are happy.'

He gave her a slow smile. 'Yes, that would be the best revenge.'

Clasping her arm again, he began to lead her off, but again she stopped him. 'Wait. I can't go yet.'

'Why? What else needs to be done?'

'This,' she said, pulling his head down and kissing him. With all the relief and pain and grief of last week, all her passion and joy and anticipation of the future.

Wrapping his arms around her, he kissed her back just as fervently, a melding of lip and mouth and tongue that sent sensation blazing through her. She exultated at the promise of this pleasure now, and the ultimate pleasure soon.

Finally, Giles broke the kiss. 'Forget banns. I'll get a special licence.'

Resuming walking, she batted his arm. 'You can't. Mama and Papa would be devastated. To say nothing of my sisters—and my friends! Especially Lady Maggie, and Lady Laura, who should return this week from her honeymoon.'

'I suppose if you're to be mine for the rest of my life, I can wait a few more weeks.'

She gave him a mischievous look. 'I'll make it worth your while.'

He returned a heated glance. 'I'll hold you to that promise. But after we see your sister and your papa, I must take you to Stratham so we may tell Father the news. He'll be delighted I didn't lose you after all. But not half so delighted as I am.'

He twined his fingers with hers. 'To duets and driving phaetons and the laughter of many, many children. To us, for finding a forever love when it appeared all hope was lost.'

She leaned up to kiss him again, this time slow and sweet. 'To our forever love.'

* * * * *

*If you enjoyed this story, be sure to
read the first book in Julia Justiss's
Least Likely to Wed miniseries*

A Season of Flirtation

*And why not pick up her
Heirs in Waiting miniseries?*

The Bluestocking Duchess
The Railway Countess
The Explorer Baroness

Get 3 FREE REWARDS!

We'll send you 2 FREE Books plus a FREE Mystery Gift.

FREE Value Over **$20**

Both the **Harlequin® Historical** and **Harlequin® Romance** series feature compelling novels filled with emotion and simmering romance.